I0846553

HEAT LEVEL AND CONTENT WARNINGS

Before starting this novel, I encourage you to first read this section to determine whether it's the right fit for your personal circumstances.

This book is closed door romance, which means there is innuendo, kisses are descriptive, and characters don't shy away from their attraction.

There is mild to moderate use of cuss words, particularly in emotional moments. However, there is no use of f-bombs, religious blasphemies, or known ableist terms.

Chapter 3 depicts a scary moment of severe turbulence during a flight. Characters are adults and there are mild depictions of alcohol consumption. There are brief narrations of sports bodily injuries.

Visit my website mariloyal.com for general content warnings that apply to my books.

CHAPTER 1
LUCKY

Tis the season of giving… unless you're duking it out for the last available chair at the VIP lounge, before a flight out of Orlando, five days before Christmas.

My foe is mighty, a woman in stiletto heels, the kind that could be used for stabbing. I suspect she's considering it by the way she stares at me, flabbergasted that I'm not being a gentleman and offering her the chair.

Normally I would—Ma raised me well—but this time is an exception.

It's almost been two months since I tore my right ACL during the very last game of the World Series, and I'm still in a lot of stinking pain. If it wasn't because I'm trying an experimental treatment at the St. Cloud University Hospital up in Connecticut, I wouldn't even be anywhere near an airport. Least of all one of the most transited ones in the whole freaking country. Thus, angry woman wouldn't have to fight me for the chair, and my record as a gentleman would be unquestioned.

"Listen," I say as I adjust my grip on the crutches again, my backpack bouncing behind me. "I realize that this is making me look like a douchebag but I really need to sit right now." Then for added measure, I point at the long leg cast encasing from well above my knee down to my foot, covered by protective padding and wiring.

"And I'm wearing heels." She folds her arms, a tiny crease appearing between her eyebrows.

I resist the urge to cringe and fail dramatically. "Sorry but that was a choice. I guarantee you that this wasn't." I point at my cast with my lips—again.

She lifts her chin, short hair brushing at the top of her shoulders. "Be that as it may, my choice has come back to make me bleed and I need to sit to assess the damage."

Of the vast range of comebacks I could've expected, none of them included her balancing against the armchair so she can toe out one of her heels. The hiss I let out attracts a good amount of attention, and a few of the onlookers who also see the issue echo the sentiment.

Turns out her shoes must've been new or something because they bit through the fabric of her tights, and also through her skin. A massive blister formed and popped a while ago, and if I had a weak stomach I'd have probably barfed the banana I had while I Ubered over.

I carefully reach up to wipe a thick bead of sweat from my forehead. I don't know if it's due to her gnarly wound or if it's because my knee feels simultaneously like burning coals, and also like ice is stabbing it. "I guess we're at an impasse, then," I say with a grimace that attempts to be a smile.

"Can I take it then?" a random man asks.

We look at him and simultaneously say, "No."

Dude has the balls to appear confused. "But no one's using it."

The woman slides her purse off her shoulder and swings it at the chair. It lands right on the seat and stays put. "There, it's taken now."

After a big eye roll and a huff, the guy turns away and heads to the bar to elbow his way into the crowd.

Now that I've confirmed that she's really mighty, I say, "I propose an armistice."

"I'm listening." Her lips pinch hard, the only proof I've seen in the past five minutes that she's actually in pain right now.

Meanwhile, I'm sweating buckets and my clothes are starting to stick to my body. I wish I could say that since I'm a professional elite athlete who is used to grueling training and aggressive games, I would be taking this in stride—though I can't even crawl these days—but no. I'm kind of embarrassed that a woman with two gaping holes on her heels is much more composed than I am.

Then again, women are freaking strong. So maybe she should have mercy on this poor, weak man?

"Option one," I say, my voice kind of breathless even though I've been standing on the same spot for a decent while. I just really need to raise my leg on the table to fool gravity for a bit. "We each sit on the armrests."

"No, you could just slide down to the middle and take the whole chair. And then you'll look like Santa and I like the child."

I blink slowly. There is nothing childlike about her. If anything she looks kinda scary. If I wasn't trying to earn a chair from her I'd be into it.

"Fine, option two: we take turns."

"Option three," she counters with absolutely no feeling in her voice. "You sit on the floor and I take the chair."

I make a face like a kid who's being ordered to eat broccoli when he wanted fries instead. "Are you kidding? On these floors that have been stepped on by billions of people per year?"

"I'm sure they clean them." She pauses. "Sometimes."

"Yeah, I'm not gonna sit on the floor but you're more than welcome to it."

"Where is your chivalry?"

"I'm afraid it died at the surgery table when I was getting my torn ACL sewn back together."

For the first time her eyes travel down to my leg and maybe I hallucinate it, what with how fast it vanishes, but a flash of sympathy passes over her face.

"What if you sit on the table?" she asks in a slightly less cutting tone of voice than before.

"I kinda need the table to raise my leg." I offer an apologetic smile because I'm not trying to be shitty—the situation just is.

She takes a deep, *deep* breath, the kind that widens her nostrils and fully deflates her when she expels it. Then she suggests, "What if I take the chair and allow you to rest your foot on it beside me?"

Tilting my head, I consider the angles and actually, the coffee table is lower than the seat. It would actually be better for me to have my foot raised higher than the other way around. There's only one concern here.

"What if I break the table?" I ask, looking at the innate object. "I'm pretty sure I weigh considerably more than you."

That's a fact. Last I checked I was still almost two hundred pounds of solid muscle and while I'm not the tallest guy in the team, I'm still 6 feet 2. Meanwhile, she's slight. Most of her weight is probably on the thick coat she's wearing and in the purse that's saving the chair.

She considers the surface space of the chair and the table like it's a math problem. Then she inspects me—like really takes the measure of me—and she says, "No offense, but my butt is probably bigger than yours, so I'm going to take the chair."

Despite the knife stabbing at my knee, I let out a big snort in amusement. "I'll take you for your word, then. It would probably be rude for me to confirm."

"It would," she confirms in a deadpan.

"Okay," I mutter to myself, hopping on my left leg and the crutches to angle myself. "Here we go." The actual motion to sit down is a walk in the park, that's the part where you can tell I move my body for a living. The part where I have to raise my leg is the tricky one. I join the two crutches and set them on my lap to free my hands, then I grab my actual leg and between arm strength and my hip flexor, I manage to raise my leg and set it on the chair. I tighten my jaw against the sharp jolt that flies from my knee to my spine.

The woman removes her coat and folds it over the chair to sit on it like she really couldn't have survived sitting on the floor. Holding her purse on her lap, she eases herself on the chair and I give her big props for how mindful she is of my foot. Now that her butt is firmly on the chair and I take in the width of her hips, I reach the exact same conclusion.

Damn, she's the one who would've broken the table.

"Anyway, uh…" I clear my throat so I don't bark a laugh, and that way I avoid having to explain myself. "My name is Lucas Rivera but everybody calls me Lucky." I extend my now free hand for her to shake.

She stares at it for a second, and right before I start to drop it she finally shakes it. It's too quick for me to glean anything from it, other than she must use very expensive hand lotion. "I know who you are," she says.

My eyebrows rise. "You do?"

"Yes, I happen to know a bit about sports," she says absent-mindedly while reaching for her heels to remove them. Her shoulders shrink at the sensation and the secondhand pain makes me stop before I spew out a barrage of questions.

Is *a bit* being modest or honest? Why does she even know an undefined bit? Does she know who I am because she was rooting for the Riders or because she's an Orlando Wild fan? After all, she's flying out of Orlando. There's a chance she's a fan. But more importantly, what is her actual name?

"Mierda," she mumbles in Spanish and my eyes lift back up to her face.

I detect an accent that's like a cousin of mine. It rules out areas like Spain, or Mexico or Argentina. I think she's from somewhere in the Caribbean.

She's inspecting her shoe, though, and I get distracted by the red stain on it.

"Yikes." I twist to look for anyone who works here. "Maybe we can find you some Band-Aids."

"I don't know if—"

The sound of static interrupts us and, like everyone else crowding the lounge, we stop to listen to the incoming tinny voice of an airport employee, announcing, "Last call for Horizon Airways flight number HA263 departing from Orlando to Miami."

I relax and am about to ask the prickly woman for her name again, until the voice continues with, "Horizon Airways flight number HA930 departing from Orlando to Mapleton begins boarding in fifteen minutes."

We both groan.

It startles us.

"You're going to Mapleton?" she asks, shocked.

"Uh, yeah. You too?"

Rather than responding directly, she asks, "Why? There's nothing in Mapleton for a professional baseball player like you."

"Actually, my—"

Her raised hand cuts me off before I can explain that my brother and his family live in Mapleton, which is really close to St. Cloud. He'll drive me back and forth for the treatments and then act as my nurse while I recover at his home. The team would've actually preferred to pay for professional in-house support but I rejected that. I don't want to rent an apartment that I'll only occasionally share with a stranger over the holidays.

Besides, I have a very important gift for my nephew. I must deliver it in person.

"No, never mind. That was rude of me to assume and I don't need to know your business." Now full on cringing, she slides her feet back in the heels and collects her things. Just as carefully as she sat a second ago, she gets up from the chair and stands. She regards me for a moment, almost like she has several things she wants to say but can't pick one. Finally, what comes out is, "Travel safe, anyway."

I guess this is it, then. "Yeah, you too." I try not to sound too disappointed but I'm not sure I succeed. Last minute I add, "Don't let them take off without me."

Her light brown eyes clock my crutches again. "I won't." And with that, she turns away and walks off with surprising firmness for someone whose feet are bleeding.

Sighing, I set about getting back up and hauling my ass back to the gate. Either it took me far too long to find the lounge, or the woman and I spent too long warring over the one chair, because I hadn't realized that time ticked by so fast.

I manage to make it to boarding by the time they're on the third group, which makes getting on the plane way clunkier than it would've been if I had just sucked it up and sat on the floor by the packed gate, rather than gambling on the lounge. But the pain's worth it, because when I make it to my first class seat I find an interesting surprise.

My former chair foe is now sitting on the seat right beside mine.

As she looks up at me in surprise, I can't help that my lips curl into a smile. Maybe I'll finally find out what her name is.

CHAPTER 2
CAMILA

"**W**ell, well, well." Lucky Rivera, World Series champion and famous enough that even I—a soccer fan—know who he is, glances first at my face and then at the seat number above me. "Looks like we're neighbors."

The worst part is that all of this catches me right as I'm taking off my heels.

Normally I would never do this. I keep my shoes on in public at all times, but that's when I don't have two holes that keep rubbing against the evil shoes of doom, sending jolts of something that is like a mix of pain and *yuck* every time I step.

I also didn't appreciate when this guy threw the truth in my face, that this was all my fault.

This business trip was just a three-day affair, so I only brought a small carryon with these heels for the event. I flew in wearing a sensible pair of flat, suede booties that I intended to wear on the way back, until they met an untimely demise. While sitting at a terrace restaurant in Park Avenue, having brunch with Audrey Winters, my former college roommate—a dog from a nearby table irreparably peed all over my shoes.

After tossing the booties, I contemplated whether to buy a new pair but I figured that thee heels would work just fine. After all, I wore them for every meeting in the past days.

Every one of which happened while I sat in a conference room, not actively walking across a busy international airport.

While he figures out what to do with crutches, a backpack, and himself, I try to massage my ankles to at least make sure I can feel something other than pain. A tiny groan lodges in my throat instead.

"Excuse me, sir," a flight attendant says, appearing next to the baseball guy, beaming with a practiced smile. "Would it be all right if I take your crutches? You'll be much more comfortable during the trip and I can bring them if you need to use the restroom."

"That would be great, thanks." He maneuvers the tools to hand them over, balancing himself on the backrest of his seat. Hopping on his left leg, he lowers himself to sit with much more fluidity than anyone else with a massive cast possibly would. Nary a huff or a complaint from him.

Meanwhile, I'm barely holding it together from how bad my heels sting.

"Oh, excuse me," he calls out once the attendant is leaving. He lowers his voice as she reaches him again, but I still catch every word. "Do you happen to have any ointment and a couple of Band-Aids?"

"Of course, I will bring them right over."

No offense, I think purely to myself, *but I don't think ointment and some plasters are going to be enough to fix your knee, dude.*

As discreetly as I can, I scoot a little away from him and pull out my iPad from my purse, clicking away until I find the weekly production report.

"Here you go, Mr. Rivera."

"Thank you," he responds with a spring in his voice. "You know who I am?"

"Absolutely, you're one of our hometown heroes. So sad what happened during the game," she says in an almost cooing way. I guess she's referring to how his knee basically snapped during an aggressive play at the final game of the World Series. "You still got the out, though. It was incredible."

"Wow, thank you for the support. Would you like an autograph?"

"I would love one, thank you! I'll be right back"

"Great, I'll wait right here." He settles back on his seat with a good-humored chuckle.

Are they going to be flirting during the whole flight? Because so help me, I will be one of those annoying people who request a seat change.

"Does this work?" the flight attendant asks as she returns, and I peep a Horizon Airways pad and pen combo that probably cost cents to procure, yet they sell to passengers for ten bucks each or something absurd.

"Absolutely. Who should I make it out to?"

"Shelley with e and y at the end." She makes the motion of tucking her hair behind her ear, even though it's all tied in a tight bun at the back of her head. Fortunately for her, Lucky's already scribbling and misses the way she blushes in embarrassment.

I feel like if our roles were reversed, she'd have given him the last chair at the VIP lounge.

"There ya go." His voice is a rumble beside me.

"Gosh, thank you. Can I bring you a drink?"

"I'm good for now." A rustling sound. Then his voice sounds above me. "And you?"

I stop in the middle of putting ointment on one wound through the torn panty hose. Slowly, I look up at the attendant who had previously ignored my existence. "Yes, red wine, please."

To her credit, she turns on the rehearsed smile to a perfect sheen. "Coming right up, ma'am."

My eye twitches. "Thanks."

Ma'am? Please, I'm barely five years older than her.

I don't complain about the quiet after that, though. Boarding must still be going on the coach section, yet this whole section of the plane is already fully boarded. I'm about to settle in to start working on my iPad when I get distracted once again.

"Here you go."

A large hand holding three small things appears in my field of vision. Two Band-Aids and a square pack of ointment, the kind that can be found in first aid kits. And it's all being handed to me.

"Huh?" I say, somehow not comprehending the obvious.

"Hopefully this helps with your blisters," he says, motioning toward my feet with his lips. "They look pretty nasty, not gonna lie."

My hand moves all on its own to receive the—peace?—offerings. "Thanks?" It comes out more as a question than a statement.

"You're welcome." His eyes dance with a smile like he finds me amusing but has enough PR training not to laugh at a stranger and catch himself in trouble on social media.

That makes me feel worse about myself as I open the pack of ointment. A dollop gushes out and I catch it on my finger, and that's when I realize that my hands aren't exactly clean. That doing this on a plane, even on first class, is probably deeply unsanitary.

Alternatively, I leave the blisters out in the open to keep catching all the germs on this plane.

Grunting, I bend forward to start the operation. There's twice the leg room space on first class than coach, but even then it's not the most comfortable to do this while wearing a pencil skirt. Of course, this is also when my drink arrives.

"I gotchu," Lucky Rivera murmurs, receiving the cup for me.

I'm torn between grabbing it with my icky hands—but then where do I put the cup?—or finishing quick. No matter how well known he might be, he's a complete stranger and I can't trust him with my drink.

But then he does another thing that takes me aback. He pulls out my seat's table from within the armrest between us, sets the wine cup on it, and covers it with the napkin that is probably intended to be used as a coaster instead.

I blink a few times, fast. Somehow this strikes me as even kinder than the first aid stuff.

This is when I get reminded that I'm extremely messed up. Where anyone else would find this as a giant green flag, my walls shoot up to the sky. The last time I went along with a nice guy who was reasonably good looking and was well off, I ended up jilted at the altar. All of this kindness can be just an act. Or perhaps, I'm just too messed up about it to take things at face value anymore.

I make quick work of the last plaster and, keeping my eye on the cup, I pluck the napkin to wipe gross ointment off my fingers. "Thank you," I tell him—polite yet frosty.

"You're very welcome." He flashes a smirk like he knows exactly what I'm doing because he can read my mind.

I might be paranoid—it's certainly among the list of insults I've received in my life—but there is something very clever in his eyes that might fool everyone with the charming way he conducts himself with, but not me. I will make sure that this is it. No awkward conversation. No further interaction.

Finally, the attendants start the safety instructions and that stops any possibility for chit chat.

I put on my Airpods before they're finished to send a clear

message to my seat neighbor. Fortunately, at this point he seems to get it because he fishes for something out of his backpack and it keeps his attention as I work.

By the time we take off, I've finally found my groove with the report I'm reviewing, and I barely feel the blisters anymore. The wine is already gone and is doing wonders. Or perhaps I'm simply less on edge because I'm finally abstracted from reality. I'll be home in just over four hours, dress my wounds properly, slip into my silk pajamas, and sleep like a log.

The plan goes marvelously for about an hour, until suddenly the light comes on to fasten our seatbelts and the plane starts shaking.

CHAPTER 3
LUCKY

don't consider myself El Frontú of the Wild players, but I've never experienced a case like this one. On the one hand, having a fan—the flight attendant—being all excited about getting my autograph. And on the other hand, sitting next to someone who clearly knows who I am and doesn't care for the knowledge.

Logan Kim, the All-Star catcher of my team, would have a blast if he found out about this humbling experience.

Speaking of, this one time when I went to bother him at his apartment, I found a bodice ripper book on his coffee table. After a solid fifteen minutes of teasing him, he admitted that his girlfriend once left it at his place and that it was surprisingly interesting. Dude's a reader so I decided to take it up for his word and honestly, this kind of literature is what's kept me sane during the knee recovery.

I take the book out of my backpack, find the bookmark—a Foxtail Coffee receipt—and pick up where I left off. Lady Arabella got lost in the woods and Lord Harrington, the Duke, is searching for her before the storm breaks out. This should be good.

Unconsciously, I try to snuggle into the seat but that just sends an uncomfortable spasm down my leg. I freeze, breathing in and out as I wait for the wave to subside. When it's gone, I feel as tired as if I had just finished practice with the team. Slacking until I lean my head back, I close my eyes and wonder when I'm going to be back at full strength.

Or if I will, at all. If I'll have a professional career after this.

Anda pal carajo, I say to my own bad thoughts. I open the book again and stubbornly focus all my attention on Lady Arabella's crisis rather than my own.

The woman next to me huffs, and for a moment I wonder if she's mocking my train of thought. But then I get another reminder that the world doesn't revolve around me, and she seems to be directing her scorn at whatever is on her iPad screen. A quick peek at it just shows some graphs and numbers that I have no hope of deciphering, which tells me a few things about her.

One, she's smart. Life has proven that I am not the demographic that smart women surround themselves with. No wonder she wouldn't even give me the honor of knowing her name.

Two, she's wearing expensive business-y clothes and is working during a flight well past eight at night, which probably means she's some high powered executive who is as addicted to work as I am to baseball.

Three, she has no chill. Probably wouldn't even crack a smile if she saw the sock I'm wearing on my left foot—a pirate's wooden leg. It kind of matches with my nutcracker sweatshirt, actually.

All of a sudden, the plane lurches and my right leg bounces off the floor like a basketball.

This time I'm unable to hold back a groan. Lights flash in my vision and I have to grit my teeth to not spew out a string of curses about la madre que lo parió that would probably make me go viral on the internet. The Duke and His Lady by Madeline Berkley lays forgotten on my lap. I hold onto my thigh as if that could offer any relief, just in time for the seat belt lights to come on.

"Attention, passengers, this is your captain speaking," a woman says over the speakers, complete with a *ho ho ho* that feels out of place. "We're running into some unexpected weather and this sleigh is about to get real bumpy."

My eye twitches. I grab harder onto my leg. I hate that I want to laugh but I can't.

"As of this moment, it is not allowed to use the facilities and you must return to your seats. Please stow your tables, sit upright, and keep your seatbelts fastened until the light goes off. Merry Christmas!"

The connection ends as another major lurch happens. This one makes someone scream. Pure reflex kicks in when both The Duke and His Lady and my neighbor's iPad fly up—by instinct I mean that I know that one of them would be a far worse projectile than the other, and I whip out my hand to catch the iPad in the air before it becomes a weapon. My book is lost after another violent shake, but that's the last of my concerns. It was easier to keep my leg stable when both of my hands were keeping it flat against the edge of the seat.

Curses start flying out of my mouth, but it's no biggie because everyone around is screaming—including neighbor lady. She's trying not to, but her hands clasped over her mouth can't stifle her terror.

This is starting to feel like a mechanical bull at the kind of dive bars in Texas that my buddy Cade Starr favors. I manage to wedge her iPad between my arm and my ribs with some difficulty, and lean forward to stabilize my knee as much as I can.

Another beep follows and the oxygen masks drop from the ceiling.

"Oh," I mutter amid the noise. Maybe we're in deeper shit than I realized. Maybe it doesn't matter if my knee gets worse because we're all gonna go up in flames.

Funny how I can see my whole life reflected on the sleek surface of the oxygen mask, since playing baseball with my neighbors in the streets of Kissimmee suburbia when I was seven, to winning my first tournaments in middle school, to getting drafted into the majors straight out of high school and buying a new house for my mom, to hoisting the World Series trophy this year while sitting on a wheel chair, to packing a baseball signed by the whole team into my backpack for my nephew.

My whole life has been baseball and it's been incredible, hard and isolating, but so rewarding.

Except I wanted more—more baseball, yes, but also just *more*. Something else aside from playing ball that is just mine and could keep me going well after my career was over. Something that looked like a family I could provide for. Is that going to stay just a dream? I can practically read the sports section headlines:

Lucky Rivera, dead before he could settle down like the rest of his friends.

The string of pessimistic crap is interrupted by a random hand in front of me. My neighbor is grabbing my oxygen mask, which I don't understand. She has one too, right?

But then I notice that hers isn't missing in action—she's already wearing it. She pulls at the mask before me and to my complete shock, puts it against my face. I feel the brush of her hand on my hair stretching out the elastic bad over my head until it snaps against my nape.

Our eyes meet. Hers are as wide as they can go, and I'm

sure mine look just as desperate. Verbal communication is impossible, but I get it. I know exactly what she's thinking.

Oh shitty shit of the stinkiest shits. This is bad of the baddest bads.

I don't know who does it, if her or me. Could be both at the same time. But in that nanosecond of understanding, it hits us that we're two lone travelers who are probably going to die alone before Christmas—and we don't want to. Die—or alone. So our hands clasp together.

She grabs my hand with shocking strength, five icicles for fingers lacing between mine and gripping in a vise. I do the same, and then I start to pray. I pray even harder than I did after my ACL snapped like a saltine cracker. Another violent shake makes the businesswoman squeeze her eyes shut but I can't. A perverse part of me wants to be fully awake for that final moment.

And yet… it never comes.

As abruptly as the turbulence started, it stops.

Somehow, my stomach churns at this moment, when we go from being tumbled like clothes in the dryer to gliding smoothly like we're skating on ice.

"Attention passengers," the captain says over the intercom again. "Due to the harsh weather conditions we're forced to make an emergency landing on Wilmington, Delaware—"

"Delaware?" my neighbor screeches.

"—Please stay seated and keep your seatbelts fastened because this may get bumpy again."

Why does the captain sound almost amused?

I swallow hard so I don't barf the banana dancing a jig in my belly. Then one hand isn't enough—neighbor and I grab onto each other for dear life as much as the wide first class armrests between us allow. My legs, hers, and every single small item in the cabin bounces up and down. I no longer feel pain, I'm not even sure I'm in my body anymore.

And then, with a deafening screech and a booming noise, the plane touches down.

CHAPTER 4
CAMILA

Is it possible to throw up one's heart?

The seatbelt digs against my hips and stomach as my body jerks upward, which can only mean one thing—we're losing height way too fast. I squeeze my eyes shut as tight as I can, bracing for a catastrophic impact.

In the next nanoseconds, my mind races with a million thoughts. I never would've thought the day would come where I'd resent the extra seating space that first class offers, but I wish I could just disappear in this guy's arms. I don't know why, but confronted with death that's the only thing I want to do. I don't want to die alone. That would suck way too bad after having spent my whole life basically on my own.

His hands are calloused but much warmer than mine, and with my eyes closed they're the only reminder that this is really happening. It's unfortunately not a nightmare.

We jerk and bounce as the plane touches ground. Something pelts me over the head and I yelp, shrinking myself as low on the seat as I can. I end up wedging my head against Lucky Rivera's side like I'm a goat trying to start a fight.

Something falls over my head and I stiffen. Except this time it's a gentle thing. And warm. A blanket?

The friction between the tires and the tarmac makes an agonizing wail that pierces my ears. I don't know if it's because of wind or ice or both, but the plane doesn't go straight. We swing from one side to the other, still going so fast that the tires are going to burn to nothing. I pray that there's nothing in the way for us to crash into and that we can make it out of this. I'll start going to mass regularly after this. I'll donate to charities. I'll even go to *SPORTY*'s Christmas party this year fully decked in an elf costume—heck, I'll wear a beard and a pot belly if they want me to.

"Please, please," I beg under my breath, drowned by the screams and the noise.

And then… nothing.

Nothing?

I crack one eye open. The first thing I notice is how both of my hands are tangled in Lucky Rivera's. Someone's breathing like a race horse. It clicks a moment later that it's me. I open my other eye and lift my head. Lucky's face is pale and he's also glancing at our surroundings to take in whatever reality we're facing.

The cabin has gone quiet as the plane continues moving, now in a normal taxying speed. Even though I have the window seat, I can see all sorts of trash strewn down the aisle, and maybe what pelted me on the head earlier is the random hoodie that is now half hanging from the seat in front of me.

Slowly, my seat mate turns to me. His eyes are wide, a little unfocused, but so very bright. They seem to tell me *we made it*, and I radiate it right back at him.

"Attention, passengers," the captain says again. "We have safely landed in Wilmington, Delaware. We kindly ask for your patience as we wait for a gate. We shall provide drinks and refreshments courtesy of Horizon Airways during the wait. Thank you for flying with us and Merry Christmas!"

My teeth gnash. A burst of energy explodes inside of me and I tear my hands from Lucky's to remove my mask. "*Merry Christmas?* Is she trying to act like this is all normal and we almost didn't just die?"

Lucky also takes off the mask that I impulsively put on his face. "I knew the ho ho ho-ing earlier was a red flag."

"I would like to wrap a garland around her neck and—"

"But on the other hand," the baseball player interrupts me. "She did land us in one piece, I think."

I clamp my mouth shut. "Hmph."

For the first time since the turbulence, Lucky's lips twitch with amusement. If it hadn't been for him—or his hands, I guess—I'd have endured this all by myself and might've crapped my skirt. So I'll allow him to laugh at my expense all he wants, I don't care anymore.

The biggest irony of all is when the seatbelt light comes off. That's when the other passengers start to come back to life. Some people jump out of their seats, overjoyed that they just can. Someone's crying. Someone else is yelling about who knows what, it's in a language that isn't in my lexicon.

"So, that really just happened, huh?" This is when I finally notice the rasp in his voice, like he did his fair share of screaming along with everyone else.

"It did." I hate how my voice trembles instead. I lean away toward the window, putting distance now that I don't need to grab onto him for dear life.

"By the way." He shifts and produces my iPad from under his arm. "Hope I didn't crush it. If I did, I'll pay for it."

My eyebrows rise. I forgot about my iPad—heck, I forgot about work for the first time ever. Where are my damn shoes? With a shaky breath, I take back the device. "Thanks."

I'm so rattled that I don't even want to fire it up to look at reports again. I just want to… sit here and do nothing but contemplate the fragility of existence—not an exercise I thought I'd be going through on a simple domestic flight that should've been a direct connection. Now I'm who knows where, who knows how far from my destination.

"I'm buying shoes the second I'm in this airport," I say aloud, surprising myself.

Is that what matters the most? No. And yet it's what I'm going to focus on.

"Good idea, you deserve a treat after this." Lucky pauses, leaning his head back. "I should get one too. Maybe pizza?"

"Hi again." The flight attendant from earlier appears by us, wheeling a cart and wearing a much more strained smile. "Can I offer you a drink or a snack?"

"How about both?" Lucky asks right away.

"Of course. We have spirits and soft drinks, as well as sweet and savory snacks."

He turns to me, like signaling me to make my request first. I lift my chin and say, "Can I just have twice the normal amount of red wine?"

"Yes," the woman says right away, past caring for the airline's bottom line when she knows anyone on this plane, but especially on this section, could be itching for a lawsuit. Lucky for her I'm too busy for that mess and am really just after getting plastered.

Her hands shake as she passes me a plastic cup filled near to the brim. I take it and immediately start sipping. Meanwhile, she turns to the famous baseball player.

"And for you, sir?"

"I'll have what she's having." He jerks a thumb in my direction and after a moment, he's also bestowed with a drink. Turning to me, he exclaims, "Cheers, to staying alive."

Nodding, I clink my cup with his. "To staying alive."

We nearly down the whole thing in one go.

"I'm going to need more where that came from," I say, wiping the corner of my lips with my thumb where a bead of wine threatened to fall.

"Don't worry, I'll flag her the second I see her."

He does good on his promise. At the first opportunity, Lucky gets us two generous refills and we're well on our way to a buzz. Especially me, being smaller than he is.

Once he sets his empty cup down, he runs his hands up and down his face and into the curls atop his head, groaning. "Qué mucho apesta esto," he suddenly says in the most Boricua accent I've ever heard. "This was already a tough trip with my knee like this. How the hell am I going to get to Mapleton now?"

I do a double take. "Wait, so Mapleton is also your destination? Not like, a layover?"

"Also?" He turns to me and blinks hard. "Don't tell me…"

Shit. That was the wine or the near death experience what made me slip. Maybe both. Usually I'm a vault.

Then again, the guy kept me sane through one of the scariest episodes in my life. Maybe I can even, erm, collaborate on making our way to Mapleton without losing our last marbles.

Clearing my throat, I extend my right hand out to him. "Nice to meet you, Lucky Rivera. I'm Camila Puig—Camila, not Cam—and I have a proposal for you."

"Gee, at least buy me dinner first."

I ignore that. "Since we're headed in the same direction, how about we find a solution together?"

He tilts his head. "No offense, Camila, not Cam, but you don't seem like the kind of person who'd be comfortable with that."

"Normally, no," I admit, clearing my throat. "But you've shown yourself to be pretty reasonable. Besides…" I pause, forcing myself to not look around. "I can stab you with my heels if you act up. As soon as I find them."

He's the first and only person in first class who laughs. It turns heads, not just because the sound is jarring in the aftermath of the drama we all just went through, but also because it's a good, solid laugh. Hearty, a little boyish, completely free and unnecessarily warm.

"Deal." He grabs my hand for a friendly shake that doesn't strangle, yet leaves my hand tingling.

CHAPTER 5
LUCKY

blow a raspberry. There's just something really funny about seeing this high powered executive walking up and down the plane aisle in her torn tights, carrying one heel in her hand while she looks for the other one. A giggle escapes from my yap and a little voice in my head tells me that the third double shot of cheap wine was probably a bad idea.

Like her, half of the passengers are ambling about looking for the shit that flew around during the turbulence. Maybe we're not the only ones who got tipsy right after, or maybe the near tragedy did one good thing in bringing out the best in people, but passengers have been trying to help each other.

So far, Camila's lone heel is unaccounted for along with a stuffed rabbit, my book, someone's Apple pen that miraculously didn't stab anyone in the eye, a pair of reading glasses, and a neck pillow that looks like a croissant. I don't know how that one remains lost, unless there's a thief who is really into pastry shaped pillows.

I can't do anything but watch. Even though an hour of waiting on this tarmac has allowed the pain in my knee to quiet down to a dull thud, the fact remains that I still have a recovering torn ACL that needs special therapy. I'm pretty much useless right now.

"I think I'm going to give up," Camila says with a mighty frown as she heads over to our row. You'd think the one heel she did find was her mortal enemy with how she glares at it.

"That's good, though. You just need one to stab me with."

"True." Nodding to herself, she resolves to give up the search and return to her seat.

I can't scoot so she has no choice but to hop over my leg, which makes me nervous every time. She grabs onto the seat in front of mine and even in my tipsy state I figure it's probably a bad idea to stare at her behind as she side steps in front of me. I nail my eyes to the ceiling, observing how she tries to avoid the oxygen masks that are still dangling from the ceiling. I think maybe we're supposed to stow them or something, but right now I have the coordination of a newborn foal.

Huffing, she throws herself on her seat. I wonder if she knows that her hair is a mess. When I met her at the VIP lounge, there was nary a hair out of place in her head. Now there are strands that have rioted at the top of her head, and there's a stubborn one sticking to her forehead. A flush has settled on her cheeks, but her eyes look surprisingly clear for someone who put just as much cheap wine down her guzzler.

"Entonces," I say, raising my phone screen toward her. "Lemme show you what I've found while you were out there playing Dora the Explorer."

"Dora who?"

Clearly she doesn't have kids around in her life.

"Anyway, I have ruled out the bus route." I show her one tab on my browser with a bus itinerary that is unrealistic for someone with an injured leg and for someone else who has two holes on her heels. "We'd basically have to take five buses and a taxi to make it all the way to Mapleton, and you'll agree that we're in no condition to do that."

"How about flights?" She raises her hand. "And before you sass me, I know that the storm is going to affect more than this flight alone. But I mean, we could take a big detour to like, Chicago or something, and then fly down from there."

I bite my lip as I switch tabs to show her. "Unfortunately, every damn flight to and from the main airports is booked. I'm talking we can't even get coach seats."

"Every flight?" She asks incredulously and I nod. "Out of hundreds, if not thousands of flights?"

"Yep."

"How is that possible?"

"I don't know if you've noticed," I say, dripping with sarcasm. "But we're five days away from Christmas. People plan trips around this time of year with months in advance. Airlines are also famous for overbooking so…"

This time the huff that she lets out makes her sound like a horse. I have to clear my throat exactly three times to not laugh.

"So then, what's the plan?" She turns a glare at me. "Do we even have one?"

Glancing around, I lower my voice because I'm sure everyone else has got to the exact same conclusion. "Car rental."

She gets with the program and also lowers her voice. "How long will it take?"

"Something like four and a half hours under normal conditions."

"Which means that in the present circumstances it can take anywhere from double that to two days."

I bob my head. "That's what I'm thinking. I don't know what commitments you have but that seems doable to me. As long as I get to Mapleton before Christmas, I don't care."

She folds her arms elegantly, crossing her legs at the same time. The pose is only betrayed by her lack of shoes. "I have a very important one-on-one with my boss in three days that I absolutely cannot miss. He also wants me to attend the company's Christmas party the day before that, but I don't mind if I miss it."

"So it sounds like we have three days to make it to Mapleton when it really should take us one."

"Right."

"The challenge is going to be right after we deplane," I keep whispering, leaning over the massive armrest. "Everybody's going to run like bulls out of the gates for the car rentals. And I don't know if you've noticed, I can't run quite as usual."

She glances down at my brace. "I'm not wasted, Lucky. Of course I remember that little fact."

"You'll have to do it. Our hopes are solely resting on your shoulders."

"But I only have one shoe." She blinks real slow. "I can't run in only one shoe."

"Give it to me straight, would you be able to run in both of them?"

After a long pause, she admits, "Fine, I'll run on barefoot."

"I'll buy you the most expensive pair of shoes in this entire airport once you've secured us a key." I thump my own chest. "It'll be my treat in appreciation for the effort."

"Socks too," Camila adds. "I will need to throw away these tights and wash my feet right after that."

I bet. There are no floors dirtier than those of an airport or a plane. I don't care if staff says that they're cleaned regularly. With so much foot traffic from all over the world, it's impossible to keep them clean.

"Deal."

We shake hands again.

"Attention, passengers." Everyone quiets down for the captain's new announcement. "We are now approaching gate D5 and will be offboarding in the next fifteen minutes. Thank you for flying with Horizon Airways, we wish you safe travels to your final destinations, and a Merry Christmas."

"Merry Christmas again, she says," Camila mumbles, sounding like she'd have spit on the floor if she could.

"Is your beef with the captain or with Christmas?"

"Neither," she says way too fast for it to be really nothing.

But the seatbelt lights come on and then the plane starts moving. We only exchange a few more ideas on how to make this work, which include her leaving her carryon suitcase behind so she can really make a dash for it. That means I'll have to take it somehow along with my crutches.

Once the light comes off, people start jumping to their feet again and attacking the overhead bins. Camila does the same, at least doing me the favor of getting her suitcase on the ground and wheeling it toward her seat so it's well out of the way. With a nod to my head, I wish her godspeed in the next leg of our journey. She nods right back wishing me the same. I watch from my seat as she takes advantage of her slight build to squeeze her way in between people.

The door opens and people start flooding out. I wait for a solid twenty minutes until the flight attendant is able to come with my crutches, and this is when things get really tricky. My left leg seems to also have forgotten how to stand. I pitch forward and catch myself on the seat in front of me, right in time to not hit my mug against one of the upright crutches.

"Puñeta," I grumble as I juggle to shrug on my backpack, use the right crutch, slide the other one on the raised handle of the carryon suitcase, and attempt one step. I put way too much weight on the carryon, almost expecting it to act like a crutch. It sends it to a tilt—and me too.

With a neanderthal yell, I catch myself against the back of my seat, saved by pure athleticism alone.

Clearly this is not gonna work. I need both crutches at the same time—or maybe this would've been possible without the extra wine. But I also can't break my promise to my new partner in crime and leave her stuff behind. I'm sure that will just lead to her driving away without me and leaving me stranded. And it's not like I can ask Mateo to come pick me up. I won't risk my brother driving in this storm if I can help it.

A new plan forms in my head. I lean against the seat to remove my belt and tie it around the left crutch and around the suitcase handle. Damn, I'm smart. I hope Camila doesn't mind that her fancy suitcase bumps into everything as I make my way out of the plane.

"Mr. Rivera?" someone asks the second I jump out of the plane and onto the ramp. I look up to a middle aged guy wearing an airport staff vest, motioning at a wheelchair. "I was told that you needed assistance, sir."

I open and close my mouth.

Now I really feel like a stereotypical jock with nothing but air in his head. I forgot this was a thing I could've booked all along, so used to traveling with the team that I am.

"Uh, yeah. Sure, man. Thanks." Then, out of curiosity, I ask, "Who sent you? The flight attendant?" She did seem very friendly.

"No, this strange lady without shoes."

Interesting. So she's capable of being nice after all.

The man helps me undo my makeshift engineering solution and sit my ass down on the chair. He wheels me with one hand, and Camila's suitcase with the other. He slips me through staff access paths that get me out in record time. Since I had no checked bags, we head straight to the car rentals area and that's when I realize the flaw in the plan.

Because while, yes, we correctly guessed that the lines to

rent cars would be infinite, it didn't occur to me to get her phone number so I could find her. And I literally can't spot her while I'm sitting on this chair.

I twist as far as the chair and my brace allow me and pin the assistance employee with a frenzied look. "I'll give you one hundred bucks if you can help me find my friend in this crowd."

He raises an eyebrow. "You can't just call him?"

"Her and I, uh, may have misplaced her phone number."

The look he gives me now can only be described as *shade*. "Do you even know her name?"

"Of course I do, she's my friend," I bluff right out of my ass, adding, "Camila Puig."

"Pew?"

"Puig."

"Pug?"

I press my lips because that one's funny, not gonna lie. "No, it's pronounced like Poo-eeg."

"That's a weird name," he says while grabbing the walkie talkie attached to his vest. He makes the request to locate one Camila Poo-eeg on behalf of Mr. Rivera to who knows who, and when he's done he extends his hands. "There, that'll be one hundred bucks."

"The deal includes finding her, not just calling on her."

But then, like magic, a voice over the speakers says, "Attention, please. Will Camila Pew head over to the information desk?" They repeat the announcement one more time, saying her last name wrong as well.

"It's Poo-eeg, not Pew." I rub my face. How will she even know this is about her? What if there's a real Camila Pew among the hundreds of people queueing up for a car?

But we only have to wait something like ten minutes until a frazzled executive appears in her otherwise impeccable fit, ruffled hair, and bare feet. Somehow she's still the most welcome sight.

"Oh, it's you," she says, almost disappointed.

"At least act happy that I brought your suitcase."

"One hundred dollars, right?" the employee says.

A deal is a deal, so I reach for my wallet and pay up. That also marks the end of his services, so I get on my foot and crutches once more.

Camila takes her suitcase from me. "Okay, I need to return to my spot in the line before someone decides to just take it. Meet me at the Emerald Car Rental booth when you can."

"Will do." She starts walking away and I call out, "And by the way, we'll need to exchange phone numbers after this to make our lives easier."

"Fine." Huffing, she turns and disappears among the crowd.

It takes me something like fifteen minutes to spot her. She's third place in line. A couple are at the counter, and behind them is a what looks like a group of five college friends. Hopefully that means just two cars and then it'll be our turn.

"I made it," I huff once I stand beside her.

"Right in time," Camila says in her businesslike tone.

And then a third voice asks, "Lucky? Is that you?"

I tear my attention from Camila, searching for the female voice. It seems familiar, which makes no sense.

But then the woman at the counter, the one who is renting a car along with a man, breaks away to face me. I squint, wondering if this is a trick of the wine or the knee pain, or if simply my brain got too rattled by the turbulence.

"Jasmine?" I ask, more out of confusion than real curiosity.

"Who?" Camila asks in just the same way as she earlier wondered about Dora the Explorer.

Swallowing down a grimace, I murmur, "My ex."

"Honey, who are you talking to?" the man next to Jasmine

asks, turning his attention away from the counter to find the source of the distraction. Going by the endearment, this must be Jasmine's new boo.

"Rupert?" Camila chokes out.

I look at her and mirror her. "Who?"

Slowly, swallowing hard, Camila glances up at me and responds, "*My* ex."

CHAPTER 6
CAMILA

This can't be happening.

Like, the bad weather thing I get. That affects everyone—probably millions of people are stranded across different airports right at this time. But this?

This feels like a personal catastrophe.

"Cam?" Sure enough, that's my ex fiancé using the nickname only very few people have ever been allowed to use in my entire life.

Steeling myself, I face him head on with a very dry "it's Camila to you."

"Is this a friend of yours?" the woman—what was her name? Janet?—asks Rupert.

Before he's able to offer some kind of excuse, I bluntly respond, "Rupert's ex fiancée that he jilted at the altar—oh, exactly three years ago today."

*

THREE YEARS AGO

Tis the season of giving—and by that I mean of giving me a headache.

Every year is the same freaking story. People's brains go on holiday regardless of what the business still needs. Every urgent request either comes back with a note about circling back after the holidays, or a shoddy out of office email that is as helpful as being ghosted.

I get it, the holidays are important for a lot of people, whether for family or religious reasons. Or simply for those who want to change scenery. Many of the people in the corporate world save their paid time off for the end of year holidays, and it's a great incentive for people to work hard throughout the year.

In fact, these are all the reasons why I booked my wedding for today, December 20th, rather than for Christmas itself. I respect people's properly scheduled days off.

If so, why is this damn supplier not joining our jointly scheduled meeting for *today* at exactly eleven minutes ago?

Huffing, I continue to pace back and forth in the middle of the empty bridal suite. I catch sight of my wedding dress in the mirror, a perfect creation of champagne silk in a mermaid silhouette that makes me look like a million bucks. Which is great because it nearly cost just as much. My tastefully made up face scrunches in the reflection as the call drops again. I wish I hadn't gone for the longer nail set, because I have to stop to tap more carefully on the phone to dial back. The dangling pearl earring stabs into my skin as I press the phone against my ear.

"C'mon, pick up, you jerk." If this supplier uses the holidays as excuse for ghosting me after all the quality issues they've been causing us, I'm going to remove them from the approved vendor list tomorrow.

Rather than the sound of the call connecting through, what cuts into the quiet is the door to my suite opening. I turn over my shoulder, somehow expecting my fiancé, but it's not Rupert.

It's my parents. The sight of them brings a wry smile to my lips.

My dad is also on his phone, angry whispering to who knows what about something that I have no doubt is lawyerly. Meanwhile, my mom does the same thing that I do—takes two steps, pauses to furiously type an email, another step followed by one more writing pause. Without getting in each other's way with the practice that thirty five years of marriage has conferred them, they manage to weave between the furniture and around each other to take seats at diametrically opposed ends of the room. That way Dad can continue his conversation, and Mom can keep focusing on her emails.

As my fifth call to the supplier disconnects, it strikes me that I'm well on track to becoming my parents.

Yes, they got married younger than I will but as tradeoff, I became an executive faster than them. And the man I chose to spend the rest of my life with is also like us: busy, important, and who values efficiency as much as I do.

Funny enough, he also agreed that marrying five days before Christmas was a statistically better choice, since people land themselves at the ER on Christmas itself more often than on the surrounding days.

Did I mention he's an attending physician at the ER, and the heir of the entire hospital chain?

That alone is like one hundred points in Rupert Montblanc's favor. But it also means that he's too busy to get upset at the fact that I'm just as committed to my work performance. We're the best match for each other.

The door opens again and for the second time, the one poking his head in isn't my groom—but the wedding planner.

He takes one look at me, furiously pacing with my phone glued to my ear, then to my parents, and sweeps his eyes around several times like he still can't believe that there are no brides-maids in this wedding.

Finally, he pulls his head out of his behind and whispers, "Ten minutes until we start."

I jerk a nod and wave at him to go organize whatever else he can in that time. For me, it should be plenty to tell the supplier where he can shove it expeditiously—but only if he picks up the damn call. I will *not* have a production stoppage right after the holidays because the leather batch for baseballs is all damaged, no sir.

After exactly nine more failed attempts, I'm interrupted by the wedding planner announcing that it's time. This is the only thing that tears my parents's and my attention away from our phones. They have the privilege of pocketing theirs—on Do Not Disturb, of course—but my dress has no pockets, and I have no choice but to leave it on the table.

"Guess I'll go sit at the pew," my mom announces with native-level English grammar, but the strong Venezuelan accent that never left her decades after leaving the country.

Her brown eyes find mine and she tries to convey some hidden meaning without the use of words, like I'm supposed to be able to read her mind. She surprises me by reaching for my hand and giving it a squeeze. Hers is much colder than mine, like maybe the heating in this church isn't strong enough for her. Without further ado, she slips out of the door to make her way through the congregation.

I cast one last look at my phone once I'm standing by the door, bouquet of white roses in hand and intricate lace and pearl veil cast over my face. It will probably be more efficient to go through the wedding first and call the supplier again after. It might also give the jerk a false sense that I've given up too, and the shock of seeing my name on the screen of his phone again might be all it takes to get him to answer.

Nodding more to myself than to my dad, I lace my hand around his arm to wait for our cue.

"Camila," Dad says in that way he has of delivering syllables in the most curt ways. "Don't forget to smile at all times, there will be cameras everywhere."

I refrain from telling him that neither Rupert nor I are celebrities, but it's still a pretty high profile wedding between the youngest executive of a sports brand that is beloved around the world, and the heir of a major chain of hospitals across the east coast.

But more importantly, it's the wedding of the only daughter to Carlos and Ludmila Puig, and if anyone expects perfection it's them.

Perfection used to mean having the best grades, graduating from Harvard, and rising up the ranks of *SPORTY*'s leadership in record speed. I guess it now means looking like the happiest bride on the planet.

"Any other advice?" I ask while practicing a placid smile that won't hurt my face.

"No, you won't need it. You do everything well."

My eyebrows twitch and I catch myself right in time to stifle the frown.

That's as much of a compliment as I'm ever going to get from my bullheaded, barely present father. And yet it's disappointing because *well* isn't enough. He's been married for longer than I've lived, and I was hoping for some inspiration from that.

But it's my fault. Why did I not think about asking about how to make marriage a success until this moment?

The wedding march begins playing outside. A side glance at my father's profile tells me that his mind is elsewhere—probably on the call he had to cut short. That would explain why he had no advice for me; he simply can't get his mind to stop working. Which I can relate to, because in all honesty I'm more annoyed at the fact that a supplier is shorting *SPORTY* on leather than I am at the fact that my dad's only going to walk me down the aisle by muscle memory alone.

I know that when I walk out into the church, one half will be packed with people—the one from Rupert's family. I'll recognize only a handful of them, the ones I've seen over Thanksgiving at his family home and a few of his med school friends, but the majority will be complete strangers.

Meanwhile, my side of the church will be half empty.

That's what happens when you're the only daughter of two parents who were also only children, of a family of high powered expats whose only acquaintances are colleagues. I could've stuffed the place with *SPORTY* coworkers, but I have a very strict policy of keeping my personal and professional lives separate.

And so I wait in this suite with only my dad for company.

Just as he's reaching for a peek at his phone, the music outside stops and murmurs rise. Dad and I exchange a glance, pulled by the same confusion. Shouldn't the wedding march be starting instead? I guess we're both living in the moment at last.

"Weird," I whisper in the quiet.

Dad's forehead scrunches and he hums a little from his throat. His attention turns to the door, which remains closed.

"Very weird," he says after a moment. Reaching for my hand at the crook of his arm, he frees himself and heads for the door. "I'll go see what the problem is with the music."

"But what if our turn comes?"

Dad glances over his shoulder. "My one and only daughter isn't walking down the aisle in silence." Harrumphing, he leaves the waiting suite.

I deflate with a sigh so profound that I can hear a tight stitch of my dress snap. That forces me to stand upright again and I grab a firmer hold of my bouquet. I pay attention to the fragrance of the roses for the first time. They're massive white buttons, stripped of the thorns that protect them, adorned with baby's breath and delicate stalks with fake pearls that are meant to imitate the morning dew. I lift the bouquet to my face and allow myself a deep inhale, and—

My phone starts buzzing.

I pick up my dress and power walk across the suite. Leaving the flowers on the table, I turn my phone to see who's calling.

"Ah hah!" I pump a fist in victory and answer the call. "Paul, this is Camila from *SPORTY*. How are you?"

"Amazed that you called me exactly seventeen times in a row over the holidays," he responds, sounding genuinely shocked.

"It's not the holidays yet, and we booked our meeting with plenty of time in advance," I correct him. "Your people haven't confirmed when we can expect the leather shipment to replace the bad batch, and we're facing a potential production stoppage."

He grunts with gusto. "Listen, we both know you have plenty of stock. My planners are already on holiday but I'm sure this is something we can fix quickly in the new year."

"Good to know that that's as much as you value our business," I return in the calmest, iciest tone of voice.

"W-Well—" the man stammers, about to deliver some half baked excuse in the hopes of not losing the massive *SPORTY* business he's about to, but that's when the door opens again.

This time it's not the party planner or either of my parents. It's my fiancé.

Vaguely, I remember that some people think it's bad luck for the groom to see the bride in her wedding dress. I don't particularly care about that as much as I do about the fact that his expression is off. And that by no normal circumstances is it normal for him to be here, rather than waiting for me at the altar.

To the phone, I say, "You better send me a confirmation of the shipment *or* of giving up your position as preferred supplier by end of business, whichever will make your holidays more enjoyable." I click off the call and set my phone down on the table.

Rupert watches me with attention but in complete silence.

"Rupert? What are you doing here?" I prod when the quiet keeps stretching.

"We need to talk."

This time it's the supplier who calls me again, how the turntables and all that. But I've said my piece and that's not going to change.

Ignoring my phone, I focus on Rupert instead. "I'm listening."

He runs his hand through his hair, ruining the styling that made him look like blond Ken. Whatever this is has him distraught. I pick up my skirt and approach, intending to fix his hair. But he pulls away so abruptly that he almost loses his balance.

We both stand suspended in shock at his reaction.

For the first time during our engagement, I get a cold tingle at the base of my spine that tells me something isn't right.

Rupert straightens up and slips a finger into the knot of his white tie to loosen it. Then he unbuttons his jacket and vest, and messes his hair again.

"What are you doing? You're going to ruin—"

But he interrupts me. "I've changed my mind."

"It's too late to go for the bow tie," I say, rolling my eyes. He's been debating about this almost obsessively the past week. "Unless you want to stop the wedding so you can go shopping for a different neck accessory?"

"I do want to do that—the wedding, that is."

I blink a few times, uncomprehending. "Come again?"

Rupert looks away from me, his eyes falling on the bouquet of white roses. "Cam, I'm not going to marry you."

Somehow my high IQ is not IQing right now.

"You *what?*"

"I'm cancelling the wedding." Now he runs both hands through his hair and I no longer move to fix it. "I'm doing us both a favor, really. We shouldn't have let it come this far."

"What the hell are you talking about, Rupert Montblanc?"

He shushes me. "Is that really the language you should be using at church, Cam?"

"Camila to you," I swipe back, folding my arms. "Forget the language and explain yourself, because I have no idea where this is all coming from."

"You don't?" I sure as shit don't—and I also don't understand why he looks so flabbergasted. "Camila, all we ever do is work. There you are, ripping a new one to your suppliers minutes away from your wedding. And here I am"—he interrupts himself to find his phone in the pocket of his tux jacket—"Getting a call for an emergency surgery."

"Oh." I relax. "That's important, though. We can postpone the ceremony. I'm sure everyone will understand that there are higher priorities."

"And that's precisely the problem!" Rupert exclaims, pointing at me with the phone. "Everything else is more important than us, and that's why I'm cancelling this damn wedding."

His words echo against the walls—and in my head, over and over until they finally click.

A dart of ice spears through my chest when I realize what's really happening. What was never a flaw in our relationship to me is apparently enough to call it all off for him.

And yet all I can say is, "Language, Rupert."

He starts shaking his head, and while doing so his eyes

sweep up and down my dress. Something akin to regret paints his features. "You really had me fooled into thinking this was going to work, huh?"

I'm a rubber band stretched too thin and finally snap. "Please, don't gaslight me. I never pretended to be different from who I am."

"You're right, my own eyes are the ones who fooled me into thinking you were wife material."

I hate that a gasp comes out of my my lips, emptying my lungs and leaving only hurt in my chest.

I hate that this hurts, that instead of proceeding with the schedule for the day, I have to stand here and listen to thinly veiled barbs that attempt to place the blame on this catastrophe on me, when I haven't done jackshit to deserve it.

Actually, who said I have to stand here and take it?

I grab my phone from the table and push past him, saying, "Have it your way, Rupert. The wedding is off." And before he can pull the same stunt as the supplier of calling back to beg, I storm out of the suite and keep going until I find myself alone in the middle of a snowy parking lot.

My phone buzzes with an incoming message and for a second I wonder if it's Rupert, asking me to come back. Instead, it's an email from the supplier outlining all the reasons why he can't expedite the shipment before the end of the calendar year. Like I'm not even worth the effort at work either.

When my parents come out of the church carrying my coat and their car keys, their faces dark like storms, is when I realize that for the first time in memory, I have failed—both at my job and at my life.

*

PRESENT

Wow, maybe the fourth cup of wine was a bad idea. I swallow with difficulty, focusing every ounce of willpower to not let it show that the memory still slices me like an unexpected and deep paper cut.

Beside me, Lucky Rivera hisses like this hurts him more than his injury. "That's rough, buddy," he whispers just for me to hear, and it gives me the lifeline I desperately needed to feign normalcy.

I glance at him and ask, "Did you just quote Avatar the Last Airbender to me?"

Lucky's eyes bulge. "*You* have watched Avatar but don't know who Dora the Explorer is?"

"Why do I detect extra emphasis?" I frown in an exaggerated way. Bless him for being a natural at tangents, I can't even tell if this conversation is real or for my sake.

"I just thought you'd watch something like true crime rather than cartoons."

Oh, so this whole dialogue isn't just to help me save face. He really had me pegged for someone who is dead serious both in her life and with her entertainment.

I still haven't recovered from the offense I fully take at that comment, when one of the dude bros in front of us says to Rupert and his companion, "Yo, you're holding up the line."

"Right." As he guides his new companion back to the counter, Rupert tells me, "Let's, uh—Let's catch up when we're done here, shall we?" Fortunately, he doesn't wait for my response.

One could say that Lucky and I are also companions because we've decided to join efforts on our quest to get to Mapleton. Yet I'm sure that's not what those two are. Spouses? Fiancés? Just a couple? Surely not coworkers. No one at

SPORTY would dare to put his hands at the small of my waist like Rupert is doing to Janine.

"What's the game plan?"

I glance back at Lucky who is balanced on his crutches behind me. "What do you mean?"

"I mean, if the dictionary had to cite an example under the word *awkward* this would be it." He points ahead with his lips, at his ex and my ex that have turned out to be very much together. "What do we do? Bail?"

"And lose our spot on the line?" I scoff and hoist the strap of my purse higher, like I'm getting ready to face a storm all by myself. "Absolutely not."

"Whew, I'm glad because I really don't want to attempt a quick Irish goodbye on these." He waves one of his crutches before settling it back down. But then something terrible happens—his expression transforms from mild amusement into pity. "Is it really true, then? That jerk left you at the altar?"

"Can you please forget you heard that?" I mutter through gritted teeth.

"Kinda can't. It was the juiciest bit of information I've heard all year and trust me, it's been an eventful one."

I kick at my suitcase with my big toe, debating whether to keep what's left of my dignity. But that's when I realize that I'm carrying one heel in my purse and I probably look like a trash raccoon. I don't have any dignity anymore.

"It wasn't at the altar per se. He called the wedding off before the wedding march started."

"*He* called it off?" Lucky grimaces in pure incredulity. "Here I was sure that you were the one who realized that you couldn't possibly tie yourself for life to someone named Rupert."

I snort. The dude bros part for a brief moment, allowing me a peek at the stunning woman holding Rupert's arm. She has luxurious long black hair and wears a stylish winter coat. I bet she even has shoes on.

"What about you and Janice? What's the story there?"

"You mean Jasmine?" Lucky shrugs. "She dumped me."

My eyebrows rise, not only surprised that her name is actually Jasmine, but also at what he just said. "You got dumped."

"Yes."

"You," I reiterate, pointing at his face. "A handsome, professional athlete who makes millions per year?"

His lips stretch into a smile. "So you think I'm handsome?"

"In the same way that I think a painting by Picasso looks good."

"I'll have you know my face is symmetrical and my mouth isn't above my eyes," Lucky teases back. When I don't engage further, he deflates a little. "And yeah, she dumped my handsome face because I'm—and I quote—too unserious."

I nod more to myself than to him. "I have noticed that too."

A corner of his lips ticks upward. "Let me guess, you got dumped because you're *too* serious."

I stay as quiet as a tomb.

"Finally our turn," one of the dude bros says, advancing on the now empty counter.

For a second I relax, thinking that Rupert and Jasmine did the whole Irish goodbye themselves, but of course life can't be that kind to me. Instead, they're heading right over, with Rupert twirling a rental car key on his finger.

"Hello again," Jasmine says, and I notice that she has dimples. Not only is her hair perfect and her outfit travel appropriate, but she also has two freaking little dots that appear on her cheeks when she smiles. Outrageous. Worse still, she offers her right hand to me, "I'm Jasmine Santos, Rupert's fiancée—the new one, I guess." She chuckles not meanly, but like she's so un-threatened by me that she just finds this amusing.

And fine, I'm not angling for her man at all. In fact, I'd rather pretend like he doesn't even exist. But it does rankle that he found a replacement, and that she's freaking perfect.

I pump her hand clinically. "Camila Puig." No nice to meet you or further pleasantries, I'm sure this conversation will be over in a minute.

"And you are?" Rupert asks to Lucky.

Before he can respond, the dude bros burst into groans and a louder voice among them shouts, "What do you mean you ran out of rentals? We've been waiting for one hour here!"

Without thinking, I grab onto Lucky's arm for support. But even if I was to faint, it's not like he could catch me—or that he would, even.

However, the move doesn't go unnoticed by my ex.

Lucky, bless him, doesn't seem to catch any of this. Instead, he leans toward me, real worry lining his eyes for the first time since the wine relaxed us. "Shit, how are we gonna get to Mapleton now?"

That is the real question.

We could line up for one of the other rental companies but we'd start again at the back of the lines, and there's no guarantee that they'll have cars left at that point. The only reason I chose Emerald is because it's the designated car rental company for *SPORTY* employees and I would've got us a nice discount. How the hell was I supposed to know that they were almost out?

"I don't—"

"Mapleton?" Rupert asks. "You still live there?"

Meanwhile, Jasmine tilts her head, looking at her ex. "Why are you going to Mapleton? Last I checked you still lived in Orlando."

Rupert turns to her. "You checked?"

"It was a figure of speech, honey." She lightly taps his arm and that's when I notice the giant rock on her finger.

I once had an enormous hunk of mineral courtesy of Rupert as well, like maybe that's his taste. The one difference is that mine was set on a gold band and hers is on a white one.

Fiancée indeed.

Complaints spread from the dude bros and all the way down the line, and as people start to disperse to find other rentals, Rupert clears his throat and turns to us again, glancing down at Lucky's leg. "Well, you guys are in luck because we happen to be heading to Mapleton as well. Why don't we drive together?"

My mouth opens with, "Absolutely—"

"Yes," Lucky cuts me off, much louder. "That sounds like a great idea, Rudolph."

"Rupert." My ex frowns.

"Sorry, yes. Rupert." Lucky grins in a cheeky way that makes Jasmine's good mood falter for just a second. I narrow my eyes, trying to discern why, but I'm coming up short especially since I might have hallucinated it. She looks normal the next second.

"All right, then. Follow us." After a pause, Rupert adds, "At your own pace, of course. There's no rush."

I roll my eyes closed.

So this is why Rupert offered to help us, because seeing a guy on crutches and obviously in pain pressed his on-duty-doctor button. It's not because of me, obviously.

And it's not like I was hoping that to be the case, I just couldn't understand why he'd even offer. After all, he kicked me to the curb so hard that he even had me mail him my big engagement rock back, as long as it meant that he didn't have to see my face again.

"This is a terrible idea," I mutter to Lucky as we follow after our respective exes.

He speaks through clenched teeth as he slowly makes his way through the airport. "Do you have a better one? I mean, other than duking it out with hundreds of people for a scarce few rental cars."

I don't, and it makes me grind my molars. I hate that this trip has gotten so wildly out of my control, it feels like a very targeted punishment.

"Wait!" Lucky puts an arm up, stopping me. "We're both out of the duty free zone. Now we can't get you shoes."

"Trust me, that's not the worst part of this trip. In fact, not even the turbulence is." I motion at the backs of our exes. "That is."

CHAPTER 7
LUCKY

have a way different take. The worst part of this trip is that I have to make all this extra effort on an injured knee. At this point, I have transcended the feeling of pain and become pain itself. Every muscle in my body is tense—so much, in fact, that I can't even use my tongue to yap as usual. I'm just focused on navigating out of this place and getting onto that rental car, where I'll take my prescription pain relief and hopefully get some rest.

Finally we reach doors. Rupert activates the sensor and the doors part.

"Puñeta!" I exclaim, flinching against the rush of icy wind.

Beside me, Camila lets out the tiniest yelp, almost like she didn't intend it. She hugs herself, her fancy business-y coat too flimsy to protect her against this weather, and tries to put one foot in front over the other to cover it from the cold.

I throw self preservation out of the window and call out, "Jasmine?"

My ex stops just outside and turns to me, almost surprised that I'm here at all. "Um, yes?"

"Do you happen to have an extra pair of shoes that Camila

could borrow?" That's when she and Rupert—I still can't get over the dude's name—realize that Camila can't take a single step outside of the airport without risking frostbite. I clear my throat, "There was a mishap and I'm afraid one of her heels is no longer with us."

Through gritted teeth, Camila asks, "Did you just make it sound like the shoe is dead?"

"Isn't it, though?" I press my lips into a semblance of a smile, in too much discomfort to muster a real one.

"Goodness, I'm so sorry for not noticing." Jasmine rushes back inside, her fiancé in tow with their suitcases. "I'm sure I have an extra pair of socks and some sneakers. Hopefully they fit well enough."

Rupert frowns in a good impression of worry. "Honey, how about you help Cam and I go get the car? I'll just drive it over and that way none of you have to walk far."

"That's why I love you, honey. You're so sweet." Jasmine presses her lips onto her fiancé's cheek, thankfully sparing us from a more invested display of affection.

From the corner of my eye, I catch Camila's expression turn even frostier.

People keep trying to come in and out the doors, so while whatshisface exits toward the car rental lot, the rest of us move out of the way for Jasmine to open her suitcase and fish for the goodies. There is not a single free chair in this entire terminal and while I could lower to the floor, I'd rather not. Getting back up is a pain and I've already been putting too much strain on my left leg with my entire body weight to risk injuring it too. I have no choice but to lean against a trashcan.

Jasmine pulls up a pair of white socks. "I hope these are fine? They don't match your outfit but they're clean."

"Yes, thank you," the other woman responds in her usual curt tone. Anyone would think she's being rude, but she sounded exactly the same when she was tipsy so it seems like that's just how she is.

"And the other pair I have are my gym sneakers," Jasmine adds as she carefully digs through her stuff. "We look about the same size, so hopefully they fit."

"I'm sure they'll be better than losing her toes," I mumble. Both women give me the same kind of look, like my very honest quip wasn't welcome. I raise my hands in the air and decide to stay out of it.

"Thank you," one woman says coldly.

"You're welcome," the other responds warmly.

It amuses me that they both have the same thing in common: disliking me.

Turns out they have the same shoe size too, so Camila does quick work of outfitting herself. A relieved sigh comes out of her once she's standing on the gross floor not on her feet. She plucks the extra heel out of her purse and motions at me to move aside. I hop out of the way and she tosses the heel into the trash, lifting her chin almost in defiance.

She has pouty lips, I notice. They make her look stern even when she's doing something as silly as throwing away one shoe.

I bite my lips but it's too late. The almost chuckle leaked out enough for her to notice. She cocks an eyebrow in this regal way that would intimidate a lesser man. Or a man who wasn't a complete clown like me. I just grin back at her.

"So…" Jasmine says, elongating the word. "How did the two of you meet?"

Camila and I look at each other. I don't know if it's just me but the chair incident at the VIP lounge feels like it happened ten years ago already. She opens her mouth to say, "It was because of a—"

"I'm sorry, that's Rupert calling. One second." Jasmine pats her pockets until she produces her phone. She answers the call with a "hi, honey. Everything okay?"

Hmm, I don't think she ever had a nickname for me. I mean, Lucky's already one but everybody uses it. She just didn't give me a special one. Granted, we were only together for about a year, but back then I really thought we'd be it. I sure had my fair share of lovey dovey names for her.

Ironically, this isn't my first rodeo with knee issues. If I have two major defects it'd be my twisted personality and my knees. Plenty of guys in professional sport are hypermobile, which is both a blessing and a curse, and in my case it makes my joints prone to sprains. About two years ago I had a bad one—though on my left knee—and Jasmine was part of the medical team who took care of me. That's how we met. She was a nurse at the hospital in Orlando that I did my offseason rehab in.

"Perfect, we'll meet you out front in a second," she says to the phone, her face glowing in absolute happiness. Like hearing the dude's voice alone is enough to light up her world.

Huh.

I don't think I've ever made someone so happy, either.

As we begin the reverse trip back toward the doors, I mull over this. I'm a pretty simple guy, I have no problem admitting that one of the reasons I got into professional baseball is because I love to entertain people. Pulling off a feat of human motion to catch a ball and then hearing the collective awe of a stadium full of people is my vocation, but so is giving my friends funny socks that tear out a laugh, or giving my nephew a giggling fit while I mimic my teammates.

And yet those were precisely the things that made Jasmine pull away.

The attention from fans made her uncomfortable—especially when a subset of them started scrutinizing her every move and look on the internet. Even worse, my humor that at first was refreshing, quickly became repetitive and then childish. It was actually the main reason she cited when she broke up with me.

Do I think it was the actual reason? No. It was probably the most convenient way of saying that we weren't meant to be.

My chest does a damn twist. After that, I went through a brief period where I tried to change, and I was miserable without the damn funny socks. Living in that lie meant that I couldn't connect with anyone new, and so I reached a very simple conclusion.

If I wasn't worthy at my clown or at my down, then at least I shouldn't keep suffering.

And so I returned to my original clown ways, and everything was honky dory until this moment.

Her new man is right outside, waiting with the trunk popped and the passenger door opened for her. He rushes over to start getting everyone's suitcases on the back, including her ex's. I hold on to my backpack, though, because that's where my prescription and the gift for my nephew are. I gladly pass him my crutches and balance myself on one foot against the car to hop in the back.

We all let out various exclamations of relief when we're safely inside the car, doors closed keeping the frigid wind away. Camila shudders violently next to me, and I figure that since I run hot I can just give her my puffy team jacket.

As Rupert turns on the heating at full blast, Jasmine turns back to us and says, "So, you were about to tell me how the two of you met. I've been so curious from the beginning."

"Is that so?" I mutter, just stalling as I finish removing my jacket and pass it along to my partner in crime.

She shakes her head but I raise the garment higher, insisting until she finally gives up and takes it. Rather than shrugging it on, she places it on her lap like it's a blanket. I guess the skirt didn't provide enough covering.

"It's not an interesting story," Camila says in her clinical fashion. "We met at the Orlando airport."

"What are the odds, huh?" Rupert mentions at the same time as he fiddles with the GPS to find the route. "That both of our exes would meet and that both of your exes would be together."

"And what are the odds that we'd all end up taking this little road trip together, huh?" I snort softly. That settles a tense silence over the group and I lean forward to find my prescription, feeling a smidge bad for making things weird. "How about some music, then?"

"Good idea," the driver says. "Honey, how about you find us something nice?"

"Sure," she responds back all peppy like.

In contrast, she selects some piano thing and I don't know if it's the boring music, the meds acting quickly, or if it's the exhaustion—but I start drifting away, leaving them to deal with the awkwardness I caused.

CHAPTER 8
CAMILA

What the… Did this guy just fall asleep in a matter of seconds?

Worse still, did he legitimately just leave me to dry like a damn raisin in the oppressive silence he left in his wake?

"So…" Rupert trails off in a way that makes me cringe even harder. "Is anyone going to tell me who this guy who everyone else knows is?"

"Lucky?" his fiancée asks, incredulous. "You don't know who Lucky is? But I thought you liked sports, honey."

"He does?" I ask, eyebrows raising even though they can't see me. I don't ever recall Rupert talking about anything sports related, other than occasionally dropping the name of the company I work for.

He clears his throat. "It's a recent interest. I can't say I know a lot of athletes—especially the ones who haven't chanced upon my ER."

"True, you're still learning." She reaches out and strokes Rupert's cheek like she can't keep her hands off him. I grimace, unable to see myself ever being that affectionate with a guy. Or anyone. "Anyway," she continues, "that guy in the backseat is Lucky Rivera, star shortstop of the recent World Series champions—the Orlando Wild."

"Is that so?"

On cue, said star shortstop releases a little snore. His head is lolling to the right side, his body slowly pitching toward me.

"We met while he was rehabbing his knee the first time," the woman says.

"What kind of injury was it?" he asks, like that's what matters and not that his beloved's previous man was a freaking Adonis.

"Just a sprain, but it was pretty obvious already that his joints are his weak point." A loaded pause. "Well, one of his weak points."

That sounds way more intriguing than I care to admit and even if I wanted to, I get distracted by the fact that said man slides all the way over. His head falls on my shoulder, the curls at the top tickling my cheek. His hand slides from his lap to fall by my thigh. Between his incline angle, the sheer size of him, and the tiny backseat of this car, there is literally no space left in between us. My nose betrays me, flaring at the warm scent of clean man's hair and expensive cologne.

Of course, this is when Jasmine chooses to turn around. The lights from the street illuminate the surprise on her face as she takes in the scene.

Lowering her voice, she asks, "How long have you and Lucky been together?"

I freeze.

My mind goes from a tired buzz to activating at full throttle, reaching the same intensity of operation as I have when I'm in a *SPORTY* board meeting or when I'm wrestling with a misbehaving supplier.

I thought it had been obvious when I said we met at the

airport that I meant we met at the airport *today*. But now I see that it could also be interpreted as meaning we met sometime in the past at an airport. Like a meet cute that was even more ordinary than the actual way Lucky Rivera and I crossed paths.

And if I go along with this, I won't appear as a loser who's still salty that she got jilted.

I haven't the foggiest clue what the story is between Lucky and Jasmine, if their breakup one-sided or amicable. In either case, I'm sure he'd also prefer to save face, right?

Tightening my fists, I say, "Not very long. Just a few months, really."

And that'll be lie number one to keep track of. It shouldn't be hard to keep track when I just have to spin a story for four hours and some change. If Lucky remains passed out through that time, even better. He'll be completely spared from the mess.

"But you live in Mapleton, while he lives in Orlando?" my ex muses aloud.

Damn it. I must still be a bit tipsy if I didn't catch that plot hole in my story.

"It's a long distance relationship," I explain with surprisingly calm for someone who is lying out of her ass.

"So how come you're both traveling from Orlando to Mapleton together, then?"

I latch onto the weird fact that he shouldn't know. "How do you know where we're coming from?"

Rupert coughs a little. "I happened to overhear you when you were asking airport staff to send travel assistance to someone who was traveling with you from Orlando."

I sit back, feeling foolish that for a second I suspected my ex from three years ago to still be keeping tabs on me. But I can't use that as any sort of ammo to attack back, especially when it still has uncovered the flaw in my logic.

This is why I hate lying. It takes so much extra work to keep things straight.

"I had a conference about advanced robotics manufacturing in Orlando, so it was the perfect occasion to visit my b-boyfriend." I hope neither of them noticed the tiny stutter. "Now we're going up to spend a white Christmas together." There, believable enough.

"Sounds like the ideal setting for you, huh?" Rupert snorts.

"What do you mean?" I ask sharply, my hands wringing on my skirt.

But rather than catching me on the lie, he says, "Mixing love with work seems to be the ideal solution for you, since all you do is work."

My face twitches and I turn away. I ask to my reflection in the window, "Speaking from experience?"

What I thought would be an openly hostile quiet is diffused by none other than Jasmine. "That's a fact. Rupert and I work at Mapleton General together and one thing led to another."

"Is that so?" I repeat Rupert's earlier words but sardonically.

The streetlights are growing more and more distant, which tells me we're starting to leave civilization. One of them at the front bumps up the classical music and I take it as a hint to ease off the pettiness pedal for a bit. The baseball guy remains out cold even as I shift around, getting my iPad from my purse. I pull up the report I worked on briefly during the disastrous flight to distract myself.

What I'm trying to do is a bit wild. Enough to border on innovative for *SPORTY* standards. I have in my hands a production report that clearly shows all of the inefficiencies that could be solved by incorporating more automation onto the production floor. It would be a significant capital investment, but it would be paid off in just five years in labor savings.

I know that's not going to be popular at all—this will

require layoffs to work—but it's the only way I can envision to save the lead factory in Mapleton and be able to compete with lower cost factories abroad. Otherwise, we'd be staring down the barrel of more than a few layoffs.

That's why I went to that conference, to get some quotes. And that's why I have to make it to Mapleton as soon as this rental can take me there. I have a meeting where I'll be presenting these initial findings to my boss, *SPORTY*'s CEO, so I can get the green light to start the formal business case.

I almost forget I have a stranger man sleeping on my shoulder until he stirs a little. I tense, hoping he doesn't wake up and reveal my lie right away, but luck is on my side—literally—because he stays out cold.

In fact, he snuggles.

Shifting his head, he buries his face into the crook of my neck and shoulder. He inhales so deeply that it drowns the sound of the placid piano.

Heat explodes in my face and I get a coughing fit all on my own.

"Everything okay back there?" Jasmine questions.

"Of course," I say way snippier than necessary, but that's only because I'm dying of embarrassment.

Well, if Rupert had any doubts on whether Lucky and I were actually together, surely that dispelled them. Even my own hormones got confused by the unexpected intimacy of a guy taking a good whiff of my skin.

Goodness, do I even smell all right? I showered this morning but I feel so disgusting right now.

If I wasn't already eager to crawl into a dark hole, never to be seen again, my stomach goes ahead and shows me up by producing a loud, violent roar. Turns out that this is all it takes for Lucky to spring awake.

"¿Qué?" he asks, bleary.

"Good morning, sleeping beauty," Jasmine teases from the front.

"Morning?" Lucky straightens up and looks around, confused when he finds that it's even darker around him than before. He doesn't seem to have realized where he was sleeping.

I clear my throat. "Sorry about that. You can go back to sleep."

"Actually, we just passed a sign that said we're two miles away from a rest stop. We should probably get some provisions for the road, then you guys can take another nap back there if you want." Wow, Rupert sounds surprisingly sensible for someone who would probably prefer to toss me out of the window of the moving car.

"That's a great idea, I'm feeling quite hungry myself," Jasmine quips all good natured like.

Lucky cracks the father of all yawns, carefree because he has no idea that no matter where we end up going to eat, I'm going to take him aside and ask him to play the part of my boyfriend for the remainder of this trip.

CHAPTER 9
LUCKY

Something happened while I was out like a light. I can't see the expressions of the two people out front, but my travel buddy is the picture of displeasure. Her arms are folded so tight, it's a wonder she's not cutting off blood flow. She's firmly turned out to the window like she can't let anyone see her face, and I wonder if she's crying.

Bleh, I don't need to know any of these people in depth to know she's better off without someone who calls off a wedding right before they were supposed to say the I do's. I'm sure dude had plenty of chances to break things off in a less humiliating way, but must've chickened out every time. And how the hell is Jasmine cool with being engaged to someone like that?

I wish I could just fall asleep again, but I can't now that I'm up and aware of my stomach. Sighing, I check my phone to see the time. If the flight had transpired as expected, I'd be at the dinner table with my brother and his family.

Speaking of, I have approximately five million texts and missed calls from him. I try to sit up straighter, but that just bothers my knee so I stay slouched as I text back.

ME

Mala mía

There was a problem with the flight

Landed somewhere in Delaware instead

Driving up with some people to Mapleton

EL BRO

Dude I was about to call the police on your ass

ME

Perdón perdón. I was so tired that I fell asleep

I'll keep you posted on the way

EL BRO

Más te vale cabrón

Don't scare me like that

Ah yeah, nothing like the love of an older brother. I shake my head and tuck my phone back in my jean pockets.

After a while, whatshisface turns us into the parking lot of a strip mall in the outskirts of a small town in the middle of nowhere. The building has just three businesses: a diner, a souvenir shop, and the larger one gas station with a car repair shop at the back. That's probably anything anyone passing by could ever need from stopping here.

"Here we are," Rupert announces with the same self-satisfaction as if he'd planned this all along and not chanced it. "Looks like the place is open."

I refrain from pointing out how the neon open sign is lit up just as bright as the Christmas lights decking the whole building.

He parks the car and says, "Let me help you with your crutches. Lucky, was it?"

I don't like how the nickname that friends, family and fans use for me sounds from his mouth, and since he's neither of those f's, I respond with "yes, short for Lucas. You can call me Lucas."

Jasmine gives me a sharp look. She knows exactly what I'm thinking, and I don't particularly care if she now understands that I don't like her beau.

"I can get them," Camila chimes in all businesslike, and before anyone can react she opens the door and jumps out into the howling wind. The couple at the front exchange a look almost in confusion, but Rupert shrugs and they also get out of the car.

The other woman opens my car door and offers me the crutches, and I can't help but notice how she shivers from head to toe at the assault of the icy wind. It takes me some maneuvering to swivel around and position the crutches without hitting the car parked next to ours, and she waits patiently off to the side, wrapping her arms around herself like that's going to help her flimsy coat keep her warm. I wonder if there's something more suitable for her to wear at the souvenir shop.

I take a step away to make room for closing the door, but Rupert gets it for me. "Ready?"

Suddenly I feel a pair of hands curling around my left bicep, and Camila says, "Actually, I need to talk with Lucky first. We'll catch up with you at the diner."

Rupert's eyes pingpong between us for a moment. "Sure. Don't stay out here too long though, or you'll both freeze."

"Right," the woman says curtly. She waits until the other two have disappeared to address me. "This is going to sound absolutely unhinged but—"

A gust of wind picks up, stabbing at everything in its path with enough violence that I rock back against the car. For a tropical boy I have a surprising tolerance to cold, but even I'm not immune to this shit. Especially when I realize I'm not wearing my jacket. She's also not wearing it, which means we left it in the locked car like two bright lightbulbs.

"Hey, how about we continue this conversation in there?" I jerk my thumb toward the souvenir shop. She clamps her mouth but ends up nodding.

Our teeth clatter as we make a slow trek across the small parking lot toward the store—all my fault, of course. I'm surprised she even keeps pace with me, when she seems to be struggling with the weather a lot more.

But she opens the door for me and as I hop along, I smile at her and say, "How chivalrous of you." Her eye twitches but she says nothing.

"Welcome to Bear Crossing Souvenirs," an elderly Black woman says from the counter, where she's sewing something. "Let me know if you need any help."

"Thank you," I respond to her with a polite nod of my head before turning to Camila. "So, you were saying?"

She's momentarily distracted by the contents of the store, her brown eyes wide and eyebrows raised like she's never been to such a place.

There's nothing too abnormal about it, racks of handmade magnets with a lot of bear motifs or the shapes of the state, postcards, kitchen trinkets that look made out of real wood, and a section for themed clothes. Those are the ones that seem to catch her interest—or rather, her disdain. Front and center is a Christmas sweater of a snowman with bear ears. It makes her lips curl and immediately makes me wonder if she'd hate it as much when she's all cozy and warm wearing it.

"Camila?" I prompt.

"Right." She clears her throat, shifting her attention back to me. "So, uh… I need your cooperation for something."

I tilt my head. "I'm all ears."

She lifts her chin, obviously ready for me to say no right away to whatever this is. "What happened is that your ex somehow seemed to think that you and I are together. Like together *together*."

Coughing, I say, "I got it the first time."

"The problem is that my ex didn't believe it, and that pissed me off."

"How dare he?" She gives me a look like she thinks I'm mocking her and okay, I kind of am. Partially. This is shaping up to be the most absurd thing I've ever heard in my life.

"Yes, it's impossible for me to get together with a handsome athlete so—"

"Don't get me wrong, I'm not fishing for a compliment, but I feel compelled to point out that you've called me handsome twice. It's going to start inflating my ego."

Her mouth snaps shut, eyebrows scrunching as she observes me like she can't quite make out what kind of sentient being I am. "The point is," she continues after a deep breath, "that I can't let him underestimate me. So I lied and said—"

"There it is." I snap my fingers. "The most absurd thing I've ever heard coming in three… two…"

She continues despite my bullshit. "I said that we're really *together*."

I blow a raspberry that erupts into a full blown guffaw. The store owner lifts her head from her needlework, pricks herself, and after a curse she decides to ignore us.

I keep laughing and laughing, too gone to even care that I'm losing my balance. I lean against the statue of a bear decked in a white beard, Santa hat, with lights strung around its body.

"Are you done?" Camila taps one foot on the floor. A foot that is now encased in my ex's sneakers.

Incontrollable giggles interrupt me every other word. "I just—I can't—believe this—this whole—mess is—happening."

"Are you going to help me or not?"

"I'll help you, woman." I try to gather my breath and wipe

the tears off my face with the back of my hands. "For all it's worth, I also can't stand your ex. There's something really annoying about him."

"You're telling me," she grouches. "Besides, I'm sure you want to show your own ex see that you've moved on too, right?"

I don't particularly care about what Jasmine thinks about me anymore. Rather, this seems like single wildest practical joke I can ever execute, and the stakes are extremely low because I'm never going to see these people again. I'd rather spend the next four hours of my life amused than wrapped up in more of that awkward silence.

"Fine, but if I'm going to pull this off as the biggest prank of my life, I have one condition."

"Prank?" She shakes her head like she's changed her mind and doesn't want any answers. "What condition?"

The corner of my mouth rises with amusement. "We have to really sell it."

"I'm not sleeping with you." I choke and she adds, "Or doing anything inappropriate."

"That's not what I was thinking at all." This time I'm coughing for real because her comment made my saliva go up the wrong way.

Once more she folds her arms tight, expression set in intimidating lines that my team's catcher would be jealous of. "Then what?"

Still struggling for air, I just point at the ugly Christmas sweater.

She stares at it for a long time, uncomprehending. "What do you mean, Lucas?"

"Lucky to you," I say, now with a raspy voice. "And what I mean is, we have to look the part."

"I fail to see how that sweater has anything to do with you acting as my boyfriend."

That last word is like a jolt to the system. It's almost as if someone had smacked me over the head and told me to pay attention. To what, I don't know. This is all a giant joke.

"Because," I say, ignoring the alarm bells going off in my head, "We're going to get couple ugly sweaters to really sell this."

CHAPTER 10
CAMILA

level him with my best penetrating look. Even my factory manager quakes at it. "You're kidding."

Lucky's lips remain curled. "Am I laughing?"

"Not on the outside, but on the inside you definitely are."

"I'll give you that one, but I'm actually serious. Think about it…" He readjusts his crutches so they dig in different spots of his armpits, and I realize he must be getting tired from standing by that ridiculous bear statue. "We can both agree that they're really obnoxious together, right?"

Reluctantly, I admit, "Yes."

"That's why the best thing we can do is be even more obnoxious than them."

"And we'll accomplish that by wearing matching ugly sweaters?" I can feel laser beams piercing my back, and I assume it's the store owner not appreciating my comment.

Lucky shrugs. "It's the tamest way I can think of to show that we're together *together*," he repeats my words back at me in a sarcastic tone.

"Fine," I agree then, because I'm not interested in exploring the alternatives. Four hours of wearing that thing in the backseat are going to be much more preferable than having to fake public displays of affection.

"Great." He extends his right hand. "Shake on it." When I don't move a muscle, he adds, "C'mon, this is how we've been sealing every deal we've struck up until now."

"Ugh." I shake his hand and try to pull mine away quickly, but he stops me.

His eyes are a reddish brown, like cherry wood, and the twinkling lights decorating the store make them look more mischievous than usual as he peruses me from top to bottom. "Tell you what," he says quite low. "I'm going to be a good boyfriend and get you a whole outfit."

I yank my hand free. "I'll pass. The sweaters will drive the point home well enough."

"So you'd rather stay freezing and wearing my ex's shoes?"

That slows my roll.

I look down at myself. My outfit was fine for the cool air conditioning of the conference hall and then for airport travel, but not for the actual temperatures outside. I also hate the fact that I'm wearing shoes shaped like someone else's feet, and I don't trust that the socks were actually clean. Not that my torn tights are any clean anyway.

I wish I could change into comfortable clothes of my own, but the fact is that nothing in my suitcase works for this abnormal occasion.

Again, I cast a look around at the store and try my best not to cringe at the assault on my eyeballs. They're very consistent with their bear theme and their love for the holiday, because every single item pays homage to both. Nothing here will fit me —my style, that is. There's just not enough black or sleek lines, but I don't really have another choice.

Expelling a heavy breath, I say, "Okay."

Right away, he turns to the store owner. "Excuse me, ma'am. Do you have this sweater for men and women?"

"Of course." Now that we're not just taking advantage of the heat in her store, she abandons her project on the counter and comes to join us. Humming as she looks at us, she guesses, "Women's size M and men's size L?"

"XL," he corrects her with a cheeky grin. "My shoulders actually need more fabric than it seems."

I stay mum because I really am a medium.

Lucky navigates by the wall of clothes, looking at various pieces until he pulls up a pair of jeans that seems sensible, until he splays them open.

Of course it has bears embroidered on the back pockets.

"No," I say immediately.

"But they're lined in fleece." He shows me the inside and sure enough, they look very warm.

I harrumph.

"They go very well with these socks," the lady adds helpfully, showing us a pair of fluffy socks in a red and green checkered pattern, with the ubiquitous bear embroidered on them.

"We'll take them. Do you have shoes?" he asks.

"My brother-in-law is a master leather worker and he makes amazing footwear. Follow me," she says and I sigh, obeying for once.

At the back of the store is a rack with different types of leather shoes, and thankfully none of them have any bears. I pluck a nice pair of boots from the rack and check the soles. They're textured enough that they'll be great for the thick of winter up in Mapleton. I wouldn't wear them for work, but they'll be just fine to go grocery shopping with.

"These will do," I tell her.

"The changing room is right behind that curtain, if you want to try things on."

"Yes, I... I think I'll just change into them, thank you." I accept the other garments from her and march myself into the changing room.

I make sure that the curtain is closed firmly so the two strangers can't peep inside. And okay, Lucky isn't a complete stranger at this point, we've been through some shit together already. But I still trust him as far as I can throw him—which is nowhere, since he's a whole hunk of muscle.

"Ugh." The complaint escapes from my lips when I realize that if I said that aloud he'd have made some sort of joke about it.

He's such a handful.

Which he'd also make fun of me for saying, according to the pattern I've detected.

The changing room is shockingly small. Even worse, once I strip off my clothes, the cold seeps right into my bones, to the point that wearing these silly clothes feels like a heavenly gift. They're very warm and soft, and I'm almost happy to be wearing them until I look at myself in the mirror.

"Carajo," I mutter. No one from *SPORTY* can ever see me in this, or I'll completely lose my reputation. Well, I'll just have to make sure that there are no pictures from this whole adventure.

Collecting my belongings, I exit the changing room and find that Lucky has also donned the matching Christmas sweater. It looks less silly on him because not only does it match the boyish smile that's always on his face, but he also does have shoulders that are a mile wide. In contrast, the sweater hangs very loose around his waist. I'm starting to get annoyed that he's so freaking attractive.

"All done?" he asks.

"Almost." I approach the counter where the woman is back to sitting with her sewing. Correction—her bear embroidery. "How much do I owe you?"

"Oh, it's already taken care of, miss."

"But…" Then it dawns on me.

"That's right, your new boyfriend paid for it." The amusement intensifies on Lucky's face. All I can do is release a shaky breath.

"Here, for your old stuff." The lady passes me a paper bag and I thank her for the foresight. I dump what otherwise was a great outfit on it that accentuated my best attributes while keeping it strictly professional. Right as we reach the door, the owner calls out to us. "Oh, and about that plan you were discussing?"

Lucky and I stop to face her.

"You didn't need matching clothes to convince anyone. All you need to do is kiss under some mistletoe and you're set." She wiggles her eyebrows at us.

How convenient that she says this after Lucky has purchased some of her goods.

"Thank you for the suggestion, ma'am," he says all polite and sweet like a church boy. El que no lo conoce que lo compre, as my mother sometimes said about my father.

I open the door, bracing against the inhospitable wind. But it doesn't bother me as much anymore. These clothes are a warm hug and I can't fault them for that.

"You heard that?" Lucky says from behind me as we walk down the strip mall. "All we need is some mistletoe."

"Don't even dream about it, Lucky Rivera."

His chuckles follow me as we walk into the diner, but one look from Rupert to Lucky's and my matching sweaters makes me realize that I'll do it. I'll kiss this stranger under the damn mistletoe if I can wipe the incredulity from my ex's mug.

CHAPTER 11
LUCKY

My situation forces everyone on the table to reshuffle, which lands us with Camila by the window so I can keep my right leg out extended without bumping into anyone, her ex across the table from me, and my ex across the table from Camila.

What is my life?

I don't know if to laugh or ask for a bottle of Don Q.

I do neither, not because I'm well behaved, or because there's no way this roadside diner has rum—but because this place is packed, and you just never know who might have their phones ready to record a drunk baseball player and go viral on social media.

Once we've all settled back on the booth, Jasmine stares pointedly at the matching sweaters Camila and I just changed into. "Looking festive, you guys."

"It was unintentional," I fib smoothly, picking up the menu to peruse it as I speak. "We just needed much warmer clothes for what this trip has become, and this is what they had available."

"I've never seen you wear something so cheerful, Cam."

Meanwhile, Ruperto or whatever coughs into his hand in an obvious attempt not to reveal how funny he finds it.

"You must not have seen all my facets," she retorts without much bite to her voice, even though her words are a whole burn.

"Camila is a lot more fun than anyone possibly imagines," I say, bumping my shoulder with hers. It makes her jolt and for a moment she seems to forget what she was doing.

"Camila?" His eyes narrow in open suspicion. "How come you don't call her Cam, like everyone close to her does?"

Both my supposed girlfriend and I freeze.

I convey the telepathic message to her that if she wanted me to play the part of her besotted boyfriend, I probably should've known something as basic as this. Unfortunately, while I don't get a telepathic message back from her, I can practically see her brain churning for a plausible excuse. I decide to spare her the trouble.

With all eyes on me, I raise my arm to bring it around Camila's shoulders and push her toward me. "That's because I'm not just everyone. I have a special name for Camila that is for her ears only. Isn't that right…" I trail off to leave them guessing.

Turning to my new partner in crime, I take advantage of her loose hair to hide my face. I pretend like I'm whispering an endearment when actually, what I say is "tenemos que hablar," and in Spanish, in case the other two still hear. Because the dude looks more American than a bald eagle, and Jasmine is from the Philippines and doesn't speak a lick of Spanish.

When I straighten back up, Jasmine is engrossed in the menu, but her guy is still watching us. To an onlooker he looks normal, calm even. But I can still detect the very strong eau de suspicion radiating off his pores.

I don't understand why this guy can't possibly believe that

his super hot and successful ex fiancée could possibly bag an also super hot World Series champion for a boyfriend. Either he thinks that I don't belong in the tightly controlled and high powered world of this woman—which, fair—or that she doesn't match his mental picture for what my girlfriend should look like. I don't particularly appreciate what either of those two things says about me, and it sure stokes my voracious competitive spirit.

Now I'm as determined to make him choke in his own judgements as I am to get my knee back in tiptop condition.

A waitress appears by our booth. The air around her tells me she's seen all the shit these roads can possibly bring to her doorstep, and she's not impressed by any of it. "What's it gonna be?" she says by way of greeting with a classic chainsmoker's voice.

"Do you guys know what you want?" RuPaul asks us.

The two women respond in affirmatives and I haven't paid a lick of attention to the menu, but I'm sure they'll have some kind of burger at least. I also nod.

He takes it as his cue to go first and he turns to the waitress. "I'll take the reuben sandwich with sweet potato fries." Then he turns to his fiancée. "And you, honey?"

My eye twitches. Did he just order before the women?

"Hmm." Jasmine, who was allegedly ready, still takes another second looking at the options. "Can I have the bacon omelet but with the bacon on the side, and replace the grits by a cup of fruit?"

"Uh huh," the waitress says with zero inflection in her voice as she jots it down. Like it doesn't matter if she thinks the order is ridiculous or the best thing since sliced bread.

There's a pause and I catch Camila staring at me like she's wondering if I'm also going to order before her. The thought of that appalls me and I motion at her to go first.

I don't know if I imagine it, but she gives me the tiniest,

infinitesimal nod that makes me feel like the most chivalrous of all gentlemen.

"Can I please have the soup of the day with a side of corn-bread? Thanks." She's curt, almost sounding more impolite than the other two, but it strikes me that she used the words please and thanks unlike the other couple.

Ironically, the no nonsense waitress offers a smile to Camila, and it clicks on me that these are two alike people. Direct, to the point, maybe abrasive to some, when they're just trying to be as efficient and practical as possible.

Meanwhile, Jasmine and her man speak in a warmer way, but they were far more impolite.

Dude aside, how had I never noticed that about my ex until this moment?

My head's still spinning as my turn comes. "I'd like to have a double cheeseburger with bacon, a side of fries, a side house salad, and Coke, please."

"Bacon on the side?" the woman asks sardonically.

I try not to grin. "Oh no, inside. And actually, let's make it double bacon."

She nods like this pleases her. "Coming right up."

Without realizing that my opinion of him gets gradually worse the longer I'm forced to be in his presence, Jasmine's man opens his mouth again. "Cam mentioned earlier while you napped that you met at an airport. How did that happen?"

Well, Ruben, we actually met some five hours ago at the Orlando airport thanks to there only being one chair at the VIP lounge. One thing led to the other and we're a couple now. Happy?

How would he react to the unvarnished truth?

But as hilarious as that would be, it would humiliate my alleged girlfriend and also me. Me because I have a very strong feeling that this dude can't imagine someone like me—the classic jock without two braincells to rub together—being with a smart and competent woman.

In a way, that's precisely what led to Jasmine dumping me. Her little quip of me being too unserious for her was code for she was better than that. And now look at her, bagged herself another healthcare professional, huh?

"It's Camila to you," the business executive repeats beside me.

I approve of that message so much that, unbidden, my arm tightens around her just a smidge.

"Right. Sorry."

"What happened was," I start, which makes her tense and the other two lean forward to hear the tale. "That a few months ago I had to travel separately from the team for a publicity commitment—"

"With *SPORTY*," Camila adds convincingly. Maybe she's not such a casual fan and knows that *SPORTY* is the Orlando Wild's main sponsor.

"Exactly," I reiterate. "And our paths crossed at the airport."

"The Mapleton airport?" dude asks, as if this plot hole was any important.

Camila immediately responds. "Of course."

I go with it. "I was just about to take a seat on the VIP lounge when she approached me."

Maybe twisting the truth with lies is enough for her to break her composure, because Camila sneaks her hand under the table and tries to pinch my thigh. *Tries* being the keyword —she discovers very quickly that it's all muscle. Or perhaps the reason for her annoyance is in me saying that she's the one who initiated contact. She's gonna love the next part then.

"And she said that she's a big fan and handed me her card." She seems the type to flirt with men through letterhead.

Giving up on pinching, Camila smacks my leg instead.

"A fan?" Rumilo or whatever raises his eyebrows.

Lifting her chin, Camila adds, "Yes, Lucky and the Wild bring a lot of revenue to *SPORTY*. Of course I'm their fan."

I'm sure that's true but it's weird for someone to point it out. Most of our fans enjoy our play, not how much money we make for a partner. I raise my free hand to scratch my head through my curls, finally losing the plot around this weird lie we're spinning.

"And anyway, I wasn't flirting," Camila says, taking back the narrative. "But he seems to have taken it that way and when he messaged me back he asked me out."

I press my lips but there's no hiding the smile forming on my face.

Clever, clever girl. She knew I was about to pass her off as the most interested party in this relationship—yeah, so I have an ego, sue me—and she flipped it back on me before I could land the punchline.

"She said no at first because she wanted to keep things professional, you know?" I shrug, falling in line with the new twist. "But eventually she fell for my charm. And my selfies."

The most curious thing happens. Everyone else on the table goes red.

Bunch of pervs.

They force me to cough so I don't guffaw in their faces.

"And here we are," Camila says like it's a period, although the confidence is a bit stripped off the words by how her voice has gone up a few octaves.

"And here I am," the waitress chimes in, carrying plates. "Soup of the day with cornbread, and double cheeseburger." She places down a large oval plate with the entirety of Camila's order, and then in a blatant display of acrobatics she takes three different plates from one arm and sets them before me. A massive burger with the juice still sizzling, a heaping mound of fries, and a whole garden of salad.

I stare at her with my mouth open and the waitress says,

"What? We're big baseball fans around here, we want to treat you."

Sometimes I forget that I'm a public figure, especially when I'm outside of Orlando or Puerto Rico. "Wow, thanks."

"And also we want to hang your picture on our wall."

My face splits into a grin. I appreciate her no nonsense attitude. "Of course."

With a nod, she disappears back between the busy tables.

The guy in front of me stares after her. "I hope she didn't forget our food."

"I'm sure she didn't." Jasmine picks up her glass of water for a little sip.

I decide that since my mom isn't watching me right now, I can toss my manners out the window. "I hope you don't mind if we start eating, right? Wouldn't want Camila's soup to get cold."

"Of course, go ahead," Rigoberto says, although his eyebrows are a pinch tighter.

The funniest part of the dinner is how their food arrives some fifteen minutes later, and since I'm done polishing my food way before them and I can't contribute to the team by driving, I decide to pick up the tab and get that picture taken care of.

Camila tags along as I make my slow, crutch-assisted way to the register. As we line up, she murmurs, "You said we needed to talk."

I barely hear her over the noise. Angling myself so that my back is toward the couple of our exes, I say, "Yeah, we're gonna need to establish a few details if we want this to work. Like, I should probably know that you go by Cam with your closest people."

She waves a hand. "You deflected that expertly."

"Guess I need to find you a nickname now."

"Don't you dare call me honey." Her brow crashes in annoyance.

I snort. "Please, I'm much more original than that."

"Nothing too embarrassing, then."

I ignore that. "I'll inform you when it comes to mind. You should probably also think of one. Plus we should know stuff like our birthdays, favorite colors, music genres, allergies… you know, the basics."

She notices that there's only one person left before it's our turn. "There's too much to cover in this short time. And besides, it's not like we can brainstorm while we're in the car with them."

"Why not?" Before she argues back, I add, "Give me your phone number."

She tilts her head. "Oh, by text?"

"You don't need to sound so surprised at me having an excellent idea."

Camila closes her eyes as in exasperation. Somewhere between paying the tab and taking pictures with the diner employees, Camila and I finally exchange phone numbers before the next leg of our little Christmas trip.

CHAPTER 12
CAMILA

n an absurd turn of events, I find myself again in the backseat of a car being driven by my ex, who is engaged to the ex of a famous World Series champion, the latter who is next to me—and with whom I'm exchanging a barrage of text messages with.

And who, by the way, demanded that I save him under my contacts as Boricua Bae.

BORICUA BAE

Fave color?

ME

Black

BORICUA BAE

Mine's purple. I blame the team

Fave number?

I grimace and turn to glare at him. He motions at my phone with those bow-shaped and full lips.

ME

Who cares

BORICUA BAE

I, your boyfriend, do

ME

Ugh

Then my favorite number is also black

BORICUA BAE

What? Black is not a number

ME

It is on a balance sheet

Black is good. Red is bad

BORICUA BAE

Fine you finance nerd, I'll allow it

It's very hard, but somehow I resist the urge to roll my eyes.

Meanwhile, our exes have moved on from instrumental music to Bing Crosby's Christmas hits. Every fiber of my being rebels against the classic crooner when I recall that it's Rupert's favorite. It makes me want to listen to death metal instead or something.

As alternative, I hyperfocus on texting again.

ME

I assume you have a favorite number?

BORICUA BAE

Of course I do

3. For three strikes, you know?

ME

You baseball nerd

His teeth glint in the dark with a wide grin. I don't need to ask but this guy's favorite thing—aside from baseball—is laughing. Or being amused. I bet if his future girlfriend gives him a book of jokes for his birthday he'd be elated. Bonus points if they're all dad jokes, he just seems that type.

BORICUA BAE

Okay, what's your absolute top pet peeve that you can't ever in a million years stand

ME

Inefficiency

He tears his eyes off his phone and just stares at me like he can't comprehend what language I'm even speaking.

Maybe it's because of the darkness, since we're driving down the highway in the middle of the night, and the only light comes from the headlights and the snowflakes catching on them. Maybe it's because this is a small sedan with a tiny backseat, which means Lucky Rivera and I are very close—much closer than we were on first class or even at the VIP lounge in MCO. But for the first time in… probably ever… I squirm.

I pick up my phone again to explain.

ME

I don't care if someone chews too loud or snores. What really makes me lose my mind is when someone purposely does things in the least effective way. Weaponized incompetence is the fastest way for me to send a man or an employee packing.

Too late I realize that I added a period, which I've been told by some colleagues makes a text message appear hostile. I debate whether to edit it out, but that would also be silly. Try-hard, even.

BORICUA BAE

That's fair

ME

Then why did you look so surprised?

I'm much more curious about the answer than I care to admit.

BORICUA BAE

I wasn't expecting an intellectual answer like that but that's on me. I'm not really an intellectual as you might've noticed

ME

You seem plenty smart to me

Not anyone would be able to assume the role of my significant other suddenly or convincingly

Lucky slowly lifts a hand and places it on his chest, giving me an 'aww' look.

BORICUA BAE

Well aren't you surprisingly sweet

Hey, what if I just call you sweetheart?

I snort a little.

ME

I thought you implied that you were more creative?

BORICUA BAE

Damn, okay. I see how it is

I do my best to prevent my lips from stretching into any sort of gesture, although the grumpy expression on his face is amusing.

Clearing my throat unfortunately catches the attention of the people out front. "How are things back there?" Jasmine asks, briefly glancing back at us.

"Fine," I respond for both of us.

As if the question wasn't actually addressed to me, she adds, "And your knee?"

"Doing okay as long as I don't move it," Lucky explains.

I'm annoyed.

It's a fact. Denying it would send me down the very inefficient spiral of denial, which only leads to confronting the topic in an even more painful way and timing.

What I don't quite understand is why I should be annoyed that Lucky's ex cares for his injury, when in fact I haven't asked him about it for… ever, actually. Not even while we were duking it out for a lounge chair.

I squirm again, the motion triggering some understanding. I'm not nice. I'm not a kind person. Thinking about others and their needs doesn't come naturally to me. I don't consider myself to be someone who puts my needs over others and makes them bend over backward for me, but not even spending the minimal energy to *consider* someone else's needs is also selfish. Because it means that I don't act accordingly, and the impact of that on other people has proven catastrophic.

Exhibit A: Rupert Montblanc at the wheel.

Exhibit B: every *SPORTY* employee who runs for cover when they see me coming.

Meanwhile, Lucky's ex who broke up with him—and for all intents and purposes doesn't harbor any feelings for him—shows with one simple question why she's a better person than I'll ever be.

It strikes me right here and now that if I wasn't stuck in a tiny car with these three strangers, I never would've confronted myself about this. I simply would've had no need. I'd have continued barreling through my life like the bulldozer I am, never understanding why everyone finds me so stinking intolerable.

BORICUA BAE

What's wrong?

The two simple works make my phone buzz in my hand and startle me.

I look up at the baseball guy, confused. He texts me again.

BORICUA BAE

You look like you saw a ghost

I'm pretty sure I'm making no facial expression whatsoever. It's what I've trained myself to do in my short but skyrocketing twelve-year-long career. Yet somehow this guy found a crack somewhere and read me like an open book.

Some alcohol might still be running through my veins, or it's the influence of the weird snowbear—is that even a word?—emblazoned across our chests. But I respond back honestly.

ME

To be honest I'm having a sudden existential crisis here

BORICUA BAE

Hmm

You do seem the type to live in your head

My cheek twitches.

BORICUA BAE

Choose the option you want me to act like right now:

A) Boyfriend

B) Friend

C) Stranger

I blink at the texts. This is probably the sweetest thing anyone has asked me in my life, and that includes when my parents asked me what I wanted El Niño Jesús to bring me for Christmas when I was a kid.

I begin typing a response but pause. My fingers move across the cellphone's keyboard, just typing in gibberish. Finally I erase everything and answer honestly.

ME

I don't know

The real life Lucky nods, like this actually makes total sense to him.

BORICUA BAE

LMK when you decide

And that is the second sweetest thing anyone has ever asked me. Just allowing me the time and space I need to figure something out, without adding extra pressure.

It takes me a moment to realize that we've been staring at each other for a while. And only because something makes our eye contact break.

"Oh, shit," Rupert murmurs over Bing Crosby and that's the only warning we get.

Next thing we know, the car goes freaking spinning.

CHAPTER 13
LUCKY

I like adventure as much as the next guy—hell, perhaps even more. I'm someone who makes a living off a ball after all. But I'm not really feeling this adventure so much anymore. I really didn't have black ice on my bingo card for my trip to spend Christmas with my brother's family and get ready for knee rehab.

Jasmine's screaming bloody murder, which helps no one.

Ruffalo grunts like a bull in heat while he tries to stay in control of the vehicle.

Camila is quiet as a tomb, but like during the very rough turbulence of the plane, her hand finds mine and squeezes in a vise.

For some reason I'm more annoyed than freaking out.

"For shit's sake, man. Stop hitting the brakes and just steer through it," I command from the back, even as being tossed this way and that sends stabs of pain up my knee and to my spine.

"How?" Rudolph shouts from the front, like he doesn't understand my very clear instructions.

"Foot off the gas pedal, you absolute—" A particularly

violent swerve saves me from calling him a very Puerto Rican, very not safe for work insult that includes the word *sucking*. But what spares him from my wrath is worse.

Dude drives us straight into a snow bank.

We jerk forward. The seatbelt catches me but my legs hit against the back of the driver's seat. And it hurts so bad that the big curse comes out of my mouth anyway.

Ironically, *White Christmas* continues to play on the sound system like nothing happened.

"Ow."

The tiny complaint comes from my seat mate. My lizard brain activates because this is a woman who showed zero discomfort despite the two gaping holes at her heels.

Pulling my head out of my own ass, I ask her, "Camila, are you okay?"

Her eyes are squeezed and she cracks one open almost tentatively. "I'm fine, I think. It's just my nose."

"Let me see." I lean toward her and, grabbing her chin, I turn her face to me. It's too dark to tell if her nose is bleeding, but it looks straight to me. "It doesn't seem too bad."

"And..." She clears her throat and slowly lifts a trembling hand to place it on my wrist. Her skin is so icy that it shocks me. "And you?"

I blink hard. The truth is that my knee was hurting more than a damn toothache a second ago, but right now the only thing I feel is the freezing cold touch of her hand, and a visceral need to warm it up. I shift my grip to capture both of her hands in mine.

"I'm okay," I murmur, feeling it as both a lie and a truth.

My knee is okay, it doesn't hurt right now. But I'm not okay. I'm in danger if I already care about this woman enough to forget about my injury.

Another grunt from the front reminds me that we have company. And also that the company really chafes me raw.

"Thanks for asking if we're fine, you guys," Rutilio grouches from the front. Neither his ex nor I acknowledge him. Finally he focuses on who he should. "Honey, are you hurt anywhere?"

"I don't think so," Jasmine says, her voice still high pitched enough that a bat could hear it. "Other than my nerves, that is."

Yeah, because if he hadn't kept hitting the damn brakes he wouldn't have driven us into a ditch, or wherever we are.

"We need to call nine-one-one," I say. That's when I discover that my phone is no longer in my hands, not just because I'm warming up Camila's, but because I seem to have lost it during one of the wild spins we executed over the black ice.

She springs to action. "I'll get it." Unbuckling herself, she stretches over to feel around the floor.

"Mine should be in my purse," Jasmine declares, also launching herself to the search.

Meanwhile, Ruggiero foolishly tries to set the car in reverse, as if it could find enough traction on and under a ton of snow. I didn't know that facepalming was a thing until this very moment, when I smack my own forehead and groan not so much because the gesture hurts, but because this guy is making my brain hurt—which is a feat.

Camila hovers over my bad knee but maybe she can't reach properly, because she all but crawls over my lap to search farther. I suck in air and turn to the dark ceiling. My eyes have already adapted well enough to the lack of light that I was able to make out the incredible hourglass shape of her body. Not something I should be noticing from someone I won't ever see again once we reach our destination.

"Ah hah!" she declares, quickly retreating back to her corner with not one, but two cellphones. "Wait, which one's yours?"

"The one that doesn't have the black case," I supply most helpfully. I bet she's glaring at me with all her might.

"Hey, Siri. Call nine-one-one," she says, using that galaxy brain of hers to bypass the issue of visibility.

The tinny voice of Apple's assistance responds that it's calling the emergency service. The rest of us hold in silence as the call connects and Camila explains the gist of the situation. Then they ask where we are and wouldn't we like to know? But whatshiface mentions the number of the interstate we were on, and that we're roughly an hour away from Bear Crossing.

"Hang in there," the operator says. "Help is on the way."

*

It takes two hours for help to arrive, and it comes in the form of a crew of firefighters wearing Santa hats and Rudolph noses.

"All set," one of them says, leaning over Rigoberto's window. "Count yourselves very lucky, because the previous accident we were called to was pretty gruesome. Right, Chad?"

Chad, somewhere behind this guy, says, "Oh yeah, that one's gonna make it to the news tomorrow." Chad sounds surprisingly chill about this.

"I can imagine," our driver says in a somber tone.

"Good, if you can then you need to turn back around," says firefighter one.

"Excuse me?"

"What?"

"¿Qué dijo?"

"Why?"

All four of us speak over one another with the same sentiment: we want to keep going forward, not the other way around.

"Yeah, you should've checked the weather app. You were

headed straight toward the worst of the storm. It's actually going to reach Bear Crossing in about two hours and there's already a state of emergency declared. Isn't that right, Chad?"

"Too right, Tom."

Ah, so firefighter one is called Tom. The piece of news I was waiting for all night.

"Do you know when the storm is clearing?" I ask from the back through my lowered window.

Chad and Tom shrug in perfect unison. "Whenever the providence decides, my dude," says Tom.

"Hey, wait a second? Aren't you that guy?" Chad points at my face, narrowing his eyes. "The one who went viral for breaking his knee during the World Series?"

"Yep." I pop the p with gusto. "That's me."

"Can I have your autograph?"

I look at him, wondering if he's for real. But there's no mistaking the excitement in his eyes over that light-up reindeer nose.

"Er, sure. Where do you want me to sign?"

"How about my hat?" He plucks the red and white accessory off his bald head.

"Hey, me too. Maybe the other guys want your signature as well." Tom grabs the walkie talkie stuck to his vest and asks the rest of the engine if they want the autograph of someone famous. To their credit, only one guy seems disappointed that I'm just a ball player and not some megastar pop singer like Celina or something.

Further to their credit, they gentle-parent us into turning back around to Bear Crossing and drive behind us, making sure that we reach the city limits safely. Jasmine looks up hotel options during the drive, and it's a very simple puzzle to solve because there's only one bed and breakfast in town. We veer right toward it where the firefighters veer left to their station, or maybe to their next call. I don't know how that works.

What I do know is that they were right. We were reckless in trying to drive through the middle of the night into a storm that was big enough to ground thousands of flights. By the time we park outside of the bed and breakfast, the wind and the snowfall have picked up drastically. We get covered in the white stuff in the short amount it takes for everyone to retrieve their luggage from the trunk.

I grit my teeth because I have to walk way slower than everyone else, and because the possibility of ice under the snow terrifies me more than I care to admit.

A lone figure stops just ahead of me. Squinting, I make out short, pin straight brown hair whipping around her face—Camila's. She waits until I reach her side and then resumes her walk, now at my pace.

"Hurry up, you're gonna freeze," I grumble, trying not to eat brow slush for dessert.

"I'm hurrying," she rebuts in that sharp way of hers, not picking up speed at all. I sigh as she holds the door open for me, annoyed that I should be the one doing that for her.

"Welcome to Bear and Breakfast, where you can hibernate and then eat an awesome breakfast," a woman who could be my grandma says as greeting. She stands behind a counter that looks straight out of the nineteenth century, with Reynaldo and Jasmine standing across from her and looking as if they had arrived a half hour ago. "I hear that you need two rooms for the night?"

Two?

The question forms on my lips but I catch myself in time before verbally blurting it out.

I don't like the look that Jasmine's man is giving me. Like he knows we're lying through our teeth and is excited for this moment to out our lie.

Well tough shit, Raymundo, I'm not gonna let you win.

"Yep," I say in the exact same way I confirmed my identity

to the firefighters earlier as the guy whose knee snapped like a toothpick on live TV. "We are most definitely in need of two rooms, one for each couple," I clarify as if it wasn't obvious enough.

The other guy's face jerks with a tiny, silent snort. He and Jasmine turn to do their check-in first and like the mature, grown ass adult that I am, I stick my tongue out to their backs.

That's when Camila jerks my sleeve and gives me a look that can only be described as *what in the chocolate fudge have you done?*

CHAPTER 14
CAMILA

I'm not a smiler, and yet there is one such thing plastered on my face as I accept the keys to what is supposed to be Lucky's and my bedroom. My head is buzzing with indeterminate thoughts, too many and too loud all at once for me to grasp a single one and follow the thread. All I can do is tag along at the back of our party as the inn owner takes us to our respective rooms.

Jasmine cracks a big yawn and even though she doesn't cover her mouth, she looks adorable. Upon checking her watch, she says, "Crap, I hadn't noticed it was so late already."

"The good news is that you'll be able to hibernate now. This is couple one's room." The little old lady sweeps her arms toward a door with a wooden sign reading Polar, adorned with dollar store Christmas garlands in red and green plastic. "And once you keep going to the end of the hallway you'll find our Grizzly room, which is for couple number two."

There are more doors, all of them named after what I assume are different types of bears. I don't recognize an embarrassing amount of them.

"Guess you better take the Polar bear room, since it's closer," Rupert says, motioning at Lucky's knee.

The owner adds, "They are very similar. Only the view is slightly different."

Who cares about the view when we have way bigger problems at hand?

It's snowing cows outside. The kind of snow that likely won't let anyone open their doors tomorrow morning—and likely means that we won't be able to continue our drive up to Mapleton for the remaining leg of our trip.

"We'll call it a night," I say through gritted teeth, grabbing Lucky's arm and trying to push him until I remember that he can't really hurry up.

He tries, though. Without even glancing back, he says, "Have a good night, you guys. Don't leave without us in the morning."

That freezes me and I turn to give Rupert my most glacial look, worse than the parting glance I gave him three years ago on this day. I silently but eloquently convey that if he dares to do drive off without us I will find him, no matter which shady corner of the earth he chooses to hide in, and I will make him regret the day he met me even more than he already does.

Rupert raises his hands and shakes his head like he's innocent of no crime. That better stay true tomorrow.

I only realize that my hands are shaking when I fail to insert the key four consecutive times. Only Lucky sees this though, since the others happily moved on to Grizzly's safe confines. Finally, the door unlocks and I stumble inside along with my carryon suitcase and my purse. The World Series champ works his crutches until he's safely inside and I close the door. And bolt it. And then glue myself to the peephole.

"Uh... what are you doing?"

I shush him and speak very low. "The hallway is kind of curved so I can see their door from here."

Something squeaks. "And why do you want to see their door?"

"I need to make sure that the coast is clear so I can go out and rent a different bedroom."

"That's smart. But maybe I should be the one to do that."

I glance over my shoulder with a frown. "What? Why?"

Lucky's sitting on the bed, the crutches propped up against the edge. That's as far as I can tell because not only is the Polar room as freezing as one of the actual poles, but it's also dark. "It's probably the most chivalrous thing to do."

"Forget about that, I bet you're in a ton of pain," I snap in a way that sounds much more unkindly than I meant. Clearing my throat, I try to soften my next delivery. "Besides, I'm also not somewhat famous. The inn keeper won't think anything weird about seeing me again."

"Wow, only somewhat famous, huh?" I imagine that he's frowning, but there are no further protests because we both know I'm right.

"I'll just…" I trail off as I start feeling around the walls by the door until I locate a switch and flip it on. Rather than a big ceiling light, what lights up are a bunch of smaller lamps distributed around the room, and they produce much softer lighting than I expected. Warm. Cozy. Almost… romantic. "Yeah. Um, I'll see you tomorrow."

"Sure." He blinks slowly, probably too tired to even muster more energy than that.

After checking the peephole again and finding an empty hallway, I carefully unlock the door and open it. The true Christmas gift I get is that the inn keepers have greased up the hinges, and I make a stealthy exit. My new boots are a lot more quiet on the wooden floors covered in ancient carpeting than my heels would've been. Maybe this is why people say that things happen for a reason and all that.

I reach the front desk again and my lucky star is still

shining on me because the owner is right there, alone and unbothered.

"Hi, dearie. Is there an issue with the room?" She pointedly glances down at my suitcase.

"No, nothing wrong with it. It's perfect." Maybe that's too thick of a lie. I actually didn't pay much attention to it at all other than that weird ambiance at the end. I continue undeterred, "I was wondering if you could rent me a separate room for the night."

Her silver eyebrows rise, blue eyes shining with the same spark of amusement that always seems to light up a certain baseballer's eyes. "Ah, I get it. Couple issues."

I—No. But actually, I'm going to roll with this because it's the perfect excuse my addled brain hadn't thought of.

"Right. Things have been difficult since…" This is *so* not the time for my brain to fart and expel the last remaining gas, but sure enough I come up with nothing.

She's the one who rescues me, though. "I get it. Every time my Marv gets sick or hurt he turns into a real bear, and not the Teddy kind, if you know what I mean."

"Totally." Not. No idea. My highly strategic and well compensated brain has finally collapsed. It only took a flight gone wrong, getting drunk, losing a shoe, depending on my ex's good will, and developing an elaborate lie with a hot stranger for it to kaput. I expected better of it.

"But I have bad news, dearie."

"Oh no." I sway, near to collapsing in body as well.

"That other couple and you two took my last available rooms. You'll have to put up with your bear for one more night." She offers me a sympathetic smile, like a woman who knows just how insufferable men can truly be.

In a final act of desperation, I ask, "Is there maybe another inn nearby that I could walk to?"

"In this weather?" She shakes her head. "Even if there was another inn in town, my conscience wouldn't allow me."

Right, this is the literal only place for visitors to stay in Bear Crossing... My shoulders sag. "Thank you, then."

"Good luck. And maybe just try showing him some cleavage. That'll surely improve his mood."

I offer another fake smile, even though showing cleavage is the very last thing I plan to do.

I retrace my steps—still very quiet—back to the Polar bear room. I peek down the silent hallway over my shoulder. I hope Rupert or his fiancée aren't peeping like I did earlier, and are none the wiser about my weird walk of shame.

Gathering a deep breath, I rap my knuckles on the Polar door and wait.

A few awkward seconds pass where I swear I can hear a ticking clock mocking me. I turn around again and of freaking course, there's a grandfather clock in the middle of the hallway, its face shaped like a bear.

The door opens. I swivel around and nearly meet my maker.

In front of me is Lucky, all right, but the shirtless version of him.

Contrary to his sense of humor, his body is very much that of a grown man's—one whose entire livelihood is based on it. When he mentioned that he had wider shoulders than average he wasn't lying, and it's because they're all muscle. Actually, *he* is all muscle... From his neck, to the thick pecs dusted in hair, down to the most spectacular abs I've seen from up close, and even the ridges of yet more muscles on his sides. Hanging from the crutches by his pits actually just accentuates his tiny waist.

Oh, good. He's still wearing pants. Bummer.

"What the hell?" I ask very subtly.

"My question exactly." He takes one careful step to pop his

head out the door and check our surroundings. "I thought you were getting another room."

"Turns out there are no further vacancies," I explain through gritted teeth.

"Ah." Lucky stares at me, still blinking slowly.

"Well?"

"I don't know, you tell me. What do you want to do?"

"Sleep," I answer right away. "Preferably near warmth."

"And you'd be okay doing so behind closed doors with a stranger?"

I frown a little. "Did you have to bring up the sticking point so clearly?"

"Sorry, I don't have any more mojo to beat around the bush tonight."

"Fine, neither do I." I sigh heavily and motion at the room inside. "Can I please just come in?"

"By all means." Lucky hops out of the way and I repeat the same motions as earlier, closing the door and bolting it. When I turn around, he's sat on the bed again and glances up at me. "Actually, maybe you can help me take this off."

"Tell me you don't mean your pants," I hiss in brewing outrage.

"No." Okay, he doesn't have to grimace like that either. "The brace. I need it off so that *I* can take off my pants."

"And then put on different pants, right? Sweatpants? Pajamas?"

"Yes, my plan of sleeping in the buff has been thwarted."

I'm not sure if he's serious anymore, but I'm honestly too tired to try to discern that. I drop my purse on top of my suitcase and drag myself toward the bed. Lucky makes an impressive display of strength when, despite his own exhaustion, he scoots back so that his legs aren't dangling. This way I won't have to bend down to help. This way I can also admire the symphony of his working muscles from the corner of my eye.

"You'll also put on a shirt, right?" I ask as I begin to work the velcro straps of his leg brace. I'm sure I'm not physically drooling over the man, but I'm beyond the point of denying that he has me bothered. Contrary to popular belief, I'm not made of ice.

"You know, normally women ask me to take off my clothes instead." The cheeky line is only weakened by the fact that he has dark circles under his eyes.

Ignoring that, I say, "I'll go to the bathroom so I can change myself and then that way you can also do your thing. Tell me when you're all set and I'll come out."

"What side of the bed do you want?" he asks.

I stop in the middle of unbuckling the last strap of his intricate brace and look up at him.

Oh, he's serious.

"You're kidding, right?"

He cocks an eyebrow. "Am I laughing?"

"No, no." I shake my head and point at the opposite end of the room. "I'll take the couch."

We both turn to the piece of furniture and this is the moment when all my hopes and dreams come crashing down, because it's not really a couch. It's a love sofa. The kind that I'd be lucky to fit my whole wide butt in, forget about my whole length lying down.

"You sure about that?" he asks.

I resume the work and yank the brace off his leg. Below the hem of his jeans I can see the white cast that is truly protecting his leg from further damage. It has innumerable scribbles and doodles, some wishing him a good recovery, some featuring jokes, many baseballs, and a surprising lack of anatomic part renditions. His jeans button is already undone, showing a sliver of his underwear—*SPORTY*, of course. We send our sponsored teams absurd amounts of merchandise. Propped on his elbows, his abs bunch in a way that is criminal. How is the light bouncing off his bronze skin this way? As in, the criminal here are my thoughts.

What was the question again?

I shake my head to force the logical thoughts to fall in place.

"What choice do I have?" I whisper, my voice trembling a little.

He pats the bed with one hand.

"No." I shake my head again. "I'm not sleeping with you no matter how inviting the offer is."

Lucky's eyebrows do the wiggly rise again. "As flattering as that is, my invitation is literally only for sleep. Not for sexy times."

"Oh."

I want to die.

"Yeah. You can even put your suitcase between us. I don't care. I just really, *really*"—here he pops his eyes open—"need to sleep like right now."

"Right. Me too. Sleep only. Nothing else."

"Glad we're on the same page." He motions toward the mattress. "Then, which side are you picking?"

"Um." I blink hard, looking at anything but him. "Left, I guess. Opposite to your injured leg."

"Good idea. Now go get changed so I can do the same and tuck in before I just straight up pass out."

"Yep." I pop the p like I've heard him do and grab my stuff to hide myself in the bathroom, where I proceed to spend the next half hour kicking myself for basically revealing that I'm attracted to his—granted, fantastic—body.

CHAPTER 15
LUCKY

'm hugging a bear.

It probably should freak me out way more than it does.

Maybe I've been living in Florida for too long if this is no biggie. At least it's not a gator, though.

Wait, why does the bear have a gator's face?

Now that's freaky. I try to free myself but it's like my arms are glued to the bear, or is the bear the one keeping me prisoner? Am I actually not hugging the bear and it's just about to eat me? I moan in protest, somehow unable to speak. This is what I get for buying those alligator leg socks. They were really funny but this isn't hardy har hars. What the hell is happening?

"Hola, Lucky," the bear-gator whispers with a female voice. There's something pleasant and sharp about it. It actually sounds familiar.

Camila?

Hold up, who was Camila again?

My eyes finally snap open.

Um… I press my lips tighter to not let a single peep filter out.

The bear-gator that I was hugging in my dream turns out

to be the real life, flesh and blood Camila Puig, whose name and last name I just found out yesterday, and who despite being someone I had never seen before in my life, is on my bed. Fully clothed. Her lips are parted and the slightest trickle of drool slides down her smushed cheek toward my arm—which is trapped under her very heavy head. That makes sense because she seems to have a brain the size of the galaxy.

My other arm is over her waist, and the reason I couldn't move it is because her own arm is over it, and her hand is cinched around my forearm. This is the third time that I recall her grabbing my arms. She might not know this at a conscious level, but she seems to have a thing for my arms. Or the rest of it, if I go by that awkward little conversation last night.

My lungs empty with a sad little sigh. The tragedy here is that I find her incredibly freaking hot—and amusing, which to me is important. If it wasn't for my leg and the pain that clings to every one of its nerves all the damn time, I'd have encouraged her advances. Or whatever that even was.

I think that was her version of flirting, with as uptight and straitlaced as she seems all the time. That's also why she looks so absurdly charming right now, with her hair a mess on the pillow and on her face, drooling on my arm.

Her nostrils expand with the kind of deep breath that usually precedes waking up. Rather than doing that, she snuggles against my arm even more. It sends tingles everywhere because the limb is dead asleep. Also because I'm a single, red-blooded man. A grunt escapes from my chest, and *that* is what snaps her awake.

Her eyes pop open and every muscle of her body turns into a plank.

It takes a second for the light to fully come into her eyes, and for them to focus on the view in front of her. Namely, me.

She blinks hard at my face. Does she not recognize me? Or she doesn't believe what her optic nerves are showing her.

Then her still very wide eyes travel down to my sweatshirt decked with the flag of Puerto Rico, my fave for sleeping when it's cold, and she takes stock of the situation our arms are in.

Frankly, it could be worse. She doesn't need to yelp and launch herself off the bed the way she does. But blood flow resumes down my arm and it doesn't exactly feel great. Groaning, I turn on my back and try to open and close my hand.

"¿Qué? Yo—" She splutters, clutching at her silk pajama top over her chest. And it's not the sexy kind either, it's the kind that looks like it's made for grandpas.

"Buenos días, mi osa," I say with a raspy voice and a smile that I know is going to grate.

"I'm not your bear," she refutes.

"Considering how you were sleeping on my arm…" I point at the sleeve. "And drooling on it, I'd say that you were taking this hibernating thing very seriously."

"*What?*" she screeches, but touching her cheek confirms that what I'm saying is the unvarnished truth. And something spectacular happens.

I have never in my thirty one years of existence seen a human being change color that fast. Camila goes from white with a dusting of dark freckles on her cheeks, to redder than Rudolph's nose. Her socks skid on the floor in her rush to disappear, and when she's inside the bathroom she slams the door shut hard enough to make the whole building rattle.

I can't take it anymore. The fact that I was able to hold it in until now is a feat in itself. My teammates wouldn't even believe it if I told them.

Finally, I burst into the loudest, most obnoxious laughter of my career as a hobbyist clown. Pretty sure I'm making the walls rattle as well.

*

"Can you just forget you saw that?" Camila hisses under her breath a short while later, while she's wheeling her packed suitcase and I'm following along on my crutches, my backpack shrugged on.

"Nope. I'm afraid I never shall. Not for as long as I live."

"Maybe I should kill you, then," she murmurs in a quite sinister way.

"If you didn't do it last night while I was out like a light, you definitely won't do it now when it takes more effort," I reason as if this conversation even made sense.

Frowning even deeper, she says, "Can't you see I'm quite unpredictable? I'm fake dating a stranger I met just yesterday, after all."

"Not so stranger anymore. We did sleep together for the first time last night." I shrug.

"Oh my word, shush!" She clamps her freezing hands over my mouth. "You're going to give us away."

Carefully, I pry her hands off. "Me? I'm not the one who bandied words like 'fake dating' about. Who even calls it that way?"

"Every single movie where two people who aren't really together pretend to be for one reason or another."

"And how do those movies end?" I ask in a deadpan, and of course she doesn't answer.

That's because I also watch romcoms sometimes—heck, I've even had the honor of watching a few of those develop in real life in front of my eyes—and I know exactly how it goes. Their lie gets discovered in the process, or they fall for each other for real, or both in the case of the really juicy ones.

Now I miss my book. I'm glad someone found it for me on the plane, because I'll hit it hard the rest of the way up to Mapleton. That way I can also get some rest from all these seasons schemings we have going on.

Obviously, Camila doesn't answer. Instead, she whirls

around and continues toward the front desk to check us out. Except we get there and practically every guest of this Bear and Breakfast is packed at the entrance. Some with the luggage and some without, but all of them looking out the front door.

Vague murmurs ebb and flow among the crowd. Camila and I exchange a look of uncertainty but we keep going. At the edge of the group we find both of our exes, also staring in the same direction.

"Morning," I say, not sure if it's going to be any good. "What's going on?"

"We're trapped," Rigoberto says, pointing ahead.

That's when I finally make out what has everybody in a trance. The snow outside pushing against the door and the windows is high enough that it would probably reach my waist, and more of it keeps dropping from the sky by the bucketfuls. From between a few people, I catch sight of an elderly man trying to push the front door open, but it's an out-swing and he can't outmatch the weight of several feet of snow with his strength alone.

Trapped, indeed.

Beside me, Camila sounds genuinely heartbroken when she whispers, "No…"

I don't know what else she has going on for her aside from her job. A boyfriend? Could be a husband—just because she's not wearing a ring doesn't mean she's single. Or she could be a mom already. Or like me, she may simply want to get some rest and family time. I wonder why she's desperate enough to ride in a car with her ex who jilted her at the altar-ish, but it must be something more important that a work meeting.

And somehow I care.

A dormant part inside of me, the one I recognize as the caveman, wakes up right there and then. I know I can't go out there and plow snow with my bare hands, especially not while I'm injured. But there has to be something I can try. Anything.

Patting my pockets, I produce my cellphone and click around until I find the local weather news. Another foot of snow is expected tonight, and that dashes my hopes of paying someone a fortune to drive us anyway. But it says that temperatures will rise tomorrow enough for the snow to start to melt. Depending on how it goes, we may be able to travel the day after.

Today we're four days away from Christmas. Worse case, we'll make it to our destination two days before the big day. It should work.

Gently, I grab her arm and it jolts her from what no doubt is a spiral of doom in her mind. I show her the screen of my cellphone and I watch her put two and two together in a matter of seconds.

Leaning to her ear, I say, "It'll work out. You'll just have to drool on me a little longer."

She smacks me in the stomach. Hard.

CHAPTER 16
CAMILA

"No need to panic, folks," the receptionist from last night says, fresh as a lettuce even though she probably got even less sleep than I did. She makes that calming motion with her hands in the air that irritates me even more. "We will cancel our reservations for the next two days and allow you to extend your stay."

"Two days," I parrot.

That's also what the weather news implies. I'm supposed to meet with my boss in two days, right before he goes on vacation for the rest of the calendar year—which in my opinion has always been an issue, because he's the main decision maker in a company that employs sixty thousand people worldwide. But he's all about work life balance or whatever, and that's well and good but I'm in charge of keeping operations running every day of the year, every year. And if I don't convince him and the board of making the changes we need before our next budget round, the schedule delay impact will have tragic consequences.

No more *SPORTY* Christmas party. No more flagship factory. No longer a top employer in the area anymore. And

I'm sure having no jobs next year wouldn't make for a jolly Christmas for so many families. It all hinges on me successfully delivering this plan to my boss.

It all hinges on me. I can fail at my private life but not at this.

"Breathe," a voice says.

Frantically, I glance all around me. Lucky Rivera, the stranger I drooled on last night, is the only one who just noticed I'm trapped—not in the snow, but in a mental spiral of my own making.

I try to gasp for air, but the claw of looming, catastrophic disaster squeezes around my throat, and when I watch Rupert put his arm lovingly around his new fiancée, I once again get transported to that moment in time when I experienced my biggest, most spectacular failure.

One thing would be to be snubbed by my fiancé. But it would be so much worse if thousands of people lose their livelihoods because I got snowed in before my boss went on Christmas vacations.

"Let's go back to our room," Lucky suggests, and all I can do is nod.

This time he's way faster than me. My legs feel like noodles under water, and I have to make several pauses along the way to lean against the walls, against the grandfather bear clock, until I join him back inside the Polar bear room.

When he closes the door, I let my purse and my suitcase fall on the floor and start pacing.

"Would it help if you talk?" Lucky asks, making his way over to the world's tiniest loveseat.

"I can't," I choke out. "It's company secrets."

"That sounds fancy. Do you work for NASA or what?"

I stop. "If I did, would I live on Mapleton?"

"Touché." He slowly lowers himself to sit, and while he sets his crutches aside he says, "The only company I know of in Mapleton is *SPORTY*."

I stare at him.

Feeling the power of my eyes on him, he lifts his head and this is finally when he realizes it. "Oh. You work at *SPORTY*. That's why you were talking about its profit and stuff."

"Yes." I wave an impatient hand and resume pacing back and forth. I stumble on a corner of the carpet around the bed but don't let that stop me.

"Ever thought that you should've told your fake boyfriend about that very basic fact before?"

"I really wasn't counting on this arrangement prolonging further."

"But now that it has, what's got your panties in a twist?" Once more I send such a glacial look his way that he raises his hands like a barrier. "Too soon after we slept together?"

I march over to the unmade bed, grab what was his pillow because it's closer, and hurl it at his face.

Except he doesn't have to make use of his baseball reflexes. The pillow drops to the floor halfway through.

Lucky's shoulders start shaking with his chuckles. "Aren't you just glad you're not in baseball?"

"Women can't play baseball because the men at the top won't let them." I squeeze my fists tight. "Do you know how hard it is for a woman to take charge of things instead?"

"Pretty hard, unless she's wielding la chancla." When he sees I'm dead serious, the playful grin drops off his face.

"Men get to have it all. Every. Single. Time." I grit my teeth. "They can be CEOs and also go on vacation and get married and have kids, because their wives are taking care of all of those things in the background without getting compensation, and sometimes no recognition.

"But my mom could—she got it all. The top job and the

family. And I was supposed to follow right in her steps. But all I have is my job and nothing else."

His eyebrows rise. "You also seem to have health and youth. Those count for something."

I ignore him. "But my boss, who is a man, is going on vacation in two days, and I need to get his approval on something important—something huge—so that I can work through the holidays to save everybody's Christmas next year." I point at my chest. "I'm the one who has the responsibility. I'm the one who has to sacrifice everything because otherwise I'll be left with nothing but failure. Again."

I only realize when I'm done speaking that my voice broke several times because I'm crying.

Me, Camila Puig. Dubbed the ice queen at *SPORTY*. I'm shedding tears. The weight on my shoulders so huge that it's squeezing even the unsqueezable out of me—tears.

"Puñeta," he whispers, tearing his backpack off his shoulders and grabbing for his crutches again.

Next thing I know, he's in front of me and his arms are coming around. The crutches clatter as they fall, and I collapse into his chest like I almost did out by the entrance. Lucky Rivera holds me as I sniffle and slobber all over his Puerto Rico flag sweatshirt, one of his hands holding the back of my head all tender like, the other running up and down my spine to comfort me, or warm me up, or both.

And it strikes me that no one has ever done this to me.

I can't remember a single time that my parents held me tight and whispered that things were going to be okay. They were too busy on their phones, with their own high stakes jobs, and I never wanted to be seen as a bother. Even when I got hurt bad enough to bleed all over the floor, I never asked for help.

What about Rupert?

We kissed. We did a lot more than kissing. But I don't

remember any tenderness in his embrace. We were both very down to the point, efficient, getting the contact we needed at any given time and nothing else.

His arms never felt like this. And I don't mean because Lucky is jacked in the way someone who trains every day of the year can be. I mean because he instinctively knew that I needed a hug—the kind I've never allowed myself. The kind that lets me cry and be messy and snotty and doesn't pull away because distance isn't its purpose.

"It's okay," he murmurs against my temple, his breath making my hair shift. "You're okay, Camila."

I give a garbled laugh. "Clearly I'm not if I'm weeping on you like a damsel in distress."

"Fair." I feel him shrug. "But it's also okay to just not be okay sometimes, and it doesn't automatically make you a failure. It just means you have to pick yourself up and try again in a different way."

I blink hard, staying quiet in case he's going to keep dropping philosophical truth bombs I need to hear.

"Take me, for example. Tore my ACL in the middle of the most important play of my life. I got the out, but I don't know if this is going to end my career." Well, when he puts it this way it's a good reminder that I'm not the only one who has pressure to perform. "But guess what I'm gonna do?"

"What?" I whisper into his chest.

"I'm going to keep trying until time tells. Because if I give up now, before even trying, then I'll really have failed."

Squirming a little, I unglue myself from him even if I don't go very far. Glancing up, I say, "But I'm already trying my damn hardest. It's not my fault that a hundred tons of snow are getting in my way."

Lucky blinks slowly, his unnecessarily long eyelashes sweeping up and down dramatically. "I have no idea what this means for the grand picture of what you're going through, but have you considered that if maybe your way doesn't work anymore, there might be another?"

"Another," I parrot again, my mind starting to churn.

"Yeah. I don't know." He raises his eyebrows. "I don't know if this would help at all, but my brother works for *SPORTY* too. It's why I'm headed to Mapleton, actually, to stay with him and his family while I try some experimental treatments on my knee at the St. Cloud U Hospital. I'm sure he could try to help if we explain the situation."

"Your brother?" I blink owlishly.

"His name is Mateo Rivera, do you know him?"

I jolt. "Oh. *Oh!*"

I clamp my mouth shut. Mateo is my production manager, and one way or another he will see the impacts of *SPORTY*'s manufacturing footprint in the upcoming years. I can't let Lucky know what I'm trying to accomplish because it'll be taken the wrong way—like I'm trying to fire people and replace them all with robots, when I'm just trying to save as many people as I can from certain doom.

"So you do know him." Lucky grins.

"I do. He's my production manager." This much I can concede.

"Your what?"

"I'm the head of operations and logistics for *SPORTY*."

"The head of..." Lucky's eyes grow wider. "You're my brother's boss, which means you're—"

"Board of directors, yes."

"Oh, shit. I can't believe one of *SPORTY*'s directors drooled on me twice."

"Ugh." I push him away from me and he hops a couple of times on his left leg to not lose his balance. Reflexively I grab onto him, though I'm not sure I'd be able to prevent him from falling anyway.

"There." Smiling, he raises a hand and when he sets it on

my jaw, my heart stops beating. Slowly, he thumbs away at the moisture on my cheek. "At least now you stopped crying. Now you can use that big brain of yours more clearly."

He lets me go and I snap my mouth shut. Displaying the athleticism that made him reach the heights he has, he bends down with one leg to pick up his crutches and settle them back in place.

"Now, while you do your thinking, I'm going to take my book and go in search of food and a nook I can camp at. If you need me, you know where to call."

"Right," I respond mindlessly. I stand in the middle of the room, watching him find his bodice ripper book and make his way out, closing the door behind him with minor difficulty.

Meanwhile, my head is not working.

I'm no longer losing my shit, but somehow I'm still unable to think—about work, at least. I keep replaying the feeling of his arms around me, the rasp of his callused thumb wiping away my tears. Neither of these things are where I should be focusing, yet I can't stop myself. For once, I don't want to.

CHAPTER 17
LUCKY

"Finally, I was about to send a search party," my brother's voice says directly into my ears via Airpods.

I made very slow progress of the buffet table at first, having to set my plate down with every step I needed to take with the crutches, until one of the guests took pity on me and just filled my plate with everything I asked for.

Now I sit on a table by the window, wolfing down my weight in scrambled eggs, a mound of sausages and bacon, grits, and buttered biscuits, while talking on the phone with my brother. Or trying to. I probably make more munching sounds than words but he understands somehow. My baby nephew, Angel, must've been the one who trained him on this art.

My caveman sounds mean, "I'm fine. We almost got into an accident on the road last night because of black ice, so we had to turn back and get a room in a local bed and breakfast, and now it looks like we're fully snowed in. We might be able to leave tomorrow but who knows?"

"Para, para." Has the moment arrived when he no longer understands? But then he says, "A room? We?"

Oh.

Shit.

On a stick.

I hadn't thought about how those key words would sound until Mateo uses his sassy voice, the kind that precedes teasing me until my ears bleed.

Side note, I respect that that's his given right as the older brother, which is why I, the youngest, seek my joy from joking with others. End of side note.

"You mentioned some people on your texts last night," he says, further goading me. "But I wouldn't possibly imagine that you'd want to share a room with total strangers…"

Sighing, I lower my fork and knife so I can massage my face while I finish chewing my bite. I peek from between my fingers but none of my travel companions are in the dining area, so I can speak. I still try to be very careful, lower my voice as much as it can go, and switch fully to Spanish.

"No te emociones, cabrón. Solo se habían acabado los cuartos, no significa nada."

"So it's a woman," he deduces even though I just explained that it was just out of necessity.

I guess that gave me away. As a straight guy who spends a large part of his time around grunting dudes who sometimes are naked, it wouldn't be a big deal if my temporary roommate was a guy. It would just be business as usual and I wouldn't have been cryptic.

"Anyway, tell your son that I'm still coming and I have a really cool gift for him."

"What is it?" he asks, letting me off the hook for now, but he and I both know that the previous topic will come back like a boomerang at some point.

"You'll have to wait to find out." Besides, I don't want to risk anyone knowing that I have a legitimate and fully appraised baseball signed by the entire World Series champion roster of the Orlando Wild. It's worth exactly one point two million dollars, and it's sitting at the bottom of my backpack.

"These are boring answers, Lucas." My brother sighs. "Anyway, I'll let you take some time to craft a proper explanation about your latest hookup—"

"She's not my—" But at this moment Ronaldinho, Jasmine's man, walks into the dining area and all I can finish with is "ugh."

"And it better be satisfying," Mateo continues, "because you know how curious my wife is going to get."

I manage to keep my groan to a minimum. Karina, my sister-in-law, is ten times more inquisitive about my love life than my brother. Her goal in life regarding me is for me to end up with someone who can bring balance to her life full of Rivera men. Jasmine was always too wishy-washy for her taste —uninterested in making a real unit with her—and Karina was openly ecstatic when we broke up, even when I was still in my feels about it.

She's ruthless. She'll interrogate every last morsel of information about Camila if I let her. Which means I can't call nor answer calls from my brother at least until I get to Mapleton. I'll have enough time to psyche myself up for them to drill me about how beautiful I find my brother's boss.

I grunt. "Bye, pendejo."

"Right backatcha." He hangs up.

Shaking my head, I resume feeding the voracious monster that resides in my midriff, but now I'm finally able to pick up my book again.

Okay, so I left off where Lady Arabella got lost in the woods. I end up rereading the page to remember what all was happening before the airplane turbulence sent the book flying off my hands. She's trying to outrun the thunder when of course her foot catches on a tree root, and she goes tumbling down a cliff. It's absurd and I love it. I bet Lord Harrington is going to lose his mind when he finds out that the woman he loves—but doesn't love him back, because of course—is in grave peril.

"Is this seat taken?"

My instinctive answer would be to say yes. The one on my left is taken by the Ghost of Christmas Past, and the other two chairs are taken by my buddies Present and Future. I'm sure he wouldn't accept that answer, though.

But since the guy standing by my table with a plate in his hands is none other than the one who is going to get me to Mapleton—hopefully in time so I can blow my nephew's mind with his gift—I shrug and motion at the seat across from me. At least that one's farther.

Thankfully, he's got enough brains to take the hint and sits on that chair. Goodbye Ghost of Christmas Present. Raul picks a buttered biscuit and takes a big bite, and I resume reading the shenanigans of a regency couple. The peaceful quiet lasts maybe a minute.

"I'm surprised you read that kind of stuff."

I lift my eyes over the top of the book. "What should I be reading instead?"

"No, I mean…" He at least squirms. "That's usually what women read."

"Oh yeah?" Lowering my book, I very casually say, "I think romance is for everybody. In fact, if you give it a try I'm sure Jasmine would enjoy it."

Roberto decides to ignore the double meaning and instead asks, "Why? Does she like those books?"

Probably not. She doesn't like fun.

"Maybe you should ask her." I spear a sausage and stuff it in my mouth.

Maybe letting the dig slide was for a greater purpose, because his eyes turn sharper, just like a corner of his mouth. "And does Camila enjoy it?" He snorts and shakes his head when I just keep eating. "Let's face it, she probably doesn't even notice. I bet she still spends her every waking moment working."

"Is that why you dumped her?" I ask, cutting to the chase. "Because she didn't dedicate enough time to you?"

Rutherford clears his throat but doesn't answer. Instead, he grabs a strip of bacon and puts it in his yap.

"And how's that working for you now that your new fiancée is also a career woman?"

"It's different," he snaps. "Jasmine and I see each other at the hospital all the time."

"Ohh…" I elongate the word in the most obnoxious way. "I get it now, so it wasn't that you didn't get enough attention from Camila. It was that you couldn't see what she was doing all the time."

"No, I mean—"

"Hey, Jasmine," I say over his attempt at explaining himself. He whirls around like he half expects me to be lying, but his fiancée really is heading our way behind him with her own plate. Fortunately for me, I'm just done eating. I don't even care that my mouth is full when I speak. "I'll leave you guys to enjoy your breakfast together. Laters."

While the guy clams up, Jasmine offers a polite smile that means even less than Camila and I sharing a room.

Speaking of, she must be hungry. She hasn't left the seclusion of the Polar bear room in over an hour, and even if she chooses to prioritize work over food, her big brain needs fuel.

I grab my crutches and after stuffing the mass paperback in my back pocket, I head over to the buffet table to see what I can get her.

The difference between Rudolph and I—I mean, aside from the facts that we look drastically different, were born in different hunks of land, and that I'm not really together with Camila—is that I'm not intimidated by a career woman.

There are a lot of guys on the team who have stay at home WAGs, and for some of them it works very well—in those cases, that's exactly what the women wanted for themselves all along. But in the cases where the women gave up their studies or their career to stay home, to dedicate themselves so that their men had the perfect home to land every other game series, with nothing for themselves that they can call their own… Most of those times it has ended up in breakups or divorce.

Everyone should have their own thing. I can't fathom making a woman that I love make me the center of her own life. I'd love her for herself and who she is, what she wants and doesn't want. Not for her deference to me. Conversely, that's the kind of love I expect too, especially after Jasmine.

And after what I saw from Camila earlier, I think it's also what she deserves.

The solution for someone who cares so deeply about their job, to the point of having a panic attack about it, isn't to force them to care less about it the way this buffoon just implied. He wanted Camila to wait for and revolve around him, when she's her own planet.

I guess he could've been even more of an asshole, married her, and then cheated on her with someone at his job. It's a good thing that he and Jasmine met instead.

But Camila… she just needs someone to tell her she's doing great. And maybe fix her a plate. At least I can do the latter.

CHAPTER 18
CAMILA

"Camila…" My boss's mouth hangs open as he leans closer to the screen. It takes me a moment to figure out that he's staring at the wallpaper behind me. I turn and sure enough, it has tiny polar bears all over it. And flowers. All pink. "Where the hell are you?"

"Bear Crossing, Pennsylvania," I answer in a deadpan.

"Pennsylwhere?" He pulls away from the camera to shake his head. "How did that even happen? Weren't you supposed to be flying in from Orlando?"

"Yes, but turbulence from the snow storm made us stop in Willmington, Delaware, from there I had the most uncomfortable car drive for an hour until black ice almost made us see our maker, and now we're snowed in on this blip of a town that is obsessed with bears."

"I take it you won't be able to attend the annual Christmas party?"

"Probably not, but that's not why I'm calling you."

"Oh?"

"You know why I went to that conference," I start, using my tone of voice that indicates an upcoming lack of small talk.

"The plan was to give you my proposal in person before you go on vacation. But now I don't know how long we'll be stuck here, so I want you to make sure to still reserve the time for me to talk via teleconference or phone or carrier pigeon if we must. Is that clear?"

"Sir, yes, ma'am." He salutes like I'm the general here and not him. Relaxing his posture but not his eyes, he says, "Now, let me tell you that I know exactly what you're going to propose —I approved you traveling to Orlando on the company's dime, after all—but if your proposal doesn't make sense in the long term, I'm not going to change things."

I frown a little. "Even if it still means losing people?"

"I would just have to find another way."

Short of coming up with the next industrial revolution even beyond blockchain and artificial intelligence, I don't know what the other way could be. Neither of us are in the tech sector at the end of the day, and for every new tech development there's also a myriad of things to troubleshoot before scaling.

"Martin, no offense but—"

He chuckles. "Every time someone says that it's because they're about to say something very offensive."

"*But*—" I make an annoying amount of emphasis that feels more Lucky than me. "Even though you're the top boss of *SPORTY* for many reasons, and I'm not, I know I'm right on this and I'm doing it to save the company, even if I look like the villain to some people."

He smiles a little, amusement genuinely showing in the wrinkles at the corners of his eyes.

One of the reasons why Martin Richter is the top dog at *SPORTY* is his sense of humor and of community. He's the one who has spearheaded the company's Christmas party as a celebration of everything we have accomplished together as a team over the year. I completely understand the practice, it's like living through a business school case, but it also makes his job exponentially harder when he has to deliver bad news—and he played a spiked eggnog dart game with the person he's giving the bad news to.

Meanwhile, even though I have a stark opposite approach, where I'm perhaps a bit too aloof and numbers focused, I know strongly that we're on the verge of disaster if we prioritize not hurting feelings in the short term for our longevity.

"Very well, I look forward to seeing this famous proposal in two days." Right before he hangs up, he adds as a second thought, "Oh, and I have a random question."

"If it's something about bears, the answer is I don't know and I also don't care."

The reason I'm able to talk so freely with Martin is because he hired me fresh out of my MBA—a fact that I enjoy throwing in his face every time he gets annoyed by my cold blood. He's put up with me since I was an intern all the way until I became an executive. Too bad for him but he's stuck with me.

Unlike anyone else faced with my rudeness, he laughs. "No, it's not about bears."

"Then?" I cock an eyebrow.

"Who is this *we* you keep talking about?" He leans forward again, a glint coming to his eyes that I don't enjoy.

"Talk to you in two days, Martin." Without further ado, I end the call and close my laptop.

Whew, good timing because I can feel heat creeping up my neck.

In retrospective, it was a very good thing that this morning was a fiasco. If things had gone to plan, I'd be stuck in the back of a tiny rental car with Lucky Rivera, whose incredibly hard arm is an excellent neck pillow to drool on. I was only able to face him earlier because I was having a menty b.

But how the hell am I going to face him for one more day? Or two?

"By burying my nose in work, that's how," I tell myself, opening my laptop again.

Someone knocks at the door.

"It's me," Lucky's voice comes from the other side.

I gasp. Then I check myself for reacting like a freaking teenager. I set my laptop aside and stand up from the loveseat. Straightening my white blouse and ignoring the bear jeans I'm still wearing, I stride over in socks to the door and open it.

Lucky Rivera stands there on his crutches, the handle of a plastic bag between his teeth and somehow still smiling. "Thought you might want breakfast."

I let my eyes travel down to the container inside the bag. "What are you, a mama bear?"

"Daddy bear." He wiggles his eyebrows.

Grimacing, I take the plastic bag from the bottom and he releases it from his jaws. "Um, thanks."

He follows me inside, saying, "I also ran into your ex at the breakfast room and he made me want to run for the hills."

"He can have that effect on people." After a pause I add, "So can I."

"Nah, you're not a jerk."

That stops me on my tracks.

Lucky's closing the door. Using his left leg to hop to the bed, he throws himself on it with crutches and all, completely clueless that he just low key said something transcendental.

Slowly, I lower myself back to the sofa, facing him. "People at work call me ice queen."

He snorts without turning my way. "People at work call me a lot of things too, trust me."

"But that's because they like you and have fun with you. In my case they hate me."

"No way."

"I dare you to call your brother and ask him."

Lucky finally turns his head toward me, and a tiny curl

bounces over his forehead. "So what? You don't need to be liked by everybody."

My eyebrows twitch at another Lucky pearl of wisdom. "Even my fiancé left me because I was so insufferable, it's that bad."

"Pretty sure that was a self projection." He turns over his side and props his head up with his arm. "Two questions, what did you even see in that asshole, and also why are you not eating already?"

"Right." I open the bag and pluck the container out. At the bottom is a set of compostable silverware, which strikes me as very conscientious for an old school establishment like this one. "I asked myself that question several times since that whole mess happened."

"And?" You'd think he's waiting to see what happens next in the daytime drama.

I sigh as I open the utensils pack. "This doesn't speak well about myself but..." His eyes widen with interest. "Deep down, I think I was looking more for a checklist than a person, because that's also how I've defined myself."

"Damn." He elongates the word for a long moment. "Once again, I really wasn't expecting that deep of an answer."

I clear my throat. "I've been doing therapy at the encouragement of some friends this year."

Rather than act judgy like many people would, Lucky just muses, "You know, I've been thinking about seeing the team's therapist. Maybe I'll do that during the rehab treatment."

He motions at the food container with his lips and I get to working. It's quiet only for a moment as I start on the warm food, until he asks possibly the hardest question I've faced.

"So what's the checklist you have defined yourself by?"

I almost choke. I manage not to. "I thought you wanted me to eat?"

"You seem good at multitasking."

Ugh. He's shockingly good at testing me. Rachel and Sierra, said friends, would be amused to learn that.

"By my career. My whole identity is tied to it, and I guess that's also how I measure others."

"At least that's honest." Lucky shrugs. "A lot of people try to measure others by standards they don't even meet themselves. So is that why you went for Rigoberto over there? Because he's a doctor?"

"Rigoberto?" I ask, my Venezuelan accent showing in the pronunciation.

"Oh yeah, I've been amusing myself by calling him by random names that start by R."

"What other options are there?" I ask before shoving some bacon into my mouth.

"Don't try to distract me, woman. It'll work too well ."

"Fine. I guess I did. I liked him because he's a doctor." I roll my eyes but keep eating.

"What about me?" I lift my eyes to him and he motions between us with his free hand. "I mean, I'm your pretend boyfriend now. Is my career compatible with your expectations?"

Covering my mouth with my hand, I say, "Pretend is the operating word there. It doesn't matter what I think about your job."

"Humor me."

I would rather not, but if I've learned something about this guy since the very first moment, is that he has the stubbornness it takes to win a historic championship even at the expense of his own body. He won't let go of this bone.

"We're nowhere near the same league," I say, his jaw dropping. "The way I see it, elite athletes like you are something like one in a million. There are definitely a good number of them, but not just everyone is one. But office employees? We're a dime a dozen."

For some reason that makes him look even more flabber-gasted. "Aren't you a hotshot executive?"

I snort. "Think about it, how many companies are there in the world?"

"A lot but—"

"And *a lot* of companies have a lot more executives, it's simple math." I wave a hand. "Think about it, why do you think we regularly feature athletes with our equipment and wear? It's because you're special and that's what it takes to sell our products, not some cranky Grinch behind a desk like me."

He points at himself. "So according to your metric, I'm more attractive than a medical doctor?"

I refuse to answer that question and just glare instead.

"Well, you did seem particularly impressed by my physique last night."

Yep, I can no longer face him.

I turn down to just look at the food. "Anyway, could you leave? I need to get back to work."

"Actually, I found a cozy nook in the common room where you could work quietly and I could keep reading my book. Wanna join me after you're done?"

I'm ready to fire back a quick denial until I take one look at the eagerness in his face, and it occurs to me that if we were two cats, he'd be an outdoors one and I'd be an indoors kind. He probably spends half of his time in the open on a baseball field, something he can't do with an injured knee. Meanwhile, I mostly keep to my office, the factory floor—which is also indoors—and my apartment. I'd be fine with working in this tiny room the rest of the day until it's time for bed, until I remember that I'm going to have to share it with him again tonight.

Suddenly, I'm just as excited to be in a different, more open space. "Okay, let's go."

CHAPTER 19
LUCKY

There's something oddly domestic about this scene.

If we were in a Regency book like The Duke and His Lady, Camila would be the one sitting on the windowsill reading a book and enjoying a warm cup of Lady Grey. I would be the one sitting by the desk reading correspondence and tallying the numbers from the estate.

But this is the twenty first century and I'm the one stretching my injured leg on the windowsill, glad almost to tears that I can finally get some weight off my knee while I read my book and chug down tea instead. Meanwhile, Camila pushed an armchair next to me and she's using a cushion as support for her laptop while she works furiously on who knows what. I just know the operating word there is *furiously* by the following signs: her stern expression, the unreal speed at which she types at intervals, and the occasional pauses she takes to roll her eyes like she can't believe what's on her screen.

She's almost as amusing as the book. Almost. Lord Harrington is about to cut off Lady Arabella's fastenings so that she can breathe after the bad fall she took. Why he's not taking care of her twisted ankle first, I don't know. Priorities.

I peel my eyes off the page for a moment to reach for my mug of tea, only to find out it's empty. I wince, still thirsty and chilly, but not really eager to get up. There's no way I'm bothering this woman either—she looks like she'd chuck me out the window if I interrupt her.

However, someone else dares to do that instead. "Excuse me, young lady, young man." We both turn to an elderly woman. She smiles warmly despite my confusion and Camila's clear displeasure. "Since we're all stuck here at the inn, the owners have kindly allowed us access to the kitchen to bake some cookies for everyone. Would you like to join in the fun?"

"I'm so sorry," Camila says, polite as ever even when her voice is sharp as a knife. "I'm afraid I must pass on the fun. Work has me trapped." She motions at her laptop.

The older woman turns to me. It takes me a moment to think of an excuse. "I would feel bad leaving my girlfriend by herself."

Camila flashes a mildly surprised look. Did she forget that we're allegedly dating? Or was I only supposed to act that way around our exes?

"I—It's okay, you can go if you want." She offers me a tight smile.

"We're set, then!" the enthusiastic lady claps her hands. "We could really use with someone strong to work the dough."

Now I motion at the near leg-long brace. "I'm not sure I can be of a lot of help, actually."

"Don't you worry, there are stools in the kitchen."

And that's how I find myself abandoning my Victorian era nook and my book, and following a jolly old lady through the inn who gets my life history from me in a minute flat. Truly a talent.

In the kitchen, there's already a pair of other older women assembled, and I'm quick to note that their average age is about forty years older than me. "Oh my, you brought us a young buck, Billie." One of them giggles, waving in an aww shucks kind of way.

Billie—the one who recruited me—pats my back and says, "Everyone, meet our new baker, Lucky."

"Er, hi everyone." I release a crutch to awkwardly wave.

"These are my sisters, Val and Nellie," Billie says, and only know is when I notice the resemblance. I had missed it because their haircuts and colors are a whole range, but they have the same cheekbones and they share the same spark in their eyes.

"Is your name really Lucky?" Nellie, the one who hadn't yet spoken and seems the youngest, asks all of a sudden.

"It's Lucas, but literally everyone calls me Lucky."

"And what do you prefer?"

I can't recall ever being asked that, and for some reason it already makes me like her. "I feel like everyone who calls me Lucas is about to give me the scolding of my life. So I actually like Lucky better."

"Lucky it is." She nods.

"Can we get him somewhere to sit?" Billie asks, and one of the sisters scrambles to drag a stool from the prep station corner, and makes room for it. The other one gets me an apron and I'm not surprised when it's decked by festive teddy bears with frills. Since I have zero chill, I snap a selfie with the ladies behind me and send it to the boys to see if it gets a laugh out of them.

HOTSHOT CATCHER

What the

COWBOY YEEHAW

Works very well for your complexion

EL CLEANUP

Agree, this uniform also suits you

ME

Don't get too excited

I'll be in Orlando Wild colors soon

COWBOY YEEHAW

Hope says hell yeah

ME

Wait did you show her the pic??

HOTSHOT CATCHER

Rose wants to know if she can send it to the
SM team

EL CLEANUP

Audrey's thinks it'd be great for the team's
brand

We'd definitely capture the senior demographic
with it

ME

So you're all hanging out together with your
girlfriends without me?!

HOTSHOT CATCHER

Oh I'm sorry, I didn't realize you were supposed
to be our girlfriend too

I press my lips, annoyed that he's shockingly funny. But if I was still in Orlando I'd be the only one in the group who hasn't found his soulmate, his media naranja, his lil boo thang. I'm really happy for these three pricks and the amazing women in their lives, and hell, helping them get together was probably my biggest contribution to society—even more than giving Orlando its first World Series title.

But what about me?

Am I just… on the shelf for being too goofy?

Is changing everything about me that makes me enjoy life the only way I can get chosen?

"Lucky," one of the ladies calls out, pulling my attention away from my phone screen and from my self-induced doom. "Would you like to start out on light duty by sprinkling edible glitter on the first batch?"

Forget everything I've ever done or said in my life. I have found my true calling.

My face splits into a grin. "Absolutely."

One of them slides a fully baked tray of round cookies toward me. "Careful, don't burn yourself."

Another presents me with white glitter. "We're going to pipe these ones to look like snowmen, so you can go ham with the glitter."

"Say no more." I snap my fingers and get to work.

For a moment, everything is blissful. I watch, transfixed, how the glitter falls in the air like snow. Two of the sisters work like professionals around a mixer that fills the spacious kitchen with noise. The third of the sisters is next to me on the table, portioning out ingredients for another batch.

"So," I hear her say, but then the mixer drowns out her next words.

"Sorry, what?"

She motions at her sisters to stop. When they do, she asks, "How long have you and your girlfriend been together?"

Oh. Shit.

I can feel the tendrils of deceit starting to tie themselves around my legs, both injured and healthy alike. This is why lying is bad—it gets complicated, fast. If I hadn't assumed that our charade extended beyond the confines of a rental car, I wouldn't be forced to lie to these sweet ladies too.

"Well," I mumble to buy myself some time as I figure out how to get out of this. I can't say we've been together a long time because then they'll press, how long is a long time? If I say it's a recent thing and somehow that reaches Jasmine's and Romulo's ears, it'll add to their suspicions. I settle for saying, "It's been a while. We actually met at an airport and we've been doing long distance since."

Still a lie, but one that's easier to navigate.

"You poor thing." Nellie's eyebrows scrunch in worry. "You must miss each other all the time."

"Any chance you'll break up?" Val, the one next to me, asks point blank.

"Val!" her sisters exclaim.

She raises her hands along with a shrug. "What? I'm just checking to see if he could become a candidate for my Sarah."

"Sarah is Val's daughter," Billie supplies helpfully. "She's about your age. Very pretty and sweet, by the way. Unlike…" Her eyebrows rise but she doesn't finish that sentence. "I guess your girlfriend is pretty too."

I bump the bottom of the glitter container to increase the flow over the last row of cookies, and they almost seem to give up on the course of conversation. Except I open my mouth again. "To be honest my first impression from Camila was also pretty bad, but…"

They all lean closer for the gossip. It'd make me laugh if I didn't find myself genuinely annoyed.

"She's actually misunderstood because of the way she talks." I recall how, despite being kind of drunk and missing a shoe, when she could've ditched me to find a rental for herself only, she stopped to talk with someone at the airport to ensure I had wheelchair assistance. It flashed through my head that it might even be the reason why she ended up so far back down the line, that the rental company ran out of cars when it was our turn. My lips stretch into a smile. "She's shockingly kind once you get to know her." Or once you get her drunk, I'm not sure.

"Aww, bummer," Val grouches. "You do look in love with her after all."

I freeze.

"Do you happen to have a brother?" Nellie asks me.

"Uh, he's married with a kid," I respond absentmindedly. The three of them groan.

Nahh. They're just caught up in the lie I spewed out with my own mouth. There's no way I'm in deep for a woman I met just yesterday. Attracted? Sure. She is *gorgeous*. Those hips make my blood boil every time I catch sight of them. And she's funny in a kind of Scrooge way. I could see myself asking her out on a date, and sitting with her at a restaurant while we both try to spin circles around each other's minds like it's a sport. She'd be interesting like that.

But love?

Love takes a lot of trial and error, and persistence more than success—which takes a long time, many dates, good news, bad news, illnesses, a negotiation of boundaries, and so on. None of that can happen in the course of a weird road trip that wouldn't even be taking place if the turbulence hadn't happened.

In that alternate reality, the one that should've been the actual timeline, we would've stayed first class neighbors, still miffed about the lounge chair, pointedly ignoring each other during the Horizon Airways flight, and going our separate ways once we reached Mapleton Airport.

"We tried." Billie pats Val's shoulder as if to offer comfort for the fact that they couldn't bag me for their niece. Turning to me, Billie says, "No worries, though. We'll continue being your fans anyway."

My eyebrows rise.

"Go Wild!" Nellie pumps her fist in the air.

"So you know who I am." I blink.

Is this why they were trying to marry off to whoever Sarah

is? Not because they deemed me a good guy, but because they probably know what my salary is.

Ouch.

"Of course we do, we've been following baseball all our lives. Our dad used to collect the player cards, you know?" Billie clicks her tongue. "He'd be so upset to know I met a player and didn't have a card on me to get signed."

I rub the back of my neck, looking at the glitter I wasted on the table with an increasing of guilt. They're just fans of the sport, this isn't about me and my insecurities.

"Would it make me look self centered if I admit that I usually have cards on me for this very reason?"

The squeals these women give off almost pierce my eardrums.

"All right, let's go get one," I say, chuckling.

The cookies lay forgotten for a moment while the trio follows me slowly, patiently, as I make my way through the entire inn toward the Polar room I share with my fake girlfriend. I'm thinking about how I can make sure to stay seated for the rest of the damn afternoon once we're back to the kitchen, when I take the last bend toward the corridor that leads to the rooms.

Camila seems to be returning from our shared room at the same time, and she stops right in front of me. "Hi."

"Hey."

She sweeps her light brown eyes down my frame to my right leg. "I thought you were supposed to be keeping weight off your leg."

I open my mouth to explain the situation, when one of my new buddies speaks from behind me. "That'll be our fault, we're on our way to get an autograph."

Another one quips right away, along with a smacking sound. "Never mind that—look."

A long pause.

I glance over my shoulder. "Please don't tell me I have a hole in my pants or something."

"No, no. Look." Nellie points up but there's nothing above her. And that's when I realize she means something above me.

I turn back around and tilt my head back. I don't know how I dare to be surprised but sure enough, that's mistletoe hanging right over the spot at the end of the corridor where Camila and I are standing together.

CHAPTER 20
CAMILA

Hell no, I know exactly how this goes in movies and TV shows. I raise the palm of my hand and say, "Not to be a party pooper, but I'm not a fan of public displays of affection."

"But that is the definition of party pooper, my dear," the older woman from earlier says, her eyes dancing with laughter at me.

Another one smacks Lucky's arm. "See? My Sarah would never waste a chance to kiss a stud like you."

I—what?

Shaking his head, the one guy in this weird little group says, "Long story short, Val here wanted to set me up with her daughter until I explained that I have a girlfriend." Here, Lucky widens his eyes and I almost think that it's to remind me to play my role, until I hear a door closing from the hallway.

Now, Grizzly isn't the only other room we share space with, but that door opening is the only one that could bring panic to Lucky's expression right now. If only I was like Spider-Man, who could see the Green Goblin's upcoming attack reflected in the pupils of Mary Jane.

"It shouldn't be that hard to kiss your beloved, you know?" the third woman teases.

Steps approach from behind me. I'm sure that with how much Murphy's Law enjoys finding me in my worst moments, it's either Jasmine or Rupert. Probably the latter, to be honest.

"Fine, just a quick peck because I have to get back to work," I mumble, searching Lucky's face for signs of discomfort. Instead, he gives me a minuscule nod.

I wish I could be as icy and stoic on the inside as I am on the outside. I don't know why, but while I've been able to tame my expressions and my movements, I've never been able to get as good a grip on my emotions. They're so intense that they often shock even me, and I'm convinced they're the real reason people can't stand me. They can sense that there's a lot of turmoil behind my icy calm.

Like right now. Even though I know that none of this is real, nor does it matter, my heartbeat still accelerates disproportionally as I approach Lucky. I have a feeling he'd meet me halfway if he could with how his upper body bows toward me. I avoid his eyes because there should be nothing intimate about this. If anything, it's like another version of our handshakes every time we add another clause to our mutual survival deal. That's what this kiss is, survival. Nothing romantic about it.

Still, my eyes close the second my lips find his. Like for a second I want to pretend that this is more than what it actually is.

Lucky's breath on my face makes me break into goosebumps. I don't even linger enough to map the feeling of his lips, and it's only when I pull away that I notice, for literally the first time since I've known him, that his upper lip is thicker than the bottom. And for some reason it makes me shiver.

"That's it?" one of the audience members complains. "Even my husband of forty one years and I kiss with more tongue."

Lucky observes my face, eyes lowering to my neck where I realize he must be seeing the goosebumps. I retreat to a safer distance, clearing my throat and folding my arms like that can preserve my dignity.

He turns to the complaining woman. "Sorry, Nellie. My snuggle bear is actually just shy. Aren't you?" He turns to me again.

My mouth opens at the nickname. His attention swoops down to it. Oh, no. I can feel heat traveling up my cheeks. "Yes, shy. If you'll excuse me." I duck my face and side step around them.

If I wasn't sure how I could face him after drooling on his arm in my sleep, now I truly can't ever be in his presence anymore. I already accidentally let out last night that I find him very attractive, but who wouldn't? Clearly those three older women are besotted with him. That alone isn't special.

But kissing him?

That's a step farther. What if he thinks I somehow orchestrated that? I could've very well been the one to hang the mistletoe, even though I saw Marv do it a few minutes ago from the armchair I have taken as my new office.

Then again, it wasn't really a proper kiss. I barely touched my lips with his. The whole thing might have lasted five seconds at most. I've been significantly more passionate eating an ice cream cone than kissing Lucky Rivera.

What a shame. I should've played along better. If my trajectory of staying committed to work stays on course, that might've been my last chance to feel a man from up close.

Rupert and Jasmine are nowhere nearby when I turn around, which adds an extra layer of discomfort. I feel so bad using Lucky to save face, and even worse that I'm starting to enjoy it.

Disappointed, I take my laptop from the armchair and plop myself on the seat with a sad little sigh. If my thoughts aren't kicking me when I'm down enough, life presents me with a new opportunity to feel like garbage when a shadow passes over me.

Rupert moves to lean against the windowsill that Lucky vacated earlier. His mouth is twisted in a way I don't like, so I try to pretend like he's not even there by firing up my laptop again. Turns out we did have an audience after all.

"So, what was that?"

My cheek twitches. I have a few messages from Rachel on Teams and I focus on those.

LEON, RACHEL - 11:31AM:

I went to your office and you weren't there??

Did you decide to permanently move to Orlando??

Is it the parks??

Or the SPORTS???

Snorting, I start drafting a reply when Rupert ahems so blatantly that I can't keep pretending he's not one step away anymore.

Lifting my eyes, I ask, "What do you want?"

He snorts. "There she is, the ice queen I knew." And didn't love, I add in my head.

"Why don't you go bother your fiancée?" Checking my surroundings, I spot no perfect long manes of dark hair nor do I hear twinkling laughs.

He shrugs a little. "She wasn't feeling so well, so she's taking a nap."

Good for her.

"Go nap with her or something," I say to him as I finish typing and hit send.

I don't even know where to begin.

Actually, it all started with the dog that peed on my travel boots. That really was the inception of every misadventure since.

"It's good to know you still value your work more than your *new boyfriend*." I snap my eyes to Rupert in time to see him make air quotes for the last two words.

Alarms go off in my head. "What are you talking about?"

"You know, I always thought I was the problem," he explains more to himself than to me because I still don't get it. It's like he's looking right through me, perhaps at a scene from the past instead. "That I had some sort of shortcoming that made you love your job more than you cared for me. But after seeing you kiss a rich and athletic guy like he's a dead fish tells me everything I need to know."

This time the goosebumps traveling all over my skin are entirely different, the ones that leave me feeling cold and wanting to shrink in on myself. "Excuse me?" The question comes out shrill.

Rupert Montblanc dares to look at me with pity. "The problem was you all along. You're just incapable of love and affection, and that's why I actually couldn't go ahead with our wedding."

His words—unexpected, uncalled for, and cruel—pierce right through the chest plate of my armor and into my heart.

But outside, I behave the way I always do—the only way I know how. Slowly, as if I was in no hurry, I shut my laptop and collect my things. I carry them in my arms as I get to my feet and stare him down, since he's still sitting against the edge of the windowsill.

With a cool voice I spit out, "Maybe I'm just incapable of loving someone who doesn't deserve it." Lifting one shoulder petulantly, I swivel on my feet and bypass the table full of middle aged people playing cards and having way more fun than I am.

There's a random guy checking his phone right under the damn mistletoe, which blocks my escape route to my room. My feet pivot before my brain can catch up with them, and it clicks as I'm walking down the staff area that there's another place I can take refuge from my ex—the same I got invited to an hour ago that I declined.

The kitchen.

When I arrive it's still empty, but there are half started batches of cookies on the prep table and two whole trays baking in the oven. I'm sure the gossipy hens will return and frankly, I'd rather be surrounded by them than near Rupert. Or near my own thoughts.

"Keep it together, Camila," I tell myself with the same harsh tone I would use on Lucky's brother when he comes into my office with issues but no solutions. The same sharky way of talking that has isolated me from almost everyone else at *SPORTY*.

But while it works very well on others, it doesn't on myself. I know the truth. Even though I left Rupert with a pretty decent burn, he did me far more damage. Because he's right.

Damn it, he's right.

I don't know what love is. And you can't give what you don't know. So while Rupert was and remains an unmitigated asshole, I was the reason the wedding didn't proceed. It was a very good thing for all parties that it didn't. I would've ruined that marriage, possibly our lives. I wonder if my therapist is going to be pleased that I'm having this realization, or if she'll be disappointed that I'm thinking this way during the holidays while everybody else is baking cookies and drinking eggnog or whatever.

"Look who's here." I stop pacing in the middle of the kitchen when one of Lucky's fans strides into the kitchen. She stops to call everyone behind her. "Lucky, your girlfriend decided to join us after all."

He's coming?

Sure enough, two other women usher him in. Lucky takes one look at my face and his transforms from amusement at whatever conversation they were having before I showed up, to something way more somber.

I hate that I have that effect on people. Just once I'd like to be the cause of someone's smile.

I blink hard, realizing that I'm about to cry.

"Ladies, excuse me for a second." He picks up the pace as much as the crutches allow him, his face tightening with the effort. I turn away from the entrance, trying to hide myself from the strangers, and when he joins me he speaks so low I can barely hear him. "Camila, what's wrong?"

"Rupert," I bite out, my eyes fixed on the ridiculous apron he's still wearing. "He found me."

His hand grabs onto my elbow. "Did he hurt you?" That makes my breath hitch. I feel him trying to make eye contact, but he can't really lean down low enough with the crutches wedged under his armpits. "Hey, look at me. Did he put his hand on you?"

"No," I choke out, shaking my head. "His tongue—"

"His *what?*"

Even the old ladies stop their chatter at the change in Lucky's tone.

Finally I meet his eyes. The brown in them looks like molten lava that could burn the whole world down. The vehemence of it ties up my brain in knots.

"No, I mean—his tongue is what hurt me. What he said. Not that he—and he also didn't hit me or anything. He wouldn't dare to…" I can't even finish the sentence.

Rather than reassuring Lucky, it makes him even angrier. His words are a dangerous hiss, "Le rompo la cara."

"No, you won't." I get in his face when he makes an attempt to go fulfill that little promise. I grab a fistful of the teddy bears apron to stop him. My hand is trembling—actually, my whole body is. I swallow hard before I can speak. "No, here's what you're going to do instead. You're going to bake cookies with me and with these women, and you're going to keep me far, far away from my jerk of an ex. Can you do that for me?" With a thread of voice, I add, "Please?"

There's a war in Lucky's face. I never would've imagined that a guy whose main hobby seems to find the funny things in life was capable of the thunder that has crashed in his face. His nostrils flare and he stares into my eyes like searching for something.

"Fine," he mumbles, and this is when his hand cinches just a little tighter around my elbow. "But you're going to tell me every single word he spewed out later, and then you'll let me decide if I'm going to sock him in the noggin. Do we have a deal?"

"No, Rupert is the petty kind who will go to the police or media with news that a professional baseball player hit him. It'll ruin your career. That's not gonna happen."

"Then what? I'm supposed to do just nothing?" Lucky is the picture of incredulity.

"Yes," I whisper. "You're not my real boyfriend, Lucky. We just met yesterday. Did you forget?"

I can tell by how his eyes widen a notch that he did, in fact, forget about that little piece of trivia. My chest does a funny flip—or it's more like the whole world flips for just a second, until I find my feet on the ground again.

"Let's just… forget this all happened." I watch my fingers as they uncurl from the apron and let him go. "We just need to get to Mapleton and then all of this will stay behind us, right?"

But he doesn't respond. And I already know that none of this is going to stay in the rearview mirror. I make a mental note of booking a therapy session right after Christmas.

CHAPTER 21
LUCKY

'm not feeling quite so cheerful anymore. In fact, my mood is downright foul.

"You do know the dough is not going to run away, right?" Nellie chuckles next to me, watching me roll the dough over the table with a lot more strength than this requires. The only reason these cookies won't be razor thin is because I'm sitting on a stool and can't use the power of my legs right now.

"I just want to make them nice and even," I say, trying for my usual levity but know I've failed spectacularly when Camila lifts her eyes and pins them on my face.

Yeah, I know we just met. But that doesn't mean I shouldn't care either. I'm not callous like her ex. And what the hell does Jasmine see in a jerk like Ralph? Why would his opinion even matter? Actually, why does he deserve to keep his face intact?

Damn it, how am I going to stay civil during the rest of the time we'll be stuck together? Should we just find a different ride? Maybe wait out the storm until the snow melts and we can rent our own car? Surely there's a car rental company located in Bear Crossing, right? Or nearby. Somewhere we could get to by taxi.

But wait, should I warn Jasmine that she's about to tie the knot with a complete douchebag?

Because if he almost made Camila cry—a woman who doesn't even mind that her heels are cutting up her skin—then that's what he is. A piece of shit who is better off alone for the sake of women at large.

"That is really good." Val cocks an eyebrow at Camila's handiwork. "Are you sure this is the first time you make cookies?"

Camila steps back to admire her piping work on the cookies that are meant to look like snowmen. "Yes, it's the first time. My family never did any of this growing up."

"Then how are you so freaking good?"

Billie responds instead, "She looks like the kind of person who is good at everything."

"Trust me, not at everything," she mumbles. Fortunately, the three sisters have no chance at hearing her because the mixer is going at full speed. But I'm a professional baseball player, I'm *great* at reading lips, and that little dig at herself didn't escape me.

I pound the dough and roll it even thinner. These are going to turn into crackers at this rate.

*

Lunch ends up being a pile of sandwiches that Marv and Lottie, the inn owners, prepared in the early hours of the morning when they realized that everyone was going to be stuck here today.

I don't leave the kitchen for lunch. My blood is still boiling even though I spend what feels like hours talking myself down. It's okay that I care about Camila, but I don't even know what words were actually said. I'm just interpreting that they were bad, based on her near tears. Why do I even care so much, though? Why am I boiling like this? Don't tell me I'm really catching fee fees.

The women return together, and I'm glad to see that at least the sisters shenanigans have cleared some of the hurt from Camila's expression. She almost looks on the verge of a smile.

"—And that's when I said: Tom, you are so screwed," Val delivers the punchline to what I'm sure is another story about her husband. Billie and Nellie cackle like hens, and Camila's lips twitch. Her eyes look much softer than before, but still a little sad.

The question hits me like a boulder. What would it take to see her smile fully?

Another thing I notice is how the longer Camila stays around them—despite keeping mostly silent—the less Val keeps trying to pitch her daughter. I noticed the shift started when Val caught sight of Camila cleaning every little mess as it cropped up, without even noticing how flour and butter stuck to her own clothes. I gave her my apron then, and that got me an approving look from the three hens.

We produce enough cookies to feed the entire nation, and we pile them on the clean baking trays to go hand them over to the other guests and the owners. But the very last thing I want to do is run into whatshisface, so I clear my throat from the back of the group.

"Actually, my knee's really bothering me right now"—not a lie—"So I'm just gonna head to my room to get some rest. Snuggle bear, wanna join me?"

Camila's jaw drops just the same way as it did the first time I used the silly nickname on her. She shakes her head. "I, uh, I'll help them out and join you in a bit, okay?"

"Okay," I grit out through a fake smile.

*

An hour later, I have calmed myself down with some stretches, turned on the electric fireplace on the wall by the bathroom entrance, and am currently sprawled on the carpet like a starfish, blinking at the ceiling and questioning my life choices.

So much for this being the biggest prank of my life. Joke's on me, because pranks are supposed to be amusing and not irritating enough that I feel like I'm going to burst at the seams.

The door opens and I tilt my head back, watching upside down as Camila walks into the room. She closes the door with her full body leaning against it, and stays there while she observes me. "Are you okay?" she asks.

No. I'm not sure. But probably not.

Instead, I say, "Shouldn't I be asking you that?"

The sigh she releases her deflates her chest. "Do you want to know what I hate the most right now, Lucky?"

"It's not that you're stuck under the same roof as your evil ex?"

"No." She picks herself up and slowly ambles over. Now that she's no longer wearing the apron, I can see flour and grease stains on her blouse that used to be pristine white. She lowers herself to sit crosslegged some three feet away from me. "I try really hard for people to not find out that I'm a mess, yet somehow you keep seeing me at my worst over and over."

I bring in my arms to lift up my torso by my elbows. "You're wrong," I say slowly and clearly. "You're not a mess, you've just found yourself in a mess."

"Semantics." She waves her hand.

"So I take it you're not okay."

Her eyes flash, and I don't think it's just because of the flames being reflected on them. "You know, it's too late to keep trying to pretend like I have my shit together in front of you." She sucks in a deep breath. "Yeah, I'm not okay. Far from it."

"What did he say to you?" I ask in a whisper.

Camila stays quiet for a moment, just watching me. "He saw us kiss."

"I know. I saw him coming from behind you and…" Her teeth scrape her bottom lip in the first sign of real uncertainty I've ever seen her display. I'm struck by the visceral need to bite her lip for her, and also to run out of Polar and into Grizzly to tell that jerk what's what with my fist.

"It didn't convince him one bit." She lets out a brief, dry chuckle. "In fact, it seems to have made him feel better about himself."

I scrunch up my face. "What?"

"Apparently he thought it must've been his fault that I loved my job better than him, and seeing me kiss you like you're a dead fish made him realize that the problem was me all along. That I'm just incapable of affection."

"He said *what?*" I hiss barely above a breath, sitting up like a bolt.

She shrugs. "And he's right. I don't know how to do any of that." She waves her hand again, and you'd think we're talking about the weather instead. "Forget about making a man happy. I don't even know how to get along with colleagues. Your brother hates me, by the way."

That twist makes me do a double take. "Wait, what?"

"He's never outright said it, but I know I'm his least favorite part of working for *SPORTY*. And I'm sure he's going to like me even less the next months. I'm going to go from the most disliked member of the executive team to absolutely hated."

"Camila, what the hell are you talking about?"

"My point is…" She trails off, eyes straying to the fireplace. "That's just how it is. The truth hurts and all that."

"Listen, I may not know you very well yet, but I can't believe you let your ex get in your head like this."

"It's not just him. It's everything. Everyone."

My eyes bulge. "So you're telling me that you didn't notice how Val stopped trying to sell me her daughter the moment she met you?"

"What does that have to do with anything?"

"It has to do with *everything*. A random old woman who knows nothing about your life got so charmed by you that she finally accepted that she wouldn't bag a baseball player as her son-in-law."

Camila blinks a few times. "That doesn't mean—"

"What about me, then?"

"What about you?" the question comes out after a moment of opening and closing her mouth.

"What if I like what I've seen so far?" I stare intently, waiting for a response that doesn't come. I push on without fear, just like I did to get that fateful out. "What if I think you're like a bear? Fierce but soft—and what if I think those two things can coexist just fine in a single person?"

Her lips part slightly, capturing my attention.

I speak to them. "See, the problem wasn't you. It was *never* you. You were trying to fit in with a man that was too small for you." It takes everything I have to tear my eyes away and find her eyes instead. "You need a man who understands how amazing you are and doesn't try to make himself big by stepping on you."

Camila sucks in air. Her eyebrows twitch. She shakes her head. "I don't think such a man exists."

"He does," I say, as sure of this as I am that my knee's going to recover. "And while you find him, I'm going to help you."

"How?" she breathes out the word.

I lean a little closer. "I'm going to kiss you properly, the kind that will melt your socks off. The kind that is going to make Randall realize he lost the hottest woman on earth."

"Right now?" Camila screeches.

For the first time in hours, I smile. I can feel like it's not my usual one—this one feels like the Grinch before making an attempt at ruining Christmas. Except I mean to do the exact opposite. I'm going to give this woman the Christmas gift she needs: understanding that she's hot as hell. That she's not lacking anything, and that her ex's opinion is worth as much as melting snow.

"No, not right now," I say slowly. "Tomorrow. Right in front of your ex."

CHAPTER 22
CAMILA

"This is the most ridiculous thing I've ever done in my life," I say with all confidence but through gritted teeth, in as low a voice as possible as I can while sitting next to a baseball player I have slept with for two nights in a row in a random small town inn.

Key word: *slept*. If the first night we shared a bed was a ten in exhaustion—on the scale from zero to ten—last night was about an eight. Turns out that working through emotions while baking cookies is draining, and we were very businesslike in getting ready for bed. He even fell asleep first, breathing so deeply that I almost thought he was snoring until I saw that his mouth was closed and it was just his chest doing all the work. This time around I woke up first, and we were at such a safe distance from each other that it was almost a bummer.

Okay, it was one hundred percent a bummer. I'll never admit it aloud.

Now we're having breakfast while plotting for the best corner and moment to make out in front of my ex.

What is my life?

Lucky takes a moment to work through his bite, to then say, "It truly is an honor to be part of such a monumental occasion in your life."

I give him a look, somehow wondering for the first time *what* is *he?* "How are you so cool with all of this?"

"Mami, I have two specialties in life." He leans closer to me, a glint in his pretty brown eyes. "Baseball and trolling."

"Ah." I reach for my cup of coffee, blowing on it before taking a sip so I can sit with my thoughts for a moment. Or rather, with the weird churn in my stomach. It's not the most pleasant feeling in the world to know that being kissed is on par with a joke.

"Ex alert," he whispers as he spears a sausage.

I check the entrance and sure enough, both of our exes are walking in hand in hand, laughing about who knows what. Probably a niche medical joke that only they understand, I don't know. Rupert looks annoyingly happy, cheeks pink and all as his fiancée delivers a punchline that sends him into a fit.

"He never laughed like that with me," I muse, a second too late realizing that I've said it aloud.

"If it makes you feel better, Jasmine mostly looked at me in annoyance."

I exchange a glance with Lucky Rivera, someone who is drastically so different from me in every aspect, that it's hard to believe he also was unable to make his significant other happy.

Frowning, I ask, "How is that even possible? You look like the whole package."

His lips stretch into a wide smile. "No need to flatter me, teddy bear. I'm already game to kiss you senseless."

Of course he says this while I'm chewing on a too dry biscuit and I choke.

"There, there." Lucky pats my back gently.

My little crisis catches Rupert's attention, which in turn

diverts Jasmine's attention to us. She's the one who sends us a little wave, before focusing on their conversation again while lining up for the breakfast buffet. It's the exact same food as yesterday but none of us mind. Snow is still piled on outside almost to waist level, and no one in their right mind would venture outside for a different meal.

I push past the block in my throat with some coffee, and once I have recovered enough I ask with the raspiest voice, "What now? Are we going to start making out right here?"

He appears surprised by my question. "I was hoping to brush my teeth first so I can give you a really good impression."

"Oh." I cast my eyes down at my scrambled eggs and my hair falls away from the its hold behind my ears. I push it back, acting like a freaking teenager with a crush. "Thank you for your consideration."

"Gee, lady. It's not a business transaction." He shakes his head but continues eating like nothing big just happened.

But it's not? A business transaction, that is. If so, what is it then?

Rupert and Jasmine pass us by with their full plates, and I breathe out a sigh of relief that they knew better than to join our table.

"Low key, I'm also glad that I don't have to kiss you when my mouth tastes like bacon."

"Hmm, that doesn't sound so bad." Lucky tilts his head, eyes fluttering to my lips.

I feel a visceral need to destroy the fantasy right away, otherwise he's going to see just how much I'm looking forward to kissing him properly. "And eggs, sausage, biscuits, and over-brewed coffee."

"Let's make sure to floss as well," he adds as an afterthought.

I can't help it—the mix of feelings in my belly bubble up

like I'm a shaken bottle of champagne that someone brought to the Christmas party.

I bark a laugh.

Lucky pauses in the middle of lifting his fork to his mouth. It hovers there as he slowly grins like he probably does after making a particularly good play on the field. It makes me self conscious enough that I slow down. "What?"

"Damn, you have such a pretty laugh."

Gasping, I cover my mouth and effectively stop laughing.

"Boo, hiss," he mumbles in a grouchy tone. "Guess I'll have to make you laugh again."

"Just—Just stick to the kissing for today, please. I can't deal with more than that."

Mierda, why did I say that?

"Hmm, good to know." He returns his attention to calmly, painstakingly eating his breakfast.

In contrast, I pour the rest of mine down my guzzler and excuse myself to return to our Polar room. I nearly run into the bathroom to give myself a professional level dental cleaning. Too bad my Waterpik is home to really ensure that my teeth are spotless.

"What the hell am I doing?" I ask my reflection in the mirror, although the question is barely intelligible as I scrub my mouth with my toothbrush, violently frothing down to my chin.

But… is it so bad if I have a little fun?

It felt good to laugh. I don't remember the last time I did— that's how infrequently it happens. And if laughter is the proof that someone feels joy, I forget most of the times that I'm capable of it.

I wash my face again because maybe I also don't want my lips to taste like toothpaste, and then I look way too pale. Without trying to talk myself out of it, I reach for my makeup bag to reapply moisturizer and then I keep going. I don't do a full blown cat eye and red lip because I might've acted a little juvenile earlier, but the guy already knows I find him attractive. No need to put a billboard on my head. I just do a tiny splash of eyeliner with brown eyeshadow, mascara, some blush, and a lip tint that makes my lips look already kissed but doesn't smudge.

There, reasonable. I made a tiny bit of effort to further dip into the moment. Let the world know I'm also a woman.

Lucky's making his way into the bedroom when I emerge from the bathroom. "All yours," I say regally, taking my laptop. "I'll meet you at the same nook from yesterday."

"Yes, ma'am."

With that we cross paths, not stopping to acknowledge each other any further.

Joke's on me, because my body acknowledges him, all right. He had a tough time this morning showering in an unfamiliar bathroom with a full cast on his leg, but my goodness, I don't begrudge him all the noise he caused because he smells incredible. The same shampoo and shower gel I used transformed into something intoxicating on his skin.

Not to be too dramatic but I think I'm going to die today. Either that's why I'm going to get kissed by such a specimen, or that itself will do me in.

As I emerge into the common room, I spot a middle aged man heading for The Nook. The only other open spots are by the table taken by the three cookie sisters, and I'd rather not have them as audience again. I pick up the pace, glad that these artisanal boots allow my banged up feet to eat ground steadily and fast. The guy catches sight of me from the corner of his eye and he steps on the gas pedal too.

Nuh uh, I think to myself, *that nook is mine.* Using my best power walk—which is this side shy of a jog—I all but use my work laptop as a frisbee to land it on the windowsill. It catches the man by surprise, enough to stop.

I park my Caribbean behind on the plush seating, my back against the frigid window. Lifting my chin, I give him a victorious look.

"Bah." He waves his hands and changes tack to camp by the sisters.

I flip open my laptop, cool as a cucumber on the outside, while my stomach does flip flops. For the first time in… all my career at *SPORTY*, I don't get immediately sucked in by my inbox. I browse it still, filing a few things away for later, deleting others, and leaving the more important stuff unread for after the kiss.

My hands hover over the keyboard, right before clicking on Teams to tell Rachel and Sierra what I'm about to do. I'm sure they'd be shocked, probably delighted as well. They'd spur me on. They've encouraged me to put myself out there over the course of the year we've been hanging out outside of work. I sure as hell am doing that right now.

But I think I want to do this on my own first. I'll tell them after the fact, once I've had a chance to process the aftermath. Right now I know I would sound like a quinceañera with her first crush.

Something tugs at me and my head lifts. Lucky's striding into the common area—or as close to it as someone with crutches can—and his eyes are trained on me. A weird reflex kicks in that makes me swallow hard.

He doesn't break the connection between our eyes even though Lottie, one of the owners, cuts into his path while carrying a blanket.

Gosh, this guy is huge.

Lucky's not the tallest guy I've ever met, but his physique is so exceptional that it makes him look larger than life. It's not bulky, rather it's so defined it could've been cut by DaVinci's chisel. Although DaVinci could only dream of achieving the perfect little curl of his hair that threatens to feel incredibly soft, and I don't think the maestro could've done any justice to Lucky's lips.

The same ones I'm going to get close and personal with soon.

As if reading my thoughts, a smirk stretches a corner of said lips. "Hey," he greets once he reaches me.

"I saved you a spot." I motion beside me like this wasn't part of the plan all along.

"Perfect." Hopping on his uninjured leg, he rests his crutches against the wall and turns around to park himself on my left. The seat seemed spacious enough until now, when he swallows it up. His arm brushes mine as he reaches behind him, and out he plucks the beaten book he's been traveling with.

My jaw drops. "Wait a second."

"Hmm?" He turns to me while cracking the book open.

"Is that what you intend to do and not to…"

"Oh no, we're doing this," he reassures, not moving at all.

"When?"

"Are you always this impatient?" His eyes dance with open mirth at my expense.

I huff. "Not impatient, efficient. Dilly dallying isn't exactly the definition of—"

Without warning, he grabs my chin and tugs gently. Somehow that registers—that even though the touch is so commanding, that his fingertips are hot and calloused—his touch is almost tender. My eyes stay popped open even as he leans over, closing the distance until our lips meet again.

Again. We're kissing for the second time.

"Close your eyes, woman," Lucky whispers against my lips, the fluttering friction making heat explode in my chest.

Inhaling his scent deeply, I let my eyes close and the most curious thing happens. Far from offering some relief, I feel positively volcanic now. The fact that the window was gelid against my back stops registering. I lean into the fire but he adds a touch more pressure to my chin, keeping me locked in place like he wants to take this slow.

And oh.

Oh.

Take it slow he does. We're snowed in on a small town in the middle of the east coast, surrounded by other strangers, with nothing to do but enjoy this moment on the windowsill—truly a first for me.

Lucky's lips deliberately savor mine, starting from the top. This is when I notice that he shaved, because not just his lips are soft. That little bit of effort is what undoes me and a tiny moan escapes from my throat.

It makes him suck in air, almost like something hurts. I try to pull away to check if maybe I'm putting my weight on his injured knee, but he doesn't let me. Instead, he angles his head to press harder, his jaw working as he maps my lips still slow, but with a lot more intent. There's a thread of vertigo in my head, like I'm falling—right into the hottest moment of my life.

My laptop tries to slide off and I clutch at it with both hands, hard enough that the plastic groans. I stretch farther into the kiss, venturing my tongue to taste that upper lip of his that drives me wild. It tears a primal, guttural sound from Lucky and two things happen. He lets go of my chin, but I only miss the touch for a second because next thing, there's a thud and both of his hands are in my hair.

This kiss rewrites every other I've had in the past right into my cells. I forget them—forget myself, or where we are, or the fact that we've only known each other for two days. When his mouth coerces mine open on the sheer power of his jaw, I'm more than happy to comply. I turn liquid as our tongues brush, hot and wet, and even though he also used a minty kind of toothpaste and probably some mouthwash, it still tastes like him. Just as good as he smells, as he feels.

I could stay in this moment forever.

A needy little mewl escapes from my chest as he pulls away, probably because I'm not an athlete with incredible pulmonary capacity and am already breathing like a truck. So not sexy.

"Easy there, osa." Lucky chuckles against my lips, the sounds coming from his mouth throatier and raspier than usual. It makes me swallow hard. "Do you want me to get thrown out into these icy streets?"

"What?" Dizzy, I open my eyes.

Lucky's are half mast, looking at my lips with such hunger that it spears my gut. He shifts one hand to caress my jaw, until his thumb finds my swollen lips again. "If you keep kissing me like that I'm going to have a real hard time behaving like a civilized man."

I gasp a little. "Me? As if you're not the one making love to my mouth?"

"Ha!" Damn it, why does he looks so radiant smiling like that? "I must not have been doing a good enough job if you could throw that jab at me."

"Trust me," I murmur, frowning. "You were doing great until I had to breathe."

Still smiling, he sucks in his lower lip and bites it, and that —*that* is what sends a stab of want all the way down to my toes. I'm angry that I didn't rake my teeth across his lip when I had the chance.

But then his eyes slip to the side and they change, losing some of the heat that was swirling between us. "Oh, good."

"What?" I try to turn to where he's looking, but his hands on my head don't let me.

"Don't. They're going to think we did it for them." The curve of his lips is more sardonic now. "Even though we did."

Them. Our exes. And a room full of stranded travelers.

Oh my goodness. What are we doing?

I'm frustrated to note that my hand shakes as it rises to his wrist, carefully prying him off. The other naturally follows the movement without my aid.

"Let me get your book," is all I can think of saying after sharing the most epic kiss of my life, and being reminded that it was fake. That it wasn't really for me.

CHAPTER 23
LUCKY

I am unwell.

At first, my pea brain figures that I had too much bacon over breakfast. But then I remember that the last time I went to the island to visit my mom I ate a whole lechón by myself, so that's definitely not it.

Pretty sure it has something to do with the fact that my skin itches under my clothes, my heart is beating at a million miles per minute, I've read the same page five times, and I'm hyper aware of the fact that Camila Puig, my brother's boss, high powered executive of a mega corporation, and basically a stranger—tastes like caramel. The minty toothpaste couldn't hide it. This woman is edible. If she let me, I'd demonstrate just how much I'd enjoy her. Thoroughly. Slowly.

However—and that's a biggie right there—the second we're able to drive out of this place, we're going to become full blown strangers again.

Now, despite Mom's better wishes, I didn't turn out to be a saint. I've fooled around—never with someone else's feelings, but certainly when we both knew it was just casual. Camila is the type of person who takes everything so seriously that I doubt she'd be interested in a bit of foolery with me tonight.

Besides, the fact remains that my leg limits me a lot right now. And it hurts worse than a toothache. And if I had the impulse of brushing my teeth thoroughly so I could impress her when we kissed, I'd also rather be recovered so I can put more effort into romancing her properly.

Except tomorrow or the next day we're going our separate ways.

I shut the book and place it on the space between us, mumbling, "Be right back."

She nods without glancing at me, her attention on a spreadsheet that she's been tinkering with for the past hour and change since we made out like randy teenagers.

Okay, I tried to apply more finesse than that. I succeeded for all of one minute before a visceral, blazing hunger took over me, and I wanted to just devour the caramel on her tongue.

My breath hitches at the memory, the air whistling through my teeth. I feel her eyes turn to me and I make as quick work as possible of maneuvering my crutches to get up and get moving. I'm starting to worry that if I look into her eyes, I'm going to lean in again and give away just how much I want her. How the hell am I going to sleep on the same bed again tonight?

"Hey, handsome." A familiar voice stops me right as I'm about to take the bend toward the bedrooms. Billie's also heading this way and her eyebrows are doing something funny. "We saw that earlier."

"What?" My brain has gone completely empty except for three words: Camila. Kiss. More.

"That was an epic freaking kiss." She covers her mouth as she chuckles. "I can confirm that Val has truly given up on introducing you to her daughter now."

"Oh."

"I don't know who's luckier, if you for finding such a good, hardworking girl, or if her for bagging the sweetest hunk I've ever met."

That tears a laugh out of me. I sound a little winded as I ask, "What am I, honey glazed ham?"

She studies me for a second, and by that I mean she gives me a more thorough full-body scan than my medical team did after I tore my ACL. "No, sweetie. You're much better." After patting my arm a couple of times, she tosses me a wink and continues on her path toward the kitchen.

Honestly, I wanna be her when I grow up.

By the time I reach the restroom and wash my face with cold water, I feel a little more like a regular guy than a caveman on the verge of making himself extinct. What would Mateo think if he found out that I have the hots for his boss?

Plucking my phone from my pocket, I shoot him a quick text to feel him out.

ME

Epa mano

What do you think about your boss

His response comes after a minute.

EL BRO

Huh???

I know what he's thinking. What's up with the left field question?

I rack my jock brain to find a semi decent explanation.

ME

Just wondering since you never talk about her

"Mielda," I say, the word echoing back to me against the bathroom tiles. Then I repeat it once more when my brother starts calling me by FaceTime. "To what do I owe the pleasure of this call?" I ask as if I wasn't about to walk straight into quicksand.

"Lucas Rivera," he starts, frowning very close into the screen like he's trying to see exactly where I am. "Don't tell me it's what I'm thinking."

I cock an eyebrow. "Wow, I didn't know you thought at all."

"Is this mysterious woman you're traveling with my boss?" I stay quiet but I'm pretty sure that I look like a deer caught in the headlights. "You are? What the——"

"How the hell did you guess that from an innocent question?"

Damn, this is why he went to college and I got into pro sports.

"It is never an innocent question from you."

"Rude." I pause. "But true."

Mateo's eyes shift around him and he lowers his voice until I barely catch the words. "Have you slept with my boss?"

"No." I look up at the ceiling, and since I'm not in the habit of lying I add, "Technically not. We've had to share the same bed, though."

"You *what?*"

I jerk away from the phone, which would've sent my ass to the floor if it wasn't for the vanity behind me. "Cabrón, you almost blew my eardrum."

"You're sleeping with my boss?" he hisses.

"Not right now. And also not the way you think. There weren't enough rooms in this place and——stop looking at me like that, I'm being honest."

Deep lines appear between his forehead. "Then why do you look disappointed?"

"Puñeta," I whisper. "Am I being that obvious?" Looks like I need to wash my face with cold water again.

"Cabrón," he spits right back at me. "You've been single way too long if you're into the ice queen."

"The ice queen?" Pretty sure the grooves are now appearing between my own eyebrows.

"Yeah, I don't ever talk about her because just saying her name makes the air ten degrees colder. She's made my life impossible at work."

That sticks to me, not fitting into the puzzle I've been assembling about her. "What do you mean?"

"The sheer amount of work she makes me do." He huffs, moving the phone farther to show that he's at the *SPORTY* facilities, his desk stacked with documents, what look like samples, and several electronic devices. "We're two days from Christmas and look at how hard she has me working."

This does align with the extremely high work ethic I've seen on her. "But is she cruel?"

"Well, she's very mean." He adds nothing further for a moment, as if that was enough explanation, until I keep staring at him. "Like, very blunt."

"Does she insult you?"

"No but—"

"Screams at you?"

"No."

"Throws things or hits things?"

"One time she almost hit me with a baseball that she was trying to test, but it wasn't on purpose," he admits. She can't even throw a pillow straight at my face while I'm sitting still, too.

"So what you're telling me is that because she talks in an authoritative manner you don't like her."

Mateo blinks. "That's not what I said."

"That's what I heard, though," I retort.

"You need to clean your ears."

"Wax free as of this morning's shower," I deadpan.

"Está bien, she's not a movie villain. But she's not the kind of person I'd ever picture with you."

"Why the hell not?"

"Brodel." He makes a face. "She never laughs. Doesn't even smile."

"That's not true," I say right away, and then I stop. I've seen her lips arch but I can't recall what her laughter sounds like. It's only made itself known once.

"See?" Mateo shakes his head. "You can't be with someone who takes life as seriously as Camila Puig does."

"Anyway." I veer the conversation drastically away. "Tell my nephew that I'll be there whenever I can, and that I miss him and only him."

He brings the conversation back around. "You know I gotta tell my wife that you're sleeping with my boss, right?"

"I'm not—I told you it's not like that."

"Right, and I'm the chupacabra."

Now completely annoyed, I say, "Good to know. I'll see if I can buy you a goat on the road."

"Laters, cabrón."

"No, you're the cabrón." We hang up at the same time like the mature adults that we are.

I'm steaming as I emerge from the Polar bedroom, but now for an entirely different reason. Like shit, I know I didn't have the best judgement when I stayed with Jasmine, even when I knew that she was sick and tired of my face. Am I making the same damn mistake by being interested in Camila? Because that's two people warning me about it, and while I can easily dismiss Roger's whiny-ex bullshit, my brother is different.

"Whoa." I stop right in time before running into someone.

Who turns out to be my ex.

She gasps a little, and we stand in the middle of the hallway looking at each other like I imagine two robbers trying to steal the same thing would.

"Hi." She tucks her hair behind her ears.

"Hey." I check behind her. "Where's Dr. Rumpelstinski?"

She huffs. "Rupert has gone out to see if by any chance we're able to move the car already."

My stomach twists. "I don't think we can. Last I checked, there's still like two feet of snow outside."

"Why do you sound like you almost don't want to leave?"

Because I don't.

I really stinking don't.

I want to spend more time here, eating the exact same breakfast every morning, having homemade cookies for every snack, chugging tea like I'm getting paid for it while I sit on a windowsill, reading a romance book next to a beautiful woman that I want to keep sharing a bed with.

I hadn't realized that in all of the exciting rush that is my regular life, especially during the ball season, I've been craving the normalcy of a home routine like this.

Rather, I've been craving a home. Like what my teammates are building with their girlfriends. I want to belong. I want to stop coming into an empty apartment after every practice, every game, and every trip.

From here I can see Camila hunching over her laptop, a mighty frown on it that arcs her mouth downward. Adorable.

Unreachable.

Not for me—and not because of what anyone says. But because she has a career in Mapleton and mine is in Orlando.

It was never going to work out.

"Anyway, I uh…" I motion with my lips toward the other woman. "I'm gonna go back to my book while I wait to hear what Rumpus thinks."

"*Rupert,*" she says through gritted teeth, knowing exactly what I'm doing and giving me the exact same expression of disgust as when we were in the middle of a fight.

"Right-o." Clearing my throat, I navigate out of her way while saying, "I'm gonna go now."

"Lucky, a word of advice." That stops me on my tracks and I look over my shoulder at Jasmine, who is crossing her arms. "If your girlfriend is anything like Rupert says, you'll last even less with her than we did."

My eyebrows rise in an attempt to look blasé even though I'm vibrating with enough anger to power the whole block. "You say it like I regret us." That makes her jaw drop, and I knew she wasn't expecting that at all. I shake my head, a sardonic smile escaping the fragile hold of my temper. "I don't. You taught me exactly what I want and what I don't, and let me tell you something, Jasmine. You and Camila couldn't be more different, and I mean that in a damn good way."

I don't wait for another quip from her—and it doesn't come even as I slowly make my way out to the common room.

My molars grind. Yes, I did doubt the hell out of myself after the breakup with Jasmine. It was my own faulty decisions what made me be with her in the first place. And I'm not sure that's not happening again.

But then Camila notices me approaching, and I don't think she realizes how her eyes soften just a touch, and how the corners of her lips lift into the smallest little smile. How pink blooms in her cheeks, lighting up her eyes like Christmas lights.

And that's when it hits me, that from someone so unused to joy, this means more than a thousand what ifs. Feeling nothing wouldn't make her expression transform upon seeing me.

That's when I decide to take a figurative leap, since I'm in no condition to be jumping for shit.

Screw Ronald. And Jasmine. Even my brother. Since when have I ever operated within other people's rules? I'm Lucky freaking Rivera. The word *play* is in my professional title, and that's exactly what Camila needs. A little more of those soft smiles, deep caramel kisses and sighs.

I'm going to see if this can go anywhere—if I can make this woman feel cheerful, even if it's only for this Christmas.

CHAPTER 24
CAMILA

By this point in my life, it turns out that work is engrained in my muscle memory. My fingers key in the right password to power up my laptop, and they know exactly which icons to click to pick where I left off. Messages pop in from Mateo Rivera, my main production manager, and my eyes snag on his last name. There's something in my mind that blocks me from delving into why that particular combination of letters seems so interesting all of a sudden, and yet I manage to respond to him as usual. Yes, I plan to attend that meeting tomorrow. I also approve his two extra days of PTO. I still need him to send me the load plan update for the next quarter. I ignore when he brings up something about the office supplies. I agree to discuss the summer internship program upon my return.

It registers a little later that I just had an entire conversation without being aware of it.

I glance at the empty seat beside me, a beat up copy of a bodice ripper being the only thing on it. Not to honor my nickname too much, but the cold hadn't seeped from the window into my bones when Lucky Rivera was sitting next to me.

Instead, I was positively swimming in lava while we were making out.

"¿Qué estoy haciendo?" I ask myself, softly touching my bottom lip with my thumb. It still tingles like it's been woken from an age of numbness.

Lowering my hand, I mindlessly move the trackpad, watching the pointer make circles over the icon for the internal instant messaging system. Biting my tingly lip, I click on it and scroll to find the chat with the other two Venezuelan women I've sort of mentored, sort of befriended. I tap the keys without really typing anything, just debating whether to go ahead with the impulse to tell someone that I just kissed a guy—one who isn't just *any* guy—and it was absolutely the best kiss of my life.

The clever part of my brain finally kicks in, reminding me that IT monitors this system.

I set the laptop aside, next to the romance book. It seems to imbue me with the courage I need to take my phone out of my pocket and find the text chat with the three of us. The last time we talked was to coordinate a happy hour after work.

Taking a deep breath, I jump right into it. I'm not one to beat around the bush.

ME

I may need you two to mentor me on a private matter

They respond right away, clearly as interested in staying focused on work as I am right now.

RACHEL LEON

Sounds intriguing

SIERRA FERNANDEZ

Eyes emoji

Here goes nothing…

ME

The snow storm changed my travel plans from Orlando

And I've ended up having to drive with my ex and his new fiancée

As I'm typing a third message, they fire back way faster than I can formulate my thoughts.

SIERRA FERNANDEZ

Wait!! THAT ex?? The one who jilted you??

RACHEL LEON

Give us the exact locations

We will go murder him

ME

No need to land in jail

He's the least of my concerns

RACHEL LEON

Then?

ME

The issue is a different guy

SIERRA FERNANDEZ

Hold on. Need to see if I have popcorn

RACHEL LEON

Side eye emoji

Do we have to beat up another guy?

ME

No

I bite my lip, glancing around—as if I didn't want to be caught typing what I'm going to say just next, when there's actually not a single person paying me attention right now. Lucky hasn't returned from our bedroom either, and suddenly thinking about the words *our* and *bedroom* together sends me into a tailspin.

ME

I met a guy at the airport

One thing led to the other and he's traveling with us

The story's pretty wild so I'll tell you the details later

He's about to return any time

But the thing is that we just kissed and

My brain draws a full blank, enough that it allows them the chance to send a barrage of texts that look simultaneously like the silliest, funniest, girliest conversation I've ever had in my life. Even Audrey Winters, my friend from college, would be far tamer—then again, we get along well because she's sardonic and I'm stoic. But these two are all enthusiasm and happiness. I almost can't stand it.

Except I keep typing.

ME

Okay calm down children

RACHEL LEON

I AM CALM

AM I NOT CALM, SIERRA?!

SIERRA FERNANDEZ

YOU ARE THE CALMEST PERSON I KNOW

The sudden appearance of laughter in Spanish makes me snort. My lips tremble, threatening to do another thing they do as often as kissing an unbearably hot guy: smile.

I shake my head. And to think that a year ago Sierra couldn't even utter a word in my presence.

Switching to a browser, I search for Lucky Rivera's name and a few pictures pop up in the results. In one, he's standing in the middle of the field during what must've been a pause in a game. The Orlando Wild uniform is the tighter kind, accentuating those shoulders of his that are to die for. Except that he's angled slightly away from the camera, and the contour of an incredible bubble butt can be seen behind him. I click on the picture and it takes me to an article from *SPORTY* magazine, listing the top ten shortstops in the league.

Copying that, I send it to the two girls and instruct them to look at number four on the list.

Sure enough, the enthusiastic responses come right away.

WORLD SERIES CHAMPION, LUCKY
RIVERA???

SIERRA FERNANDEZ

Serious question for the culture

Does he kiss as good as he looks?

Ducking fully from sight, I respond right away.

ME

Better

SIERRA FERNANDEZ

KKMASDNOÑIAONÑDOIINAÑ

RACHEL LEON

AAAAAAAAAAAAAAAAAAAA—

Wait

You said two problems

I'm not seeing a single one

ME

Of course there's a problem

You know how I am

I need to add nothing further for them to talk back.

RACHEL LEON

Fierce and incredible?

SIERRA FERNANDEZ

With fashion style to die for?

RACHEL LEON

A complete knockout?

SIERRA FERNANDEZ

Your ex's worst nightmare?

And I mean that as a compliment

He's always sounded like a tool

ME

Well, thanks. But I mean

My nickname isn't ICE QUEEN for no reason

RACHEL LEON

Maybe this is the perfect opportunity to change it to HOT QUEEN

SIERRA FERNANDEZ

Where's an emoji snapping fingers when you need one

Could I?

It's not like I need anyone's permission. And actually, I'm not even in my usual environment, surrounded by people who judge my every move. The only one here who does that is Rupert and like Sierra said, he's a tool. His opinion matters not one whit.

I could just… have fun. More than once.

The novelty of that concept hits me so hard, the phone almost slips from my grasp when it vibrates with more texts. Their words blend into a single take away: encouragement. If they were here right now, I bet they'd push me toward the guy as if we were college girls at a bar looking for dance partners.

Slowly, I lift my head and find Lucky Rivera standing under the mistletoe where I gave him a tiny, quick kiss, and he's watching me in a way that makes me feel like I'm the only one in the room.

Everything inside of me flutters, like I have butterflies in my veins. His lips curve and I'd swear I can feel them against my own all the way from here.

I put my phone away. I don't need any pep talks anymore.

"Hey," is his soft greeting once he reaches me.

I take back my laptop and his book to allow him enough space to sit next to me. Not that I want him to—Actually, I really do. I just hope I don't seem overly eager.

He radiates so much heat that I nearly sigh when he sits back down. I reach toward him with a busy hand, but instead of his book it's my laptop. I switch quickly, hoping he didn't notice my momentary glitch.

The glint in his eyes tells me he very much did.

His hand is big enough that it brushes mine as he takes the book. We both stop moving. It takes me herculean effort to raise my eyes from his thumb over mine, and to his pretty brown eyes that seem to hold all the joy in the world.

"Hey," he repeats.

With an airy voice, I say, "You already said that."

"I did, didn't I?" Lucky doesn't sound at all embarrassed, though he finally retrieves his book and frees my hand. "So, I ran into Jasmine just now."

"Oh." Crap, did I sound disappointed at the sound of his ex's name coming from the lips I tasted earlier?

"She said Rudolph went out to see if he can safely drive the car."

No.

An invisible hand squeezes my heart like it's a sponge, and it's trying to drain every last bit of warmth from it.

Perhaps Lucky can read my mind, because he adds, "I don't think it'll work, though. The two feet of snow outside are still too fresh and it's anybody's guess how fast they're able to plow in this little town."

"Do you think we'll have to stay longer?" I try to not show

any signs of hope through the cracks of my voice, but I'm not sure I succeed.

"Probably." Lucky's eyes roam around my face, pausing at my lips for long enough to revive the tactile memory on my nerves. Slowly, his eyes move to find mine again and he holds them so intensely, it almost feels like a tight hug. "I hope so."

My breath catches in my throat.

The tip of his tongue runs across his thicker upper lip. "Camila, I—"

"May I have your attention, please," a voice interrupts. It quiets down the easy chatter of the guests around the common room, and one by one everyone turns to the source. Marv, one of the owners, stands in the middle decked in full winter gear fitting of the North Pole. Behind him, a couple of men also walk in with clumps of snow clinging to their clothes, and one of them is my ex. "A few of our guests and I ventured outside to assess the situation, and we have some news."

Sighing, Lucky mumbles, "Perfect timing, huh?"

I feel solidarity for his sarcasm.

"Bear and Breakfast's grounds are still covered"—I curl a fist in silent victory—"However, the authorities are beginning to plow the main roads. I believe you'll be able to leave by tomorrow should you desire."

Damn it.

Meanwhile, one of the three cookie sisters exclaims, "Excellent news! We'll be home in time for Christmas."

The thought of that fills me with dread.

There is no Christmas waiting for me at my downtown Mapleton apartment. I didn't even decorate it, because I have no one to celebrate with. My parents are in Spain, working over the holidays just like I intended to do.

But now it doesn't feel enough. It feels wrong.

I turn back to Lucky and find him already watching me. "One more day, then," he mutters.

"Right."

Then, he sets his book aside and offers me his hand. I stare at it because it's not positioned like we're going to make yet another silly deal for survival. Rather, it almost looks like he just wants me to hold it. With mine. Like people who are dating do.

"Huh?" I ask very eloquently.

"Do you want to make the best of our last day at Bear Crossing?"

Rachel's words pop up in my head. This is my opportunity to become a hot queen—er, or more accurately put, to step away from my normal routine. From the person I've become, and that I'm starting to shed.

I slide my smaller hand into his, enjoying how his fingers curl to hold tight. "Let's do it," I say, not even stopping to think about what he might have in mind.

CHAPTER 25
LUCKY

"We're going to play in the snow."

I can tell that's not at all what she's expecting when her jaw drops like she's the star of an old timey cartoon. "We're going to what?"

"Play in the snow," I confirm with a nod full of gravitas.

"No offense Lucky, but…" She lets the words hang in the air and pointedly stares at my right leg, encased in a massive cast that reaches mid-thigh, and a brace that cushions the cast from impact and would allow some mobility if I still wasn't in this much discomfort.

"I know what you're thinking but I have a plan." Ish. I have a plan-ish. That's good enough for me.

"Does your plan include getting us proper winter clothes? Because there's no way we're going out in this." She motions between us in general, and at least on this point she's right. I'm wearing the bear Christmas sweater, jeans and one boot. She's in a similar outfit—two boots though, hurray—a blouse, and her fancy dress coat that couldn't warm an ant up if it tried.

"I'm sure we can borrow coats from someone."

One of her eyebrows twitches. "Fine, let's say that works

out. How are you going to make your way into two feet of snow?"

"Easy. You'll see." I offer my cheekiest grin. "But first, we must find gear."

"Then let's split to find people about our size, it'll be more efficient that way. Especially considering your injury."

"That's very chivalrous of you," I tease, even though it's true.

She lets out a little snort and gets up to begin the quest, except our hands are still joined and her motion pulls at our arms. Her frame freezes for a moment, and it takes her physically looking at our hands to realize what's going on. I guess I should let go, but I don't wanna. She tugs a little, and I hold her hand a little tighter.

Hmm. Is that a blush on her face?

Camila clears her throat. "Excuse me, I kind of need my hand."

"Do you, now?" I run my thumb across the skin at the back of her hand. It feels softer than I imagine a cloud to be.

And sure enough, the heat on her face intensifies.

When she catches me grinning like a fool, she tugs hard enough to free herself and leave with a little harrumph. Chuckling, I grab onto my crutches and put my book in my back pocket, ready to also go on my side quest.

The first guy I see heading my way, is too long and narrow for me to fit into his winter coat, should he lend it to me. Moreover, once he reaches me he says, "Are you vacating the windowsill?"

"Uh, yeah?"

"Good." With that, he bypasses me and plants his ass on what a moment ago was my seat. The fact that he looks at me smugly makes me think he was probably angry that Camila and I dared to exist on his preferred spot.

The owner of the inn finishes a conversation with some

guests, including Rigoberto. The latter stares at me as I approach and I can't make out the exact expression on his face, since I'm only clocking him on my periphery, but he's so intent that it gives me the heebiejeebies.

Despite that, I approach Marv. "It's me again," I start, reminding him that we almost ran into each other this morning while he was bringing in a tray of fresh bacon and I was making my way to the buffet.

"Hello, Mr. Rivera. What can I help you with?" Dude looks like he probably moonlights as a mall Santa in his spare time, complete with the beard and beer belly.

"I was wondering if maybe you have lost and found storage, and whether a proper winter coat that I could borrow would be found in it."

He strokes his beard. "And what would you need that for?"

Conscious that I'm being watched, I explain, "You see, my girlfriend and I are tired of being cooped up and we want to go out to play in the snow."

"Are you out of your mind?" Richard asks, no longer willing to pretend that he wasn't eavesdropping. "You shouldn't be putting your leg at risk just because you're bored."

"Yeah, maybe listen to the good doctor," Marv says.

I don't stoop to glaring like a petulant child the way I wish to, out of respect for Inn-Santa. "Thanks for the concern, man, but I have a plan."

"And what's that?" The doctor folds his arms. I'm not going as far as calling him good when I don't like him, even if he might be the best physician on the east coast.

"You'll see," I respond rather than saying nunya. See? Growth.

Santa raises his hands. "As long as you don't hold me liable if you get hurt, I can even lend you my own coat. I'll even pitch in with gloves and a hat."

"Please tell me you have a Santa hat," I beg, clasping my hands together in hope.

"Well, don't call me when this goes wrong." Whatshisface turns around and screws off, which is good news indeed.

"Ignore him," I tell the owner. "He's a professionally trained party pooper."

Marv gives me a look. "He might be right, though."

"Eh, it'll be fine."

Some fifteen minutes later, I'm outfitted with a yellow winter coat that squeaks every time I move—which is how I know it's the good shit—a white and red Santa hat that was clearly not made for messing around, with how much it warms up my head, and some black waterproof winter gloves I can barely move my hands with. I look like a festive bumblebee.

"I also got you this," Marv says. Since he helped me shrug into his coat without me losing my balance, or my teeth, I only notice now that he had propped another object against the wall by the entrance. "I figure it's safer than you attempting to use crutches in the snow, and it'll spare me the lawsuit."

I blow air out of my nose. "I appreciate that your legal concerns led to this wonderful idea." It truly is one, because we're talking about none other than a sledge. It looks like it'll barely fit a butt cheek and a half but hey.

"Okay, I'm here."

We both turn to the other voice. Unbidden, I blow a raspberry that turns into a giggling fit—straight up giggling, not even a manly chuckle. Camila is draped in a thick coat the color of Barbie's bubblegum, and I don't know if it was the same person and if they had a vendetta against her, but they lent her one of those furry hats that look like she has a dead beaver on her head.

"I am so gonna take a selfie of us out there," I say.

She ignores that. "How are *you* getting out there?"

"Do not worry. No Yelp review of the Bear and Breakfast

has ever said that we're a boring place to stay at." Marv places his hand on top of his sleigh.

My original plan was to launch myself at the snow and then crawl over it, but now that there's a path shoveled out of the inn it makes it pretty easy for him to drag me out into the open. Easy, I say, being the one whose only effort is to stay on the sleigh. Meanwhile, the poor old guy huffs and puffs from the effort of hauling all my muscle.

"You doing okay, grandpa?" I ask from behind him.

He wheezes out, "Just tell me you'll give us a five star review when you check out."

"I'll give you a ten, how about that?" I laugh as he picks up speed.

Meanwhile, Camila is making her way behind us much slower, which means I'm facing her as she treads as carefully as she probably would if she was walking on an iced over lake.

"There you go, kids." Marv leaves us at a nice spot not too far from the building, but also not close enough that we'll still feel cooped up. "And Miss Puig? Feel free to call me when you're ready to come back inside and I'll haul your man for you, free of charge." He winks at her.

"My—" Her eyes bulge but she stops herself right in time. "Got it, thank you."

For a moment, we watch the old ox head back into the inn, shivering against the frigid breeze he's unequipped for, what with me wearing his coat and all. He closes the entrance door and it strikes me that Camila and I are now alone.

The most alone we've been so far.

Yes, there are a bunch of people in the red bricked building with a bear shaped sign hanging over the entrance, and I can spot a few of them peeking out of the windows at the two weirdoes who came out in the snow. And in theory, one could argue that we've been alone in our bedroom, even though there were people next door and above us on the second floor.

But out here, it's just us, the thick carpet of barely disturbed white snow, the bare trees capped with frost and flakes, and the bluest sky we've seen since leaving Orlando three days ago.

I dig my hand into the snow and scoop up a decent amount. I pack it into a neat but not too tight ball, and I prove my theory that Camila's reflexes are made of noodles when I launch the ball at her, landing it square on her stomach, and seeing her react only then.

"You did not just—"

"Oh, but I did." I close my hand around yet more snow. "It didn't hurt, did it?"

"Only my pride." She watches me as I make a second ball and then it finally happens—Camila Puig agrees to fool around a bit. Leaning down, she grabs onto a much bigger mound of snow and starts to work it between her borrowed, neon green gloves.

I'm much faster. This time I aim for her right hip and she yelps when I pelt her right on the spot.

"You're gonna get it now, Lucas." The threat in her voice comes to no fruition when she launches the projectile and, instead of it flying forward, it falls right over her shoulder and behind her.

Laughter explodes from my chest. "Wow, that is hands down the worst throw I've ever seen."

The sunlight reflects on the snow and bounces off her face, clearly casting her embarrassed blush into view. "Not all of us have elite athlete genes."

"Or..." I lean to the side, digging for more of the fluffy snow. "Perhaps you just need someone to coach you into having fun."

Camila cocks a defiant eyebrow. "I thought that was what we were here for."

I've met many grumps in my life, but none of them have

ever made me want to laugh half as much as this woman does. It's like she doesn't realize it, but every time she's grouching about one thing or another she looks freaking adorable.

"Right, come closer so you can learn." I wave her over and she complies even as she tosses me a frown. "If you want to make it hurt, you press hard on the snow so it becomes more solid. But in our case, you just need to shape it a little so it doesn't disintegrate in the air before you throw it."

"That makes sense." You'd think I just taught her how to fly an airplane responsibly. "But my question is, how do I even throw it."

Since she's clearly never thrown a baseball in her life, I give her the basics on how to hold a ball and the movement of her arm and hand to release it. I'm not gonna get too nerdy here and bring up how important the swing of her torso is, how she can get power from her legs, or how she'll eventually start to be able to read the direction of the wind and how much resistance it'll give. We'll need a lot more practice than just one morning of playing in the snow.

But the mini class is sufficient to get us going. Even though I'm sitting on the same spot, half a butt cheek falling off the sleigh, she still doesn't manage to pelt me accurately. In contrast, I'm about to turn her into a snow-woman.

"Hold still," she demands, trying one more time.

"Woman, I'm not going anywhere. You should just aim better." I laugh and then I get what I deserve—a snowball finally lands square on my face.

"Yes!" She pumps a fist in the air and releases a new sound, one so girlish and cheerful that it stops me from wiping the snow off my mug. "I got you good, Lucky Rivera!"

Clumps of snow fall as I grin up at her, and it feels both as though I'm melting and as if I was floating. "Did you just laugh?"

Unfortunately, that stops her. She presses the ugly green

gloves against her mouth, eyes as wide like she was just caught doing mischief. "No."

"Yes, you did," I singsong back.

"It's all in your head."

"Do it again," I counter.

She bends down to gather more snow. "I'll try but I'm pretty sure that was the best shot of my life."

"Not that, laughing."

She holds the awkward position as she looks at me. "I don't… quite know how. It just came out."

Shit, that makes it all the more precious that I managed to get it out in the first place. I rub at my chest, where my heart is doing things I'm not used to anymore.

Packing a very loose snowball, I launch it at her face and find the bullseye faster than she can process. An outraged sound comes out of her throat instead, and she throws all the basics I taught her out of the window to come and drop a heap of snow on top of me. I'm laughing so hard that I fall over one side of the sleigh, and after that we descend into maturity levels only seen in five-year-olds as we start splashing snow onto each other like we're swimming at a pool.

Something makes Camila squeal in delight—maybe because she got me again before I could roll over. And then we're both just giggles. It's the best thing I've ever heard in my life.

Her breath is coming a lot more labored so I plop on my back to give her a break. "Have you ever made a snow angel?"

"No, but this one seems easier than besting a baseball player at a snowball fight." She sits back and I watch as she sweeps her limbs over the snow. The tip of her nose is red enough that it makes me want to warm it up by kissing it. "You know, this all seemed very silly in movies but it's actually quite fun."

"Life is fun when you're with the right people."

Her limbs slow down until they stop. Slowly, she turns her head toward me.

A strand of her hair is caught between her lips, and for once she doesn't seem to mind that she's not tidy and tastefully dressed. Her brown eyes sparkle, and it's not just because of the bright sun above us. It comes from within. This version of Camila is the most beautiful I've seen so far, even better than the Camila I had just kissed senseless.

"You're right," she whispers.

Voices sound somewhere behind me, people spilling out of the inn to join us in playing with the snow. But I don't care. A meteorite could be hurtling our way and I wouldn't pay it any attention either. Not when I'm too busy caught in the feeling that maybe I've found the right person, the one I could make happy.

CHAPTER 26
CAMILA

can't recall the last time I had a goofy ass grin on my face, but Lucky flashes me one and I feel the muscles of my face shifting to mirror it. I probably look like someone else entirely and I don't care.

"Have you ever built a snowman?" he asks me, his chest rising and falling with his rapid breathing.

"No," I admit, breathing way harder than the professional athlete.

He snaps his fingers and sits up. "Let's do this."

I also sit up, sinking a little into the fluffy snow. "Here we are. What do we do?"

"First, we decide what kind of snowman we want." He folds his arms, the coat straining against powerful shoulders, and I'm so busy drinking him in that I miss a few words. "—baseball player, or we could build a businesswoman with a laptop. Wait, why is it always snowman and not also snow-woman?"

"You tell me," I wheeze, and not necessarily because of the exertion from throwing snowballs at him, or attempting to duck his extremely accurate shots.

It's because of him. He's making me lose my breath. I can't stop looking at his upper lip.

"Let's make a snow-woman." He nods to himself, leaning forward to scoop up some snow around his hands. "She's going to be a sexy executive with a sharp tongue, a mean glare, and luscious hips."

Heat explodes in my face. I clear my throat. And again. "Is she inspired by someone in particular?"

The little jerk just flashes me a smoldering smirk, the kind that ratchets up his attractiveness from one thousand to one billion. I check to make sure I'm not melting the snow all around me.

"Now," he speaks with a deep voice even though it's directed at the snow. "What should we accessorize her with?"

Man, I don't know. I don't care about the snow-woman. How do I get him to kiss me again? Maybe grab my allegedly luscious hips at the same time. I guess in order for that to work out properly we wouldn't be able to stand, as that could risk his leg even further. I could, however, straddle his lap and kiss him.

I make my own breath falter at that fantasy. When it makes his attention shift back to me, I get a sudden, visceral fear that he might be able to read my mind. Looking away, I scramble to my feet and babble—me, Camila Puig, better known as the ice queen, babbling like a teenager with a crush.

"I don't know but I'm sure someone can come up with something. Maybe I'll just take a quick tour of the inn asking people if I can borrow their items? I wonder if anyone has heels we could use. I could also find something to give her red lips with, instead of the typical carrot nose you see in the movies. I'll be right back!"

I leave him chuckling, which further increases my suspicion that he knows I wasn't having exactly innocent thoughts about him.

Other people have also made their way outside. An elderly

couple is on one side of what I assume is normally a garden, the man taking pictures of his wife and smiling at her like he can't believe such a pretty lady is still giving him the time of the day, even after a lifetime together.

I duck into the building, my heart racing—yearning, I admit to myself, for something like that for the first time.

My parents have never looked at each other that way. Frankly, they don't look at each other that much, period. They're too busy with work, just existing near each other without much friction… and also without much passion. And it occurs to me right now, after playing in the snow with a guy who is all passion and heart, that maybe I don't want exactly what my parents had, that it's what I'd have gotten if I had married Rupert three years ago.

Speaking of, he gets in my way while holding a steaming mug of what smells like coffee. He sweeps his eyes up and down my frame, eyebrows slowly rising. "And what are you up to?"

My real desire is to not answer him and keep walking, but we still depend on him to get us to Mapleton. I put on a smile I know makes me look like a shark about to pounce, a far cry from goofy teen-like grins, and say, "Just having fun with my boyfriend. See ya!"

I go as far as skipping along, and I'm pretty sure he's laser beaming the back of my head as I make my way into the inn.

I find the cookie sisters lounging by the window with more steaming mugs in their hands. Since they're the ones who lent me my amazing getup, I have no doubt that they won't bat an eye at my next request.

"There you are." Billie grabs me by the arm and brings me to their circle. From here I have a perfect view of Lucky's back as he works on the bottom of the snow-woman. "I am so jealous of you, missy."

"Huh?"

"Just look at him." Val shakes her head, eyes narrowed. "Even while sitting on the snow he's a sight for sore eyes. How are you possibly not jumping him every second of the day?"

"I—erm…" I don't know how to answer that. I've technically never jumped him in any of the senses they may mean. But I sure as heck want to.

"You don't have to be coy." She wiggles her eyebrows at me. "We saw that kiss earlier, mama mia."

"I nearly fainted." Nellie fans herself.

Um, me too.

I'm also about to pass out from embarrassment right now.

"I was actually coming here to ask for another favor," I say in an attempt to steer them away from the topic of Lucky and I making out in public.

"Don't tell us you need tips on seducing that man?" Billie throws her head back to release a hearty laugh, and still in the middle of that she adds, "That man is so clearly in love with you already, you don't need them."

"What? No, he's not!" I screech.

"What are you talking about, dearie? He looks at you like you hung the moon for him." She leans closer to me. "And you look at him like he hung the sun or something."

The cookie sisters break into girlish giggles.

Meanwhile, I'm drenched in cold sweat. "N-No. You don't get it. We're not—He's not—"

Val puts her hand on her chest. "Don't tell us you two are just friends with benefits or something scandalous like that?"

I didn't know anyone who used the word scandalous anymore, but even a friends with benefits situation would make more sense than what Lucky and I are doing. Heck, even the fake dating to save face in front of our exes made more sense too. I don't know what ground we're treading anymore.

"Anyway." I straighten myself, hopefully to let them understand that I'm through with their line of questioning. "I was wondering if you have other accessories I could borrow for the snow-woman we're building."

"A snow-woman, huh?" Nellie's eyebrows lift.

"Perhaps a scarf? I'm afraid I didn't bring any because I was supposed to travel from Florida and to my car parked at the Mapleton airport." I huff, frustration attempting to crawl back out of the hiding hole it has been this entire, absolutely freaking dreamy morning.

"Come, let's go to our room and see what we can find."

All four of us move as one unit again, the sisters surrounding me with chatter about how we can beautify the creation that Lucky is focused on. At the last second, I glance over my shoulder to see what kind of progress he's made, and instead meet the eyes of my ex as he watches me over the rim of his mug. The hairs at the back of my neck stand in alarm, and I turn away to ignore him like he deserves. He won't ruin my day.

"—The fake eyelashes?" one of them asks me and I blink like an owl. "Or perhaps they won't be visible until you get very close to the snow-woman."

"But we could make fake eyelashes if we find paper, a black marker, and scissors," another sister bounces back, and maybe I'm completely freed because that makes me laugh with my whole chest.

Billie takes her key out and opens the door to a bedroom called Red Panda. Inside, it looks like a tornado has gone through it and spread various clothing items across every piece of furniture. I'm about to call the police because they must've been robbed, when I notice that none of them find anything amiss. The two queen beds are also unmade, and that's what makes it click that they're just messy. Or maybe they decided to also take a vacation from organizing.

"Let's use your scarf, Nellie," Billie says, plucking said item from a floor lamp.

Val marches over to the night table between the beds. "I'm pretty sure I saw a notepad here. Now we just need to find a marker and scissors."

"How about your bangles?" Nellie asks Val. "We can just find some good sticks for the arms and put your bangles on them."

The latter nods enthusiastically. "And it would look so good with Billie's pink jacket."

"This one?" I ask, pointing at myself.

"No, silly. Her lighter one."

I place a hand on my chest. "Of course, how could I have mistaken them." That makes them laugh.

Unfortunately, that and collecting the items around the room aren't enough distraction. Billie zeroes in on me again. "So tell your aunties here, why are you so embarrassed about your relationship with your gorgeous boyfriend?"

A groan escapes from my throat. It's to no avail, as the three vultures abandon the task and descend on me, looking for crumbs of gossip to entertain themselves. And frankly, I can't blame them. This is probably the most entertaining chapter of my life.

"It's just…" Ugh, I want to tell them everything. I need the opinion of complete strangers who don't know anything about my life to tell me if this thing with Lucky makes any sense. I glance around us, but it's only us in this room anyway. "This is pretty new and I don't quite know how I'm feeling."

Billie tilts her head, a white curl falling over her forehead. "Wait, how is this new but he's your boyfriend?"

I trip over my own words. "I mean, he's newly my boyfriend. It's not like we've been dating for years and already know we're headed for marriage or something like that." What the hell am I saying?

"Ahh."

"I get it."

Nellie sighs. "I miss those early days when everything feels so tender and beautiful."

"Yes." I perk up. "That's exactly how it feels."

"And now I'm jealous all over again," Val grouches, putting her hands on her hips.

But Billie, being the sharpest of the cookie bunch, once again pins me with her eyes and spears me with another question. "So if you're in that stage where everything's perfect, why are you stepping on the breaks?"

I turn into a snow-woman myself.

"Right. You should be bragging to everyone about what a catch you made." Another sister says and they all nod off tune, proving that on this topic they share a single braincell. I want to be them when I grow up, accosting a younger woman about her love life for fun with my girls, except I have no sisters.

But I have some friends. Three of them, to be precise. And they all would be having a blast here.

I sigh and kick at the floor. "I mean, I wish I could. But I don't really have a right to brag about Lucky."

"What?"

"Why not?"

"When I say this is new, I mean it." I grimace a bit. "As in, we met at the airport in Orlando on the way here."

Nellie's jaw drops.

Val shrugs one shoulder. "You've done well. I just met him yesterday and was already planning his wedding to my daughter."

"To be fair," Nellie continues, "If I was your age I also would've put my grabby hands on him right away."

"Ohh…" Billie elongates the word like something just clicked with her. "Is that why that kiss under the mistletoe yesterday was so lackluster?"

I'm pretty sure my face is redder than Rudolph's nose now.

My voice comes out choked as I respond. "Yes, that was our first kiss."

"And then this morning?" she asks, leaning closer.

"Our second," I admit.

All at once the three sisters start squealing, one of them clapping, another pushing at the third sister, and the last one laughing uncontrollably. You'd think they're back in middle school, talking about the cutest boy in the class. I can't help but join in the giggles.

Me, Camila Puig, ice queen. Giggling *again*. And cherishing every second of it.

"You have to invite us to your wedding." Billie clasps her hands in front of her. "Oh, and make it a winter wedding so that we can remember this day."

That tears a snort from me. "Please, you're getting too ahead of yourself. I just told you that I have no idea what we are—"

"—Perfect for each other, is what you are," she says.

"Agree." Val harrumphs. "Unfortunately."

Nellie glances at her. "Maybe don't invite Sarah to the wedding. She'd be so upset to see what she missed out on."

I stare intently at Billie. "What makes you think so? That we're perfect for each other, that is."

"Because I know that look in his and your eyes. You both look at each other like you found the person that brings the light out of you."

I gasp.

All at once I can hear my heart beating furiously in my ears, and every color around me grows sharper.

Somehow I can see Lucky and I tumbled on the snow, making snow angels while looking at each other and laughing. Except in the scene, it's not the two of us on the yard of the snowy Bear and Breakfast, but in front of a white house with a wraparound porch and rocking chairs.

And I want that. I want it so more that it hurts and almost makes me double over. Because I know I can't have it. Once he recovers from his injury he's going back to Orlando where it doesn't snow, and I'll be staying in Mapleton working my ass off so that *SPORTY*'s shareholder value doesn't drop.

"Well, he must be waiting for me," I say with a thread of voice.

"Right!" That spurs the three sisters to grab all the miscellaneous things we may need, and together we leave the room.

But once we make it outside, we stumble upon a figure outside. It's Rupert, leaning against the wall by the Red Panda room.

He looks at me all smug. "I knew it." And that's when I realize that the bedroom door was open all along, and he heard everything.

CHAPTER 27
LUCKY

Should the snow-woman have boobs?

I'm sitting on the snow, legs spread wide as I build the base in between them. There will definitely be hips, the same spectacular kind that the real life Camila has. That is nonnegotiable.

But wait, aren't hips part of a typical round base? Then there won't be anything special about this construction other than whatever accessories she's able to find. Unless we make boobs. I have a feeling I'll have to negotiate that with her, though.

Where is she? I twist to glance over my shoulder. Aside from other guests strewn around the yard, there is no sighting of a woman wearing a bubblegum pink coat with radioactive green gloves, and a dead fox atop her head.

Biting the tips of my glove fingers, I free my hand to palm around my borrowed coat pockets for my phone. Rather than calling her, I send her a text first because I'm not a monster. This gets me no answer, not even the word read shows below the text, leaving me with no choice but to call her. And when that also yields no result I start to wonder if something's wrong.

Realistically speaking, she could just be in the bathroom. Or perhaps finding things to decorate the snow-woman with is proving a bigger challenge than anticipated. If that's the case, I'm better off helping her than freezing my ass here by myself.

"Excuse me?" I call out to the nearest people, an elderly couple taking pics. "Do you mind calling Marv for me? I need help being sleighed back indoors."

The two of them take one look at my leg in a massive brace, then the sleigh that lays abandoned nearby, and they put two and two together. "Tell you what, young man, we'll help you," the old man says.

I debate whether to turn down the offer. He looks more frail than Marv, but the determination on his face tells me that I'd be hurting his pride in front of his beau—and you know what? I'm a lover and not a hater, so I say, "That would be amazing."

The woman brings the sleigh over to me, and I help along by easing onto it with the strength of my arms. To my surprise, both of them pull at the sleigh together, grunting about how teamwork makes the dreamwork, and wheezing out giggles amid the effort.

Without realizing it, they get me thinking. Somehow I was expecting the guy to do all the work—but as an athlete in a professional team, no single guy carries the whole team. Everyone on the field has a role and that's how we back each other up every step of the way. Maybe being a couple was supposed to be like that all along, like Camila and I making snow angels together instead of me building a snow-woman alone.

Instead of me trying to carry the spark of the relationship all on my own.

My crutches are waiting by the entrance, and I have to use some serious balancing skills to rise from the sleigh so I can grab them. After thanking them and getting my cheek pinched by the old woman like I'm just a cute five-year-old, I begin my tripod travel back into the inn.

I pop my head into the common area, my eyes immediately falling on the windowsill where we shared our first proper kiss. The dude who was so eager to steal it is still there, sitting across it with his side to the window like he's a fairytale princess, reading a newspaper that is legit made of paper. My mind superimposes the image of Camila and I leaning toward each other, and you know what? Screw the snow-woman, when I find her I'm going to ask if I can kiss her again.

Now with an extra pep to my step, I veer toward the hallway to see if she's in our room—and my pulse does a thing at those last two words—but a lone figure there stops me.

"What's Ronald doing there?" I mumble just under my breath.

That's when I notice he's like stalking a bedroom door. Is it ours—I mean, the Polar room? Is he harassing Camila again?

I try to pick up speed but I'm not even halfway when people start emerging from the bedroom door by whatshisface. The three cookie sisters are followed by Camila and my teeth grit at the confirmation that yes, that asshole is probably up to something.

And then he utters some words, and Camila's entire face blanches to the point that she looks ill.

"Camila," I call out before I can think better of it. All five pairs of eyes turn to me, but I only focus on her. "Are you okay?"

Her head shakes in tiny jerks, eyes widening almost in horror. That spurs me on even faster, but the more I approach the more apparent it becomes that what she wants me to do is to go away.

That's when Rigoberto gets in my way. "There he is, the fake boyfriend," he says with obvious glee.

I freeze. I don't need to be a rocket scientist to figure out that the ruse is up. Camila mouths at me to go, but I can't just leave her to be eaten by this vulture.

"And there he is," I retort with a raised eyebrow. "The jerk who broke her heart."

He snorts and folds his arms, looking for all intents and purposes like he has the upper ground here. "At least I never played her and was always honest."

That snaps Camila out of her stupor. Temper brings color back to her face and her eyes flash dangerously as she glares at the back of his head. "Do you define as honest only telling me how you really felt on the day we were supposed to get married?"

"Oohh." One of the sisters leans to the others. "This is way more dramatic than I imagined." Another one shushes her.

The guy whirls around to Camila. "That doesn't mean you can lie to me with some random guy."

"And just who are you to say that?" I scrunch up my face. "What Camila does and with whom is none of your damn business."

"That's right." Billie pumps her fist.

Nellie adds, "You tell him."

"Well, it is when I'm being lied to!" Dr. Ridiculous shouts.

A door closes nearby, followed by a familiar voice. "Honey?"

"Great," I mutter, watching as Jasmine emerges from the Grizzly room at the end of the hallway. She takes one look at the scene and immediately knows that something's up.

"Honey, can you believe this?" Ruperto jams a finger in the air first in Camila's direction and then mine. "These two were lying. They're not dating at all."

For a moment, there's no reaction from Jasmine. There's no surprise or even disinterest in her face. It's like she's just watching a particularly disinteresting scene on TV. But then she says, "Yeah, I figured."

"What?" her fiancé asks, and my eyebrows rise.

Jasmine shrugs delicately, tucking her long hair behind her ears. "It's just, there's no way that a woman like that would go out with Lucky for real."

And there it is. My worst fear confirmed.

It would be impossible for an incredible, accomplished, razor sharp woman like Camila Puig to seriously consider going out with me.

The world tilts and I have to reposition my crutches so I don't pitch from my axis.

The one who responds is precisely the executive. "What the hell is that supposed to mean?"

"Don't get me wrong." Jasmine lifts her hands as a barrier. "I mean it as a compliment. You seem like too much for someone like Lucky who's only ever interested in having a good time."

"There." Jasmine's man lifts his chin. "That's precisely why I never believed your act."

Val whispers loud enough to be heard in Japan. "One would wonder, then, if he has such a high opinion of Camila, why did he let her go?"

"He must not be so smart himself," Billie answers.

"Excuse me, I'm a medical doctor," he snaps at the old ladies.

"And that's all you had going for you," Camila slides in like a sharp knife trying to cut through a soft piece of bread. It makes his smugness falter. "You know, it took me a long time to realize that in every little interaction, you were always looking for ways to feel superior to me. Here's a perfect example." She motions in general at us. "You just had to dig and dig until you proved that yes, your relationship is real and mine is fake. Is your ego satisfied with humiliating me once again?" She grabs the furry hat with a fist and takes it off to run the other hand through her hair. "Damn, I'm so glad I didn't get shackled to someone like you."

Her feet unglue from the floor and we watch in silence as she walks over to the Polar door. While fumbling with the key, she pauses to turn to Jasmine. "Maybe you should reconsider too, unless you're happy being with someone with a superiority complex." With that, she unlocks the door and walks inside, slamming the door hard enough to make the walls rattle.

Bile rises up my throat and it takes everything I have to swallow it down. Through gritted teeth, I say, "Congratulations, asshole. You hurt her again."

"Me?" He scoffs. "I'm not the one who forced her to play an absurd charade. That's all on you."

"Rupert." Jasmine sighs. "Did you stop to think about why they did this?"

"It's pretty obvious that it was to kill two birds with one stone," Billie says. We all turn to her and she adds, "To show you two fools up"—she points at Rudolph and Jasmine—"And because they're into each other."

Except… My brain's a lot slower than my body is, because this is when the ball finally connects with the bat.

I wouldn't have given two shits about what Jasmine and her beau thought about me if I had been by myself. But I couldn't stand the thought of them gloating about Camila, not when it was so clear that seeing them together reopened old wounds for her. And that's because I cared about her all along.

I don't know when it was—if when we were staring down at each other at the VIP lounge, feuding over the only available chair. Or if it was when I realized her feet were injured by her heels. Or if it was when she put on my oxygen mask for me during the severe turbulence. Or maybe when we were getting drunk together after surviving that scare. Or the first time we made a deal to survive together and shook hands, my skin touching hers and feeling at home right away—like it wasn't the first time we held hands in this life. Or perhaps it was when she gave me a hasty kiss under the mistletoe with a trio of old ladies watching us like hawks.

If it wasn't for that, I wouldn't have cared about her feelings toward her ex fiancé. I wouldn't have agreed to the funny scheme of pretending to be a near stranger's significant other.

I liked her from the beginning. I like her even more today. I think she might like me too. I don't want to stop liking her.

"That's right," I say carefully. "At least I am. I'm so into her that it scares me, and I don't give a shit what you or you"—I glance at whatshisface and my ex in turns—"Think about it. I don't care if Camila and I don't make sense on paper, if she's too good for me or whatever. I'd be a complete fool if I let her go."

Billie snaps her fingers. "Go get her, tiger!"

"Yeah!"

"You got this!"

I barely refrain from flipping the bird at the annoying couple, and I turn my back on them with as much dignity as my injured leg allows me. Camila locked the door on the inside, and it takes some serious work to find my key and get inside.

The room is empty.

For some silly reason, I check that she hasn't escaped from the window, but the curtains are neatly drawn and there goes that theory. Which means she must be in the bathroom. My steps make three different thuds, probably warning her that it's me.

Sure enough, once I get to the bathroom door and am about to rap it with my knuckles, she says, "I need a moment." Her voice sounds odd, too thick and garbled—like maybe she's crying.

I grit my teeth hard. I'll kill her jerk of an ex. But later. Right now, she needs me more.

"Okay. I'll wait out here," I mutter, leaning my forehead on the cool wood.

CHAPTER 28
CAMILA

Ugh, I hate crying.

Like, why even should I be crying? None of this matters. Rupert has mattered less than litter on the sidewalk for years now. And as for Lucky…

I wasn't expecting anything. What started out as a farce can't possibly turn real. This was just the reminder I needed that whatever has been going on between the two of us is just the same as momentarily leaving the warmth indoors to go play in the snow. Once we get to Mapleton there will be no more reason to play anymore. We'll go our separate ways. Finito.

I lean over the sink, my face dripping after having washed it. My eyes are red and puffy, and there's no hiding that I had a lil cry. I can't stay locked up in the bathroom forever, though. Not when Lucky's outside waiting. Perhaps he needs to use the bathroom too, or we're about to have an awkward conversation where this little arrangement of ours finally comes to an end. After patting my face dry, I take a deep breath and step out into the room.

Lucky's once again on the floor, the crutches discarded

against the loveseat sofa behind him. He pauses in the middle of stretching and looks up at me. There's something somber in his expression. It tells me everything I need to know.

I fold my arms. "Let's get this over with, then."

"What's over?" His eyebrows rise, even though that doesn't dissipate the weird seriousness in his mien.

"This." I motion between us. "Our fake dating deal. We got caught, so it's over."

"Hmm." I don't know what a hum from his throat means, and instead of clarifying he returns to his stretches. He lowers his torso back to the floor between his legs, not even making a peep if his right knee hurts as he gets a full extension in.

Dang, all that muscle is strong and flexible. The thought makes my entire body flush with ideas I shouldn't be having about this guy. Especially now that our deal is over.

"Is that what you want?" he asks, rising back to sitting and twisting to one side, then to the other.

I shrug. "It is what it is. I made the mistake of telling the cookie sisters about our situation and the door was open. I got what I deserved."

Lucky closes his eyes and his nostrils flare with a deep inhale. When his eyes open, they're dark with barely contained anger. It's startling to see, when most of the times his eyes are lit up with amusement, or liquid with seduction.

"Sit," he says soft but clear.

I tilt my head, confused. "Wait. Are you angry at me or something?"

"Not at you. On your behalf." He points at the floor with his lips. "Sit."

"Please?" I cock an eyebrow.

Tilting his head back to look up at me, Lucky Rivera pierces me with heated eyes. His voice turns deep and grave, wrapping around me as he mutters, "Please."

Welp. Next thing I know I'm kneeling on the carpet and

sitting on my hunches. My heart races and I swallow hard a couple of times, trying to calm it down. He observes me for a silent moment, eyes roaming around my face, searching for something. Finally he expels a big sigh that deflates his chest.

"Fine, we'll stop the fake dating."

I squeeze the hem of my ridiculous snow-bear sweater.

"How about we start real dating instead?" he asks.

Silence.

Actually, that's not true. There's a lot of buzzing in my ears. I'm not sure about what I heard. "Sorry, what?"

"I know this isn't super conventional," he says, bringing his legs closer together so he can lean on his left thigh. "We met just days ago, but I've been thinking about this for a while now. Why would it be any different from seeing an attractive stranger across a bar and asking them out?"

"Wait." I hold out a hand, stopping him to wait until my whirring brain catches up. "Are you seriously asking me out right now?"

"Am I laughing?" Lucky asks with a sly expression on his pretty face.

"No, but it could be the set up to a punchline."

"Then here's the punchline. Camila…"

I gulp. "Lucky?"

"I'm severely, viscerally, and intellectually attracted to you." His lips curve a little when my jaw drops. "I confess that at the beginning I looked at this whole arrangement as the most elaborate prank I'ver ever pulled, thinking it was on our exes, you know?" He stops himself to shake his head. "It was on me all along, though. I fell for it. Actually, I'm pretty sure that I fell for—"

"*Don't say it.*" I jump to my feet with surprising agility, and I stand there awkwardly, watching the confusion on his face. I hug myself and take a few steps back. "There's no way that's true."

"Why not?"

"Because… Because—" I cut myself off to make incoherent sounds, then a scoff. I drop my arms and roll my eyes. "Lucky, it's only been—what? Two days and a half since we met? You don't really know me. This whole trip? Everything has been abnormal, including me."

Lucky leans back, propping himself up with his hands on the carpet. "What if this is actually the real you? The woman who sometimes gets flustered like now, but who can also throw it down with words sharper than knives, and who also helps strangers in need even when she's missing a shoe."

"No." I sound like I'm pleading. "That's not the real me. The real me is the most disliked person wherever she goes. Uptight, neurotic, and definitely a party pooper."

"Is that what people tell you?"

"Yes." I wave my hands around. "All the time. And you've seen it too."

"All I've seen is your ex trying to make you feel that way so that he can feel better about his own smallness." Lucky glances away for a second, his jaw ticking with the same anger from earlier. Not at me—on my behalf. He faces me again. "Wanna know what I think?"

Yes. Desperately. I've never wanted anything more in my life.

I stay quiet.

"I think," he volunteers in a soft voice, "that you're like looking into the sun. Too big and radiant for most people to be comfortable with. But I'm not most people."

My voice is but a thread. "You're not?"

"No." A corner of his lips rises. "Mami, I work under the sun everyday. I'm used to it. Look." He pulls at the collar of his own sweater until the tan line around his neck is visible.

Unbidden, a snort rises from my throat. The thing morphs into a hiccup when I really just want to cry. Again. Collapse on the floor weeping, feeling sorry for myself openly for the first time in my life. For turning out so unlovable that this is the first time anyone ever says something like this sweet to me.

Lucky spreads his arms wide, just watching me like he knows that no matter how long it takes me, I *will* go into his arms.

But I know it too, and I don't waste a second. Overriding my earlier instinct of putting distance between us, I eat it up with two big leaps and drop in front of him. Lucky doesn't wait, he tugs me against his chest with one hand, with the other grabbing my legs to rest them over his left one, and then I'm in the circle of his embrace, so close to him that not even an air molecule separates us.

He guides my head until my face finds the crook of his neck and shoulder, and finally I wrap my arms around him. My chest convulses with a great sob.

I feel his nose search into my hair until it finds my ear. Lucky whispers, "I saw you, Camila. I saw you every time you helped someone, and every time you worked harder than anyone else and found solutions. I saw you when you smiled and—shit, it was the most beautiful sight. I can't wait to see it again."

My hands fist around the fabric of his sweater. How I want to believe this—that someone can feel this way for me. But it's so hard when it's coming from him, a freaking World Series champion, someone who has women hanging from his every word and move.

"You have bad taste, Lucky Rivera," I say into his warm skin that smells like cologne and warmth and all male.

"On the contrary." His hand brushes my hair aside, and then his lips are on my neck. It's funny how that paralyzes me, even as it lights me up on fire. "I think I have the best taste."

A gasp interrupts my weeping as he kisses my neck, and I'm not talking about a little peck. I'm talking hot, open mouthed. Like he craved a taste of the salt in my skin. I turn into jelly in his arms.

"Hmm, yes, I do," he muses as he peppers kisses up toward my jaw. "You taste just like you were made for me."

Groaning, I tremble all over as I push away from him. His half mast eyes skewer me, and the jerk runs his tongue across his lips like he can still taste my skin on them.

"I don't do this," I pant, embarrassingly out of breath. "I don't do flings."

"That works perfectly, because it's not what I'm proposing." He reaches for my face, his hot hand falling on my cheek to wipe the moisture there.

"Then what?"

"I want to give us a chance." His eyes lift to mine. "Camila, I think we could be really good together. Me showing you how to make snow angels. You putting on my oxygen mask."

I swallow hard and squeeze my eyes tight. More tears fall and this time he catches them with his thumbs. Softly, I admit, "My heart wants it, but my brain resists."

"Then, can I try to win over your brain this Christmas?" Lucky asks.

Leaning into his hands, I say, "You can try."

CHAPTER 29
LUCKY

'm pretty sure a cat climbed onto my chest in my sleep and
is making biscuits.

It's still fairly dark when I crack an eye open, expecting
a fifteen pound ball of fur to be staring down at me. Instead,
it's Camila's head on my left shoulder, and the biscuits are
being done by her hand on my right peck. Even with my brain
foggy from sleep, I find it hilarious that her subconscious seems
so entranced by my man boob.

Wait, am I fondling her too?

I check myself. Right hand tucked under my sweatshirt
over my stomach—safe. Left hand curled around her shoulder
in a quite chaste way—safe. Other body parts are where they
should be—also safe, whew.

Meanwhile, her hand splays open wide and grabs a good,
solid feel. She makes a sound most frequently caused by delicious food and snuggles even deeper. Her nose brushes against
my jaw and a little whine comes out, probably because of the
stubble I no doubt have. Her leg wraps around my left one as if
to make sure I'm not going anywhere.

Joke's on her. Even a tornado wouldn't make me move. The problem is that I'm a red blooded man, in bed with a seriously beautiful woman who smells like everything good and worthy in this planet, who feels absolutely incredible and soft against my harder body, the latter which is turning into burning coals because I'm wishing I could be a very, very naughty boy.

I fix my eyes on the dark ceiling above us, imagining that both our guardian angels are giving me warning looks, like my wits better prevail over my hormones or else. Fortunately for them, I have a busted knee and pain is my constant companion since. Makes it a tad less enticing to get very physical without expecting her to do all the work. And when—*if*—Camila and I ever get physical, I want to properly show her how much I want her. Every delicious and soft inch of her.

Because I do. So freaking much that I'm breaking into a sweat just thinking about it.

"Hmm?" she mumbles in her sleep and then her hand starts moving.

I turn into a statue—imagining several scenarios about where that hand could be going—but all it does is travel from right pec to left, close to her face. Her touch is firm like she has complete ownership and yes, I approve. I want her to own me.

Her hand presses a little harder, finding no give but not giving up anyway. She repeats the same humming question but it sounds different, more confused than curious.

Then she jerks up, twisting until her face hovers over mine. My body might be fully awake but my brain isn't quite processing, and I blink slowly. "G'morning, snuggle bear," I slur.

Her attention lowers to her hand fondling my chest and the funniest part is that she doesn't pull away. "Oh." The spot between her eyebrows crinkles a little. She also sounds sluggish as she says, "Your heartbeat woke me up."

"Your fault for fondling me."

This makes her gasp and attempt to pull away. "I'm so sorry! I won't—"

I don't let her go too far. Bringing her back to half lay on me, I say, "It's okay, I give you permission to feel me up."

"Lucky." She smacks my chest softly. "We barely just… I don't know. We're not even going out officially."

Chuckling, I turn to face her and bring my right arm over her. I can't hold this position for long because it strains my knee but shit, I can't wait to get better so this can be a permanent fixture in my life. Burying my face in her hair I say, "Your mouth can't tell me you don't enjoy the snuggles when your body already confirmed it."

"Ugh." Her hands close around the fabric of my favorite sweatshirt.

"You smell amazing." I sigh.

"My hair's dirty," she grouches.

"It's okay, your pheromones make the grease smell like flowers."

She snorts. "My breath also smells like sewer."

"Hmm, let me kiss you to confirm if that's true."

"Absolutely not," she says sharply. "Not until I brush my teeth."

I groan. Clearly I set a bad precedent yesterday when I mentioned that I wanted to brush my teeth before kissing her. Those were my own nerves speaking. "Listen, I don't care about that. None of your body odors are ever going to be as bad as a clubhouse full of sweaty and farty men who just did a workout together."

She stays quiet for a moment. "Fair point."

"Conversely," I add on the verge of laughter. "It's your nose the one that's at risk here."

She nods a little, as much as my chest and my face allow it. "That's true, men can be really gross."

"Do I stink right now?" I ask, worried with the turn of the conversation.

"No." A pause. "You could bottle this up and get rich."

"Whew. Thankfully my pheromones work on you too." I laugh through my nose. "See? We have undeniable chemistry. That's a sign that we're meant to be."

"You're laying it a bit thick, Lucky."

"I'm not above groveling if I have to." I place a soft kiss on the crown of her head. "What are your plans for Christmas?"

"Working." After a moment, she adds, "Maybe in my pajamas."

"What kind of pajamas?"

She answers dryly, "Baggy sweats, you perv."

"Okay but can I watch anyway? I can finish reading my book while you work. I had to pause once again at the part where Lord Harrington is taking care of Lady Arabella while she's bedridden with fever."

She chokes a little. "Are those seriously words that just came out of your mouth?"

"You're not judging my literature choices, are you?"

"No, but…" She shakes her head. "I'm in awe at who you are, Lucky Rivera."

I jolt a little. "What does that mean?"

"I've also seen the video of your accident, like everyone who is on the sports side of the internet. I know that you're tough and hard working and loyal—that's the only way you could get that out despite the nightmare that was unfolding for you. And even after that, you've kept your sense of humor and your… your whimsy. Those aren't qualities I have, but I deeply admire them."

Somehow I can feel my face heating far more at this comment than when she was feeling me up earlier, and that's saying something.

I clear my throat, ready to refute the praise or turn it back on her many great qualities, but she's officially rendered me speechless. My friends and family will be stunned to realize that they day came where this finally happened.

"I like you a lot," she sighs into my chest. "I just don't know how this thing between us can possibly work once we leave Bear Crossing."

She doesn't have to explain it. I may be bordering on himbo but I've been mulling over the same issue. Camila lives in Mapleton and that's where her job is. I technically live in Orlando but my job takes me all over the country for the majority of the year. The only reason for me to go to Mapleton on a normal occasion is to visit Mateo and his family. Our paths won't cross after I recover and go back to playing— because that not happening is out of the question.

"The real reason I'm going to Mapleton is because I'm signed up for some experimental treatments at the St. Cloud University hospital, so I'll be staying with Mateo for a few months and we can see how things go between us during that time," I reason aloud.

"And what if they go really well?" she asks as if that's the worst case scenario. And honestly, it might just be. "Do we do long distance? Because that doesn't really work in the history of ever."

"I know that ball guys have a really bad reputation but I'm not a cheater," I say softly, tightening my arms around her just a notch. "You can ask everyone on the team. Hell, even Jasmine will confirm."

"That's not it." She pauses for a long moment. "What if I miss you too much?"

My chest squeezes but this time it's not her hands making biscuits out of my pecs, it's just a stab of pain in my own damn heart. "We'll FaceTime every day, even if it's just to breathe next to each other."

"I can't watch every one of your games in person. I have way too much work to travel that much."

"Nor would I expect you—"

"But isn't that what baseball wives and girlfriends are supposed to do?"

"No, that's up to each couple." Caressing her hair, I travel my hand until I find her jaw and gently guide her face up so I can look into her eyes. "I'd just be happy knowing you're on my corner, no matter where in the world we are."

"And what about the snuggles?" Camila asks with a surprisingly serious expression.

My face splits into a grin. "I'd need a hit of those every so often, yes."

If anything, she frowns even harder. "So you want to do this?"

"Hell yeah." I stare into her unfathomable eyes. "You?" I stay still like she's a lioness in a cage and I'm but a man armed with nothing but a rare steak.

The room has gradually turned brighter, light filtering through the heavy curtains signaling a new day—two away from Christmas, to be precise. Today is the day when Camila has to return to Mapleton for the important meeting that has robbed her of peace and quiet the past few days. And I have to resume my life and see where it takes me the next few months.

I wish we could stay in the cocoon of these blankets in this bear-themed inn forever, hibernating in each other's arms for the rest of our lives. What I'm proposing to her isn't quite like that, but if I can get a few moments like this throughout the year, then it'll be worth it. Much better than not being in each other's lives anymore.

"There will be conditions," she enunciates slowly. I do my best not to wag my tail in excitement.

"Like what?"

"Our jobs are a very important part of our identities, we have to respect that."

"Of course." I nod. "Respect is always both ways. I'll always cheer on your accomplishments."

"I'm not a social butterfly so if I'm expected to join the WAGs for events, know that it's not going to happen."

"That's okay, the only event I want is you in my bed."

That earns me a smack. "And I'm also not the sweetest, most affectionate of girlfriends, so if you're expecting that then this is a no go already."

"Girlfriends, huh?" I run my hand up and down her back, leaving tiny shivers on its trail. "You seem plenty affectionate to me."

She grouches again, "Lucky…"

"It's okay, I can be affectionate enough for both of us."

I roll her on her back, gritting my teeth a little as the bedsheets tug at my cast. There is no comfortable placement for my leg so I use my arms to prop most of my weight as I lean over her. She lets me bury my face in her neck and I take a good, deep whiff of the warm spice in her skin. She may not mean to, but she smells like Christmas—cinnamon and pine and marshmallows and warmth.

"I'll never get enough of you," I whisper in her skin, sliding one hand under the curve of her back and finding skin. "I'll agree to whatever deal you propose just so that I can stay around you." I kiss the side of her neck, slowly finding my way to her jaw, to her chin. "And I'll text you how much I want you and miss you every day."

Her hands come to my shoulders and she sighs. "That sounds too good to be true."

"I'll show you." I reach her lips and they're so warm. "You'll see."

I kiss her and it's nothing like the other times. This is hungry and bruising, and she meets me halfway with the same kind of urgency that's moving my body. Logic says that we're about to embark on a challenging journey, even more than this trip from Orlando to Mapleton has been, but every fiber of my being tells me that it's right.

That my place is in Camila Puig's life, and that she's the reason why all of this has happened—the injury, the VIP lounge chair, the turbulence, and the rest of this messy trip.

CHAPTER 30
CAMILA

push the curtains open, not because I'm super interested in checking the weather outside like I'm pretending, but because my lips are bruised and throbbing to the beat of my heart, and I need to calm down. Or else there's no getting out of Bear Crossing today, and I'd really rather meet with my boss in person to talk about investments and head counts.

Outside is still a white landscape, but the snow blanket is no longer perfect. Between a handful of guests, including Lucky and I, playing in the thing, and someone or something shoveling it, it no longer looks impenetrable. It's still the early hours and the sun isn't fully out yet, but I can't find a single cloud in sight. The weather apps said there'd be no precipitation today, and it looks like it might be true.

"Looks like we're going to—" My words die in my mouth as I turn.

Lucky's in the middle of the bed, yawning wide with his arms stretched as high as they go. The motion pulls at his sweatshirt, revealing a swath of extremely toned stomach and hip. I don't know if that's the natural placement of his sweatpants or if they're riding low because we just made out like our lives depended on it. The line of muscle over his hipbones and down his front makes my knees weak.

He savors the last of the yawn and lets his arms collapse back on the bed. Turning his head, he sets his sleepy eyes on me and pats the bed.

My traitorous body takes one step forward until I remember that we're on a schedule. Shaking my head hard, I say, "No, I'm going to shower and then I'm going out there to figure out how to get us to Mapleton."

"I take it we're not driving up with our exes anymore?"

"Hell no," I confirm. "I'd rather we crawl on our elbows all the way there."

"Me too." He slides his arms up until he cushions his head with his hands. "Go shower. I'll close my eyes for another moment and imagine you're still straddling me and eating my mouth at the same time."

Pretty sure I'm about to become the first case of spontaneous combustion.

Grabbing my stuff quickly, I dash into the bathroom and get myself under the shower spray in record time. Apparently when men are turned on and they need to behave, they have to take a cold shower. Not me. I boil myself and scrub hard enough to forget the feeling of his hands searching the skin under my shirt. Or how he felt under me while I kissed him with an abandon that I never knew myself capable of.

Once again, I ask myself, "¿Qué estás haciendo, Camila?" I can't believe I'm doing this—whatever this is shaping up to be—with a professional baseball player I didn't know last week.

Yet, when I emerge from the bathroom completely clean—head to mouth to toes—I find said player fast asleep on the bed. His chest rises and falls softly, and it feels apropos to note that even unconscious, the guy has a tiny smile on his lips, like he's happiness personified at every moment of his life. It's almost criminal that I have to wake him up.

"Lucky," I whisper, laying my hand on his chest again. I can't help it, apparently I have a weakness for pecs of steel. "Wake up, you also need to shower."

"Hmm, why," he mumbles them like they're the same word.

"I'm afraid your pheromones may not work on everybody else," I tease.

A caveman-like sound comes out of his throat. Before I pull away, he grabs at my hand and keeps me half crouched for a minute. When I try to tug, he lifts my hand and brings it up—and up still until his lips meet the palm. My skin tingles everywhere, not just at the point of contact.

"I'm going," he mumbles, barely opening his eyes.

Snorting, I slide my hand free, the friction intensifying the butterflies fluttering in my stomach. Goodness, this can get addicting fast.

It takes Lucky two more tries to finally get out of bed and make his way to the bathroom. Meanwhile, I make quick work of packing my suitcase, making sure that my laptop is in my purse and doesn't go the way of shoe-gate, since this is the only depository of the strictly confidential business case that is going to save *SPORTY* in the long run.

Once I hear the shower running, certain mental images start appearing in my mind and I decide that the best way I can continue functioning is by changing scenery. I'll wait for Lucky to have breakfast together, but in the meantime I head over to the reception. Now that roads start being accessible, there's a line to check out and I have no choice but to join it.

"Leaving by yourself?"

I roll my eyes until they close and do not turn around even as Rupert gets in line behind me. "What's it to you?"

"Just wondering what's next after your little deception." He chuckles, the sound hitting me so different compared to anyone else who isn't a slimy jerk. How his 'doctor' title was enough to con me into thinking he was the best option, I don't understand. "Are you still driving to Mapleton with us?"

"Absolutely not," I spit out, still facing forward.

"C'mon, this whole thing doesn't have to—"

Whatever he was going to say gets lost in the ether as the cookie sisters also descend upon us. For once, the three of them appear serious—even annoyed. "Good morning, dearie. Is this oaf giving you trouble?"

It takes me a moment to realize that I'm the dearie and my ex is supposed to be the oaf. I know for a fact that he would describe us the exact opposite way, and it's good to see that a third party is validating my perception of him.

"Yes, actually. His presence alone is very unpleasant," I respond.

"Hey—"

Billie snaps her fingers and cuts him off. "You heard the girl. Off you go."

He scoffs behind me. "Excuse me, but I'm not a dog to be shooed."

"Actually," Val cuts in. "You *are* a dog. The way you behaved yesterday proved as much."

"Dang…" Nellie elongates the word, punctuating it with a dropped jaw.

"Whatever." The normally composed and amiable Rupert sounds sick and tired of this. He spits out a *blah* and I feel him step away. Glancing over my shoulder, I find him retracing his steps back toward the Grizzly room, where his equally bad-person fiancée probably awaits.

"Good riddance," I mumble under my breath, happy if this is the very last time I ever see him.

Val shakes her head. "Men. Can't live without them but also not with them."

"At least Lucky is so much better," another sister comments.

Out of curiosity, I ask, "How do you know that?"

"Unlike that fool that is your ex, Lucky has kind eyes," is the initial response, followed by, "And they turn absolutely scalding when they're on you. That's how you know he's a keeper."

My cheek twitches. That is a shockingly accurate way to describe the phenomenon that is Lucky Rivera.

"Speaking of." Billie leans closer. "How did things go with him yesterday after the whole debacle?"

"Yes, we're dying to know." Nellie rubs her hands.

"Good morning," a different voice cuts in with a lot of cheer. The cookie sisters's faces turn positively foul at the interruption but Lottie, one of the inn owners, pays them no attention as she addresses me. "Ready to check out now that the roads are cleared?"

"Hopefully, but first I wanted to know if there are any car rentals available in town."

Her demeanor gives very strong *oh honey*. "I'm afraid not. Bear Crossing is too small for that."

I mutter a tiny curse in Spanish.

Someone taps on my shoulder and it appears to be Val. "Where are you headed?"

"Mapleton, Connecticut," I respond. "Any chance you guys are also going that way?"

"We're headed to Philly. How about we give you a lift to a car rental there?"

I didn't lie to Lucky this morning when I said that I'm not an affectionate person, and yet I'm so overjoyed at this news that I wrap all three of the elderly sisters in a tight hug. "Thank you, thank you, thank you." I pepper my gratitude on each one with individual hugs too. "You lifesavers."

"We need to leave ass up, though," Val says.

Nellie bursts out laughing. "It's not ass up, it's ASAP."

The other sister scrunches her face. "What does that even mean?"

"As soon as possible, you stooge," Billie explains with a laugh.

Okay. Who cares about breakfast. If I can get us on the road and as far away from Rupert's mocking and Jasmine's condescension *ass up*, the better. I'm sure Lucky would agree.

"Got it. Then I'll go tell Lucky to cut his shower short."

They wait until I'm at a few steps away to say, "And don't join him, or we'll be late!"

As the attention of other people turns my way, I duck out of sight and rush toward the Polar room.

He's still in the bathroom but I don't hear the shower running any longer, which has to be a good sign. "Lucky!" I knock on the door. "You need to hurry. I just—"

The door swings open and the first thing I notice is that his wet hair weighs it down so much that the stretched curls get in his eyes. He paws at his face twice until he can see me—and see me he does, with eyes as wide as saucers. "What? What's happening? Is something wrong? Are you okay?" He grabs me with one hand, with the other keeping himself upright against the door frame.

I forget how to talk, which makes him even more concerned. But it's not because something is wrong, but because he's just wearing a towel—oh, and a long plastic bag that covers his cast.

"Um…"

"Camila, what's wrong?"

I manage to point at him. He looks down at himself. Freeing me, he grabs onto the towel right before it was about to unravel. "Well?" he asks me like he didn't just accidentally show me what his momma gave him.

Words tumble out of my mouth. Neither of us understand

them, so I clear my throat and try again. "I found us a different ride, but we need to leave ass up."

He tilts his head and blinks. "What?"

"ASAP, I mean." I could smack my forehead.

His chest deflates in relief. "Got it. Let me just dry my hair quickly."

"And also put on some clothes," I spew out.

"Is this bothering you?" He motions at his bare chest dusted with a smattering of dark hair that turns into a little trail south.

"Yes," I confirm with a nod. "Very much. And unless you want to get the cookie sisters all hot and bothered—and also catch a cold—you're better off wearing something."

Nonplussed he focuses on the most innocent thing. "Oh, so they're going to drive us to Mapleton?"

"Just to Philadelphia, and from there we'll rent a car and I'll drive us all the way."

"Perfect. So long Rodrigo and Jasmine."

I would laugh if it wasn't for the water drop slowly trickling down his stomach between the ridges of muscle. "Aren't you cold?" I ask absentmindedly.

"Not when you look at me that way," he mentions with a little smirk on his face that I'm afraid I love.

I lift my eyes to his and I see exactly what the three old ladies described in him. Enough sweetness to rival a chocolate candy bar, but also as much heat as the sun itself.

"I'll check us out and wait for you outside," I manage to wheeze out and my legs quiver like jelly as I wheel my suitcase back out to the reception.

CHAPTER 31
LUCKY

"And that's how I met my husband," Val finishes saying, after nearly an hour of every nuance around the event.

I'm at the backseat with Camila and Nellie, while Val drives us to Philadelphia with her sister Billie snoozing on the passenger seat. Either she finds the story boring or she's conked out after a few days of shenanigans at the Bear and Breakfast.

"Fascinating," I say, because it kind of is. I doubt that a lot of people find the love of their lives while swimming as mermaids for an aquarium. Camila has been busy typing away at her computer from the middle of the backseat, comfortable with my arm around her shoulders but not paying me any attention otherwise. "So what brought the three of you to Bear Crossing?" For all that we've chitchatted during the past three days, this has somehow not come up until now.

"We came to visit our parents," Nellie responds from the other side of Camila.

The latter speaks absentmindedly. "That's nice."

"Yes, I bet they were happy."

"What do you mean?" I lean forward as I ask.

Val answers from the front, "That's because they can't really tell us as much, what with them being interred in neighboring plots and all that."

Camila lifts her head at that. She turns to me, mirroring the same cringe that's now on my face.

"I'm sorry to have brought it up," I mumble, sending an apologetic look to the one sister who can see it.

"It's all good, sweetie. They passed when we were kids." Nellie waves a hand. "It was five days before Christmas, so we've made it a tradition to come visit them every year that we can."

"Sometimes only one of us can make it," Val adds, "but they never spend Christmas alone."

Camila leans back, her hands still on the keyboard but no longer attacking it. "I guess I'm not the only one with a sad Christmas story, huh?" She's referring to whatshisface having jilted her, and it annoys me anew.

"No, dearie. But now we're also not the only ones rewriting happy stories on top, huh?" Nellie nudges her and sends me the most indiscreet look in history.

I bite my lips, very casually running my hand up and down Camila's arms. The nickname that I gave her when everything was an act is going to stick, because she leans against my side and snuggle-bears the heck out of me. And since it can't go unreciprocated, I search for her intoxicating scent with my nose into her hair, and place a little kiss wherever I can land it.

Seems like Billie wasn't asleep the whole time, because she sounds quite perky as she asks, "So, when's the wedding and are we invited?"

I choke. Camila reacts the opposite way—she freezes.

The cookie sisters start cackling like hyenas.

Val breaks off from the hilarity. "We need some credit for helping you get together, especially after I gave you up for my Sarah."

I thump my chest, coughing until I can breathe again. "Sorry," I manage to spew out.

"We…" Camila clears her throat, lowering her attention to her screen. "We just started this, whatever it is. Marriage talk is too early."

"True," I muse, watching as the scenery turns deeper into the city. "It's not even clear what we are yet, or where we're going."

Nellie starts humming the wedding march.

"We won't ask to be maids of honor, we'll be delighted to just be there for the big day," Billie explains as if this was even in the picture. "Bonus points if it's in Bear Crossing, five days before Christmas."

"Oh, my." Nellie gasps. "Your babies are going to be so beautiful."

Val wonders, "Now, will their babies be professional athletes or professional businesspeople?"

Slowly, by increments, Camila turns to look up at me like maybe, just maybe, she would've preferred driving up to Mapleton with our condescending exes. My lips twitch and I can't help but releasing a booming laughter that immediately sets the sisters off.

*

"Don't be strangers." Billie hugs me like I'm her long lost son. Once she pulls away, she snaps her fingers. "Oh, that's right. We have something for you two."

As she sticks her head back in her car, the next sister—Val—parades in front of me and also gives me a motherly hug. In my ear she whispers, "Let me know if you two break up, and I'll get you a perfect new girlfriend right away."

I shake my head both at her antics but also because I have

no plans of replacing Camila. I'm too busy thinking about how to make us work instead.

"Ignore her." Nellie pushes her sister away from me to also wrap her arms around me. Each of these ladies is a tiny little thing but squeezes the living lights out of me. Unlike the others, she pats my cheek like I'm a five-year-old kid. "You get healthy and be happy, okay?"

I smile. "Thank you. And you too."

"Ah ha!" Camila's exclamation brings our focus to her. She raises up a car key as if it was Excalibur and we all ohh and ahh. "Finally we will be able to make it to Mapleton."

"I would clap if I wasn't balanced on crutches," I explain.

"Ah ha!" a different voice echoes. Billie emerges from the sisters's vehicle with a bundle in her hands. It seems to be a red bag with—is that mistletoe what's tying it closed? "Here you go." She extends it toward Camila, whose hands are free, other than the car key.

"What's this?" she wonders even as she receives the gift.

"Cookies for the road."

Camila and I exchange a look. We truly could expect no less from the cookie sisters.

Damn, I'm gonna miss these old hens.

Camila's lips curl into the tiniest, sweetest smile. "Thank you—not just for the cookies. For everything."

"Aw, of course."

Now Camila gets squished by all three of them, and if it wasn't because she has places to be, I'd guess she also would like to hang out with the sisters some more. But it's time to part ways, and after transferring our luggage to the rental car, we wave goodbye to our new, unexpected friends.

"That was something," I say with a grunt as I swing my stiff leg into the space between the passenger seat and the console. I end up having to move the seat as far back as it goes so I can fit in.

"It sure was." Camila turns on the trusty Corolla rental. "This whole trip has been."

"Is, uh…" I lean against the door all casual. "Is that a good thing?"

"A very good thing." She falls quiet for a while as she drives us away from the rental parking lot and into traffic. The GPS guides us through to the highway, showing that we're one hour and fourteen minutes away from Mapleton. I almost forgot what we were talking about when she resumes. "My perspective has changed a lot the past few days."

"Oh yeah?" I prompt her to say more, and she does.

"I've always operated on the principle of *my way or the highway* but, how should I put this… Maybe life has its own way, and I just need to learn to cruise along the highway."

"That's deep." My eyebrows rise. "But actually, I get it."

"You do?"

"Think about it. If I hadn't torn my ACL in the final game of the World Series, we wouldn't have duked it out for the last chair available on the VIP lounge."

Camila gasps a little. "That's true. We would've passed each other by."

"To be more precise, I would've given you the chair and then gone on my merry way," I clarify.

"Right. You're a gentleman. Unless your ACL is torn."

I nod gravely. "Yeah, sorry. I'm not the perfect book boyfriend."

A second too late I wish I could just physically put my foot in my mouth. That would be way easier than dealing with the silence that falls between us after dropping the b-word this soon.

"I didn't mean to imply…" I wave my hand awkwardly, not knowing how to finish the sentence.

"That aside," she says, now fully recovered from the surprise since she's using her characteristic businesslike tone.

"I want you to know that I don't expect perfection from you."

For some reason that almost makes me bubble out a giddy laugh, but I manage to contain it by lightly coughing into my hand. "Is it because you already saw how bad my breath smells in the morning?"

Ruthlessly she says, "That and because you're just a normal guy."

"Um, excuse me. I'm a professional sports champion."

She flashes me a quick side eye. "I mean, you're not a checklist."

"Ohh." I blink, remembering what she told me about how Rutilio fit her perfect idea of what a husband should be, yet look at what a piece of dung he turned out to be. "Wow, that's the sweetest thing anyone's ever said to me."

She smacks my arm. "I'm serious."

"I know." I grab her hand and slide my fingers between hers until we're intertwined. She's the one who closes her hand, gripping mine hard. "What if you ticked all the items of my own checklist for the perfect woman?"

"Hmm?" Instead of finding it amusing, she frowns like she's trying to put a puzzle together.

So I start ticking off items. "She has to be smart, with a tongue as sharp as a razor to really challenge my wit. Also, with curves that absolutely boil my blood and make me forget my name."

Camila clears her throat.

"Her smile has to be the most special sight, even if I'm not the one that caused it."

That earns me another quick glance, this time in surprise.

"Wait." I lean forward. "There's one thing I don't know about you."

"Only one?" she asks sarcastically.

"Well, aside from your bra size, I mean if you can dance."

After spluttering for a second, she says, "How are those two even related?"

"Listen, I don't actually care about your lingerie. Bachata yes or no?"

"Are you going to dump me if I say that I haven't danced much?"

"Well, no. But I'm gonna teach you." I pat my leg brace gentle. "After this bad boy comes off."

Gripping the steering wheel harder, like she's already stressed, she asks, "My parents put me on ballet when I was a kid, will that help?"

"Don't worry, *I* will help." A corner of my mouth lifts. "And trust me, you're going to enjoy it very much."

"I have no doubt," she mumbles before shaking her head. "But Lucky, you also need to understand that I'm not perfect. Your own brother can't stand me."

I don't deny it. "You're his boss. Your job is to be disliked by your subordinates."

"I am particularly disliked by almost everyone in the company."

"*Almost* being the keyword there, of course."

She sighs. "*Almost* because now there are two and a half people who can stand me."

"And a half?"

"The boyfriend of one of the two."

"And now three," I say, shrugging. "Even though I'm not a *SPORTY* employee."

Silence.

I tug at her hand, fishing for a response.

"I heard you, I'm just processing," she whispers.

Lifting our joined hands, I place a kiss on the back of hers. "There's no hurry, snuggle bear. We're not under pressure anymore." And that earns me a real smile.

CHAPTER 32
CAMILA

Never have I had a harder time to stop myself from laughing. "Let me guess, this other one is also about the lechón," I say to Lucky once another Christmas song from Puerto Rico plays on the sound system.

"What can I say, it's a really important part of our lives."

"I have no right to make fun of it," I add gravely, "We have quite a few traditional songs that mention hallacas."

I feel him turn to watch me and I wish I could meet his eyes too, but I have to keep them on the road. "What are those?"

"Hmm. I guess they're like a cousin of the tamale? Basically corn dough filled with some kind of stew, wrapped in a plantain leaf and then boiled."

As if on cue, Lucky's stomach roars like a savage beast. I can't help but tearing my eyes off the road for a second to glance at him. There's no embarrassment in his expression, instead he's rubbing his flat stomach and looking wistfully into the distance. "Man, that sounds right up my alley."

"Did we run out of cookies?"

He grins. "No, and I can't believe I'm going to say this… I think I don't want sugar anymore."

The truth of that also resonates in my very fiber. I check the GPS and it indicates that we're very close to Mapleton now, some twenty minutes to go. "Do you have somewhere to be once we get to Mapleton or should we stop somewhere for a meal?"

"Why, Camila Puig, are you asking me out on a date?"

I choke on my own saliva. "No—Well, I…"

"Yes, I would love to go out with you," he teases me and then he does something wild—he slides his hand to my nape, fingers through my head, and softly kneads.

A groan comes out from the deepest recess of my chest and we both freeze.

"Um." He clears his throat. From the corner of my eye I catch him squirm, but he doesn't remove his hand. "Should I stop or keep going?"

I mull this over with as much seriousness as I've poured onto the business case I'll be presenting to Martin this afternoon, thankfully rescheduled to accommodate my travel schedule.

Honestly, the heat and the weight and the callouses on his hand feel amazing, way better than the hand held massager I keep in my desk drawer for when I have a tension headache. On the other hand, I wonder what he means by the words keep going. As in, massaging the same spot? Or moving to a different locale of my body?

In either case, do I trust myself to keep driving us in our lane, or would my limbs turn into noodles and make us crash into our dramatic demise on the highway?

"Maybe let's not make us crash?" The last word comes out in a lilting question once he gives one final, delicious squeeze.

"Good to know that it affects you," the evil guy says with the calmest, smoothest voice, deliberately sliding his hand off with as much friction as possible. He breaks into a chuckle watching me shiver at the sensation.

My eyebrows squeeze. "Just so you know, I'm not the kind of person who takes things like this lying down."

"Looking forward to your revenge, then."

How does that sound like he's also going to win that round?

*

Revenge comes when we're sitting together at a booth in the same café I came to almost a year ago with Rachel and Sierra. This time I don't focus on how sticky the table is—clearly they still don't clean this place properly—when there's a whole baseball player sitting next to me with his beefy arm around my shoulders.

A waitress tries with all her might to take our order professionally, but she can't stop staring at Lucky. I'm pretty sure it's not because of how many items off the menu he rattles for his order, but rather because he fills up this entire place with his presence and the undeniable charm in his smile. I narrow my eyes at him, wondering how I was capable of fighting him for that lounge chair.

Finally, done ordering half of the menu, he lifts his pretty brown eyes to the stunned waitress and says, "That's it, thank you."

"Um… of course." She stares at the notepad in her hands, probably realizing she only got a fraction of what he ordered, and deciding to scurry off anyway because being around the gorgeous man is too much.

Felt, I think to myself.

If he insists on calling me snuggle bear, I'm going to own up to it. I lean into his side, resting my arm on his left thigh until my hand falls on his knee. I feel him tense but he doesn't pull away. Slowly, I lift my face and find him already watching me.

"Is this your revenge?" he mumbles in a deep voice that sends my heart into a tumble.

"Maybe?"

"Look at you." He brushes a finger on my chin. "Blinking all cute and everything."

"Is this okay?" I ask in a wheezy way.

"More than okay." He slides his hand down my arm to my elbow, bypassing it altogether to land on my waist. "So what are you doing after this?"

It takes some abnormal effort to find an answer. "Ah, I have that meeting with my boss. You know, the life or death one."

"You never said what that's all about." He immediately picks up on the hesitation on my face and adds, "If it's anything confidential, you don't have to say anything."

"It kind of is but also… it's just striking me that it may make you dislike me."

In a somber way, he counters, "I would only dislike you if you make fun of my mom."

"I would never!" I gasp.

"There ya go." Lucky's face splits into a grin.

It makes me shake my head. "No, I mean, I'm afraid that we need to make some unpopular decisions to ensure that the company can continue to exist, period."

"So, layoffs," he guesses cleverly. I stay mum. Lucky reaches for a strand of my hair and tucks it behind my ear. "Listen, if my brother has to lose his job I can keep him and his family afloat."

"I can't confirm or deny anything." I press my lips tight. "But I'm pretty sure he's never going to like me, regardless."

His lips curl. "And here I was thinking of inviting you to Christmas dinner tomorrow with everyone."

"I'm afraid I would make it way too awkward." I reach for

the glass of water on the table when a thought strikes me. "Wait." I turn to him. "Does the fact that your brother hate my guts mean we can't date?"

"Nahh." He pauses, then shrugs. "He'll get over it."

"That doesn't sound quite promising."

"You know what would help him start coming around?" he asks and I imagine that he's going to tell me something like *not firing him* or *giving him a raise.* Instead, he says, "If you come to Christmas dinner tomorrow."

"Lucky…"

"Do you have other plans?" He raises his eyebrows in curiosity.

"Well, no—" I shut my yap tight, trying to resist his puppy eyes with a mighty frown. I can feel how little it's working. "I don't think there's an employee in the world who would be comfortable with having his boss at his home on Christmas eve."

"You wouldn't be going as Mateo's boss, though. You'd be going as my hot date."

I snort. "I think that would be the most shocking part of all."

"Not really. I already told him."

My eyes widen. "You told him… what?"

"That I have a huge crush on his boss."

Butterflies explode in my belly. "You do?"

"Excuse me, I thought it was obvious."

"No, no." I raise a hand. "I get that. I'm just processing. A year ago something like this was completely impossible."

"Why not?" Now he's the one snuggle bear-ing me, nuzzling my neck with his nose.

"Excuse me," I repeat after him, except in a much squeakier voice. "Have you not seen how neurotic I am?"

"Yes, and?" He places a soft kiss on my neck. A sweet one, compared to how it immediately sets my body on fire.

I open my mouth, trying to get some breath into my lungs. "U-Uh, men don't like that."

"The wrong men don't," he retorts with confidence that either comes from having won a professional sports championship, or because he can feel that I'm turning into putty against him.

"M-Maybe," I stammer again, and I try to steel myself against the consuming want to make out with him like a randy teenager in this public establishment. Mapleton isn't exactly the smallest of towns, but everyone here knows someone who works at *SPORTY*, and one thing is if word gets around that I was seen getting cozy with a guy, a different one if the gossip includes tongues. "Anyway, men weren't exactly lining up around the corner for me."

Thankfully, Lucky pulls away to a respectable distance. "That's okay, you don't need men. You just need me." His eyes dance.

The food starts to arrive then, a tomato soup and grilled cheese sandwich that Lucky courteously allowed me to order first, and a whole parade of dishes for him from quiche, to salad, to soup, and bread, and the best looking roasted vegetables I've ever seen. He catches me eying them and slides them over to my side of the table, motioning at me to tuck in.

I can't articulate why that tiny, probably inconsequential gesture reaches the depths of my frozen soul and starts thawing it. No one has ever put my wants before their own that way—in *any* way. I'm glad that he's already stuffing his face and it keeps him busy enough to miss how my eyes are tearing up.

Sure enough, he ends up having to order more food. I excuse myself to use the restroom while he's polishing off the last of his meal, and when I come back I find that he has already picked up the tab and is ready to go.

"We could've split the bill," I grouch as we make our way

back out to the cold fresh air. "I have a pretty good salary, you know?"

"Didn't you pay for the rental?" Lucky cocks an eyebrow at me.

"Yes…?" I sort of ask.

"Then consider us even."

"Fine." I harrumph, which just makes him chuckle, and makes it impossible for me to pretend to stay grumpy.

I help him get in the car, not missing how he winces when he has to swing his injured leg into the vehicle. I put his crutches in the backseat and skip my way toward the driver seat, trying to warm myself up against the the winter bite.

"So what now?" he asks once I'm in the car, strapping my seatbelt on.

"Now I take you home and drive to the company. Then I drive to the airport to leave this car and get my own and then I go home to shower, change into clothes that don't have bears, and try to get some work done."

His eyes crinkle with a soft smile. "I don't mean to sound too needy, yet I have to admit that I'm not ready to go our separate ways."

Me neither.

The vehemence of that understanding hits me not like a ton of bricks, but like a soft, feather pillow that is enough to jolt me. "Is this how it's going to be every time we have to part ways?" I whisper.

"Probably," Lucky responds with sincerity. He extends his hand to me and I grab it without hesitation.

"You could, uh…" I squirm. "You could wait for me at *SPORTY*'s lobby."

"And let a whole company of sports apparel know that you're dating a hot professional athlete? Sounds fun, let's do it."

"There's a tiny voice in my head telling me that it's probably a bad idea. I have a reputation to uphold," I explain as I set the car in motion.

"Camila, it's time for you to do what you want. Screw what others think."

I narrow my eyes at the slushy road. "You know what?" I brace to say the single wildest thing I'll ever utter in my life. "You're right. I'm done living the way other people expect me to live."

"Hell yeah!"

And that's how, for the first time in a week and a half, I walk into the doors of my workplace with a gorgeous man next to me. We'd be holding hands if it wasn't for his crutches, but the sentiment is there.

It's not the most dramatic entrance anyway, because only the security personnel are there to greet us. They obviously recognize me but not Lucky, so I sign him up as my guest and get him a temporary badge so he can stay in the premises.

"How's your leg?" I ask as I put the badge around his neck like it's an Olympic medal.

"Holding up, why?"

I leave my hands on his chest, delighting in the steady drum of his heart. "Would you like to wait for me outside my boss's office? He has a pretty nice seating area, and his assistant can probably get you a coffee."

"And after that?" He leans closer to me.

"I go into my meeting."

"And after that?" Lucky repeats, now resting his forehead against mine. He's almost a full head taller, but the crutches allow him to reach my height comfortably.

"After that, um… do you want to come to my place?"

With the thickest voice I've heard on him, he answers, "I'd love nothing more."

Suddenly, I'm more motivated to get this meeting done and over with than ever before. "Then, come with."

Now, reaching the top floor and emerging out of the elevator with *the* Lucky Rivera does attract every available pair of eyes.

He's recognizable around these parts, whether by the viral video of the moment he tore his ACL, or by past pictorials with the magazine. Martin's assistant—a grown man who is married with kids—opens and closes his mouth like a fish as I help Lucky get installed on a lounge couch that is all for him. A steep improvement from the crammed chair of an airport lounge, or the uncomfortable seat of an airplane with or without turbulence.

"Wait." Lucky grabs my hand right as I'm about to pull away, tugging gently. I allow him to lead me down until our lips meet, and the dreamy sigh that comes out of me makes him smile.

When we pull away, someone clears their throat behind me. Martin Richter, my boss, stands with the door to his office open and his eyebrows in the sky. No doubt he just saw this little amorous episode. Screw my old reputation, indeed.

I straighten up and nod at Lucky as if he was just a coworker I just shook hands with. Instead, he leans back on the couch, looking me up and down like there's literally no one else around us. Pretty sure my face is redder than Rudolph's nose as I walk into Martin's office with him.

"Will you take me to HR if I ask what all that was about?" Martin asks while taking a seat at the conference table inside his office.

"Let's just say this trip has been eventful," I tactfully say, skirting around the fact that a week and a half ago when I went to Orlando, I was more single than a cheap paper tissue. "Anyway, I hope you got my pre-read document?"

"Sure did." He leans back, lacing his hands over his belly.

We're both busy so there's no need for me to run through the whole thing like I'm an intern. "And?" I prompt.

He tilts his head. "Last time we talked you didn't mention starting a new line along with the automation change."

"I didn't—because that's an addition." I fold my legs under the table and swivel around to point at my boots. "I got the idea from these."

"I don't recognize the brand," he says.

"That's because I bought them at an artisanal shop on the side of the road in a small town called Bear Crossing." I reach over to pat the leather boot. "These have been so comfortable that I haven't even noticed the raw welts at my heels for days."

He blinks. "The what?"

"I made the mistake of wearing heels while I traveled—it's a long story." I wave my hand. "My point is that these hand-made boots made me think that we can ensure *SPORTY*'s future through automation, while also honoring our grassroots past. While we automate the large scale product lines, we can produce certain products the old school way, by hand, and keep employing local crafts-masters. There would still be some redundancies, but not as drastic as in my original proposal."

"And the capital investment we'd need for this?"

I rest back against the seat. "Sales for our standard products will recover the capital expenditure in just three years. Meanwhile, our traditional line could potentially see a return on investment in ten."

He does a double take.

"But," I add, "the social capital we would gain from it will be immediate."

"Social capital, huh?" he throws the business buzzwords back at me not because he's mocking me, but like he can't believe I just mentioned them.

"Despite my 'ice queen' nickname, I do care about our employees, Martin. I'm hoping that the traditional line can keep a lot of them still employed with us, and that the commu-nity outreach by involving local artisans in the design can demonstrate our commitment to remaining an employer of choice in this region."

Martin stays quiet, just staring at me like *I* am the presentation full of estimations and timelines.

"I'm glad I postponed my vacation for this meeting, or I'd have missed the moment when you finally became the manager I've been training you to be."

"What?"

"Start the two projects in January," he says, flooring me even more than with the previous compliment. "But before that, I want you to take some time off to really get some rest and enjoy your new boyfriend."

I splutter. "He's not—We're not—"

"Then go make him your boyfriend. Happy employees do excellent work, and I'm going to need you to really ace it with this plan so that I can retire with a prosperous company."

"Retire?" I exclaim.

"*And* make you my successor," he says casually, as if he wasn't contributing to this being the best day of my life.

CHAPTER 33
LUCKY

José Feliciano's Feliz Navidad plays in Mateo's home. I'm on the sofa with my right leg propped up on some cushions, finally having reached the last chapters of The Duke and His Lady while waiting for Camila. Angel, my nephew, sits on the carpet with his back propped against the sofa while he reads a picture book—though his is baseball themed and not a Regency romp. Mateo and Karina are in the kitchen, the former glazing a massive lechón and the latter checking in on the arroz con gandules.

The house smells amazing, like all of the childhood flavors that were a comfort when the whole family was together. Usually we spend the holiday on the island with Mom, but the knee treatment got in the way of that tradition. She'll join us for new year's, though, so at least we'll have that.

We all know who's on the other side when the doorbell rings.

"Does your boss like music?" Karina asks her husband with the same nervous manner she adopted from the second I broke the news about our dinner guest.

My brother grouches, "I don't know. I've never known her to like anything."

"She likes *me*," I chime in as I try to slide to the edge of the couch, but my nephew's not moving from his spot. Clearly he has no interest in meeting the newcomer.

"Stay." My sister-in-law gestures at me to not move. "I'll get it."

I press my lips. "But I'm the one who invited her, I should get the door for her."

"Surely she'll understand?"

"I don't know." Mateo grunts as he straightens up again after putting the lechón back in the oven. "I've never known her to be understanding."

His wife tosses him a look that very clearly reads *shut up or else*. This is why I like her, she telepathically communicated what I was about to say and saved me the trouble.

She makes her way to the foyer, leaving him to mumble who knows what. A dividing wall hides the view, but I hear the door unlatch and then another voice. "Hi, you must be Mrs. Rivera," Camila says in her curt businesslike manner. I bet she's offering her hand for a handshake too.

"Er, yes! But please call me Karina. And you must be Camila… or should I call you Miss Puig? Or Dr. Puig? I don't mean to presume, I just—"

"Camila is fine," I yell from the living room.

Mateo makes a face as he washes his hands that tells me he doesn't think Camila or her presence are fine. I have to work really hard to not roll my eyes.

"Please, come on in," Karina says, and a moment later the door closes. "Can I help you with your things?"

"If you don't mind…"

After some rummaging, Karina emerges from the foyer back to the living room with a bundle in her arms. It looks like a log that's been wrapped in tinfoil.

"Ito," I tell my nephew, short for Angelito. "Dame un permiso." He slides over to the side, allowing me to finally sit on the edge of the couch. I stifle a curse when I notice that one of my crutches fell over the carpet.

That's when Camila rounds the corner and sees me. "I'll get it." She leaves her purse on the floor and trots over to get my crutches. I watch her with a silly smile. "Here you go." She straightens them out for me and catches me acting like a lovesick fool. Her lips twitch.

"I missed you," I say with a sigh, sounding very much like Lady Arabella.

In contrast, Camila is as serious as Lord Harrington when she says, "Me too."

Mateo clears his throat. "Hi. Welcome to our humble abode."

Humble, he says, as if the place wasn't decked with probably thousands of dollars worth of Christmas decorations, and impeccably selected furniture.

There's a gigantic natural fir dressed in cheerful twinkling lights and crystal ornaments in a corner by the fireplace, which aside from being decked in garlands, is guarded by a life size nutcracker—if by life size we interpret the height of my nephew.

There are probably a hundred gifts of sizes that range from pocket to jumbo spilled all over the tree skirt, wrapped in glittering paper that will leave us all glinting like fairies for days, no matter how much we scrub in the shower.

Every room in the house is as festive as possible—and I mean that literally, even the bed sheets in the guest room have a print of little red and green gifts—and the finishing touch is the bunch of mistletoe hanging from the archway toward the dining area.

"Your home is very beautiful, thank you for having me." Camila unwinds her scarf and offers a nod to both Mateo and

Karina. The latter returns a smile. My brother still can't quite seem to believe that his boss is here right now.

I clear my throat. "Hey, snuggle bear, let's go put your stuff in the guest room."

"Uh, sure."

I point in the general direction of it for her to go ahead. My brother mouths the words *snuggle bear* like it's the most shocking question he's ever asked. In return, I mouth famous words from our mom: *pórtate bien o te voy a dar*.

Inside my room, Camila whirls on me. "I should just go. I'm going to make it awkward for everyone and—"

"Shh." I close the door behind me and lean against it. I motion with my lips at the bed. "You can leave your coat there."

Sighing, she sets out to do that when she notices I left a little mess on the bed.

"Oh, shit." I spring, trying to get to it faster than her but it's a lost cause. "Don't open the red box."

Camila side eyes me. "Did you get me a gift?"

"Yes, but you have to wait until tomorrow." I snarl in frustration. "I was trying to get you alone so you could feel me up for a bit. I forgot I left all the presents out there."

Sure enough, there are five of them on the bed. One for Mom that I'll save for when she flies in. One for my brother and sister-in-law each, and the signed baseball I've been hauling all along for my nephew. That's the only one I tried to do before getting ready, but even though I know how to do many things with my hands—including giving Camila neck massages that melt her like a candle—wrapping isn't my forte.

Since she's someone who walks the narrow path of right-eousness, she ignores the gift meant for her and instead picks up the badly wrapped one for the kiddo. "What's this?"

I sigh dramatically. "It's a collectible item I brought for Angel, my nephew—a baseball signed by the entire Orlando

Wild team that won the World Series, valued at one point two million."

With a yelp, she drops it back on the bed. "Dollars?"

"Yes, not hugs."

"Shouldn't that be in like, a museum?" she squeaks.

"Nah, it's no big deal." I shrug.

"Wait." She raises a hand, eyes lost in the distance as she recalls something. "You brought it here, which means... you had one point two million dollars in your backpack all this time?"

"Yes, but—"

"Uninsured?" she screeches.

That one gives me pause. "Hmm, you have a point there. It would've been a big problem if I had lost it."

Strength leaves her and she drops to sit on the bed. "Lucky..."

"Yes?" I swallow hard and paint on an uncertain smile, somewhat feeling like I'm about to get scolded.

"Thank you so much for not telling me about this ball until now. I don't think I'd have been able to handle the stress otherwise."

My eyebrows rise. "Um, you're welcome?" It comes out as a question because she's staring at me like she can't quite comprehend what I am.

"I'm so glad you're a way more relaxed person than I am," she says at last, completely silencing the buzzing in my brain. "I actually think we'll balance each other very well on this regard."

A full smile blooms on my face. "Absolutely. And once Mateo sees that, he'll come around."

"Maybe," she still sounds doubtful, but she casts one more look around the bed. "Should I teach you how to wrap properly?"

"Yes, please."

Rather than embarking on a well deserved and much anticipated make out session, we sit together on my bed and she shows me how to wrap one of the boxes, the one for Karina, while I copy the instructions to wrap Camila's gift. I tuck it away into the bedside table drawer before moving onto the next gift.

We finally walk out a few minutes later and Mateo gives me a look like he thinks we were up to what I wish we had been up to.

"This looks great," Karina says, unwrapping the tinfoil from the log looking thing. As I approach, I notice it's some kind of bread. "What is it?"

"Pan de jamón," Camila explains, glancing at each of our faces in turn. To Mateo, she may not seem nervous because she sounds the exact same way as when she's doing business. But I've learned in the past few days that she adopts this serious persona when she's nervous. It's the disguise she uses to hide behind. And I can tell that she's quaking in her boots—the same ones we got her at Bear Crossing. "It's a traditional Christmas food from Venezuela. I um, baked it myself so I can't guarantee it's any good. But I had help, so I don't think it'll be too terrible either."

Her little rant makes Mateo's eyes pop, his head tilt, like he needs a different angle to get acquainted with this new version of his boss that he hasn't seen before.

Karina stares her dead in the eye. "If it tastes as good as it smells you'll have to give me the recipe."

That finally breaks through Camila's stiffness and she smiles that sweet, fleeting little smile that feels like a flurry of snow. Mateo's jaw drops.

"Of course," she says in return before glancing around. "I heard Lucky mention a nephew. I didn't know if you allow him sweets or if he had dietary restrictions, but I made one end of the bread without any of the stuffings for him if necessary."

Karina places her hand on her chest. "That is so thoughtful of you." And with that she's been fully won over by her husband's evil boss.

My brother's foul mood fades as Angel comes into the kitchen following the lovely scents, and stops at seeing the stranger. Camila offers her hand out like she's meeting another executive rather than a kid. "Hi, I'm Camila. Nice to meet you."

Nonplussed, my nephew grabs her hand and shakes it with all the sobriety a six year old can muster. "I'm Angel, nice to meet you. Are you going to be my friend?"

"Yes," she responds in all seriousness and without hesitation.

I blow a raspberry and burst out laughing, and my sister-in-law joins me because this is both ridiculous and so adorable, I wish I had caught it on camera. But the memory will live on in my mind forever, and it'll be just one more of the first Christmas spent with Camila—a woman so different from me that it makes her my perfect match.

EPILOGUE: CAMILA

ONE YEAR LATER

Conor and Sierra Mahoney sway in each other's arms in the middle of the dance floor, sharing their first dance as a married couple.

Beside me, Rachel sniffles in a feeble attempt to contain her tears. My advice to get waterproof makeup comes in clutch when a couple of tears escape. I was prepared and snatched some napkins earlier, knowing that one of my companions was bound to cry no matter what.

"Isn't this so perfect?" she whispers as she accepts the paper napkins and blots her face with them. "They fell in love during Christmas and are now marrying at Christmas. How sweet is that?"

"Very sweet." I nod, stoic as usual.

She nudges me with her elbow. "Does it bother you?"

"Hmm?"

"I mean, with your history and all…"

Oh. She's referring to the fact that I was jilted before what was to be my perfect Christmas wedding four years ago.

Now, I have enough perspective to understand that yes, that was my failure—but not because there was something wrong with me. Rather, because I was looking for the wrong things in a partner. It would've been the biggest mistake of my life.

"No," I respond in all sincerity. At the last second I try for some levity. "I'm even cheerful during Christmas now. I no longer find it the most foul time of the year."

"I'm so glad." She grabs my arm and gives it a gentle squeeze. "You deserve only wonderful things, Camila."

I return the nudge. "So do you. You should get your famous brothers to find you a hot soccer player."

Even in the dim light I can see her nose wrinkle. "Ugh, absolutely not. They put me off all soccer players forever. Besides, my son hates the sport." This is always a source of much back and forth between her son, Adrian. He's into American football, an inexplicable preference when he comes from soccer royalty on his mom's side.

I chuckle under my breath. "It's okay. Unlike Sierra, I won't pester you to also find a significant other. You can just devote your nights to baking and I'll support you."

"Thank you." Her brilliant grin flashes in the dark. Something beyond our little circle catches her eyes, though, and she whispers, "Incoming."

I turn around, my heart skipping in sudden excitement. But it's just my parents coming over with champagne flutes to watch the happy couple's dance.

The lovebirds were very kind in allowing me to bring well beyond a plus one. My parents were in town, for the first time visiting to spend Christmas as a family. It felt weird to leave them home to themselves where they probably would've got back to working, while I was at a wedding as one of the maids of honor.

I snort a little through my nose when I realize how much my

life has changed. Two years ago, Sierra and Conor couldn't even meet me in the eye, and I had no interest in partaking of Christmas traditions I had never experienced. And here I am, with family and friends, building new memories to look fondly upon.

"Champagne?" Dad passes me a flute and I accept it.

"Thank you."

My mom stares at the newlyweds intently. She doesn't have to say it, but I can practically feel her thinking that it could've been me instead. But if she's picturing Rupert in that scene, she'd be absolutely wrong.

"I'm happy for them," I say, leaning toward Mom and Dad. "And I'm also happy about how things are going for me, if you were worried about that."

My parents, as poised and unflappable as usual, look at me like they're seeing me for the first time.

I have friends. Audrey hang out more often, what with the *SPORTY* branch we've opened in Orlando to centrally manage the traditional line. It's been super helpful to now that we have taken the helm of two massive enterprises. And when I'm here in Mapleton, I also have Rachel and Sierra. They keep my feet on the ground, and even feed me when I forget to eat because work has absorbed me. Also—

"Would you like to dance?"

The champagne sloshes as I whirl around, and it's a wonder that it doesn't spill over my hand. Lucky Rivera stands before me, extending his big, calloused hand toward me. I drink him up in his black tux, tailored to hug his delectable shoulders to perfection. A curl has escaped from the hold of his hair wax, defiantly claiming its place over his forehead. His eyes alone could light up this entire space.

"I would love to, but…" I look down at my champagne.

"Here, let me hold that for you." Dad takes it right back and goes as far as nudging me in the direction of the professional baseball player. I catch Mom fighting back a smile, and it fills me up with so much happiness that I could burst.

"Get it, girl." Rachel laughs a little.

Shaking my head, I hold my boyfriend's hand. Lucky was supposed to be my only plus one, but once he heard that my parents were flying over he was willing to give up his spot. That's how kind this man is—he would do anything to make me happy.

Funny, because I'd do the same in return.

As other couples also blend into the dance floor, Lucky leads me along through the people. One hand holds mine, and the other sets dangerously low at the small of my back. There's no way I'm moving it.

Finally, he twirls me around until I'm right in the circle of his arms, pressed against his chest. Lucky rests his forehead on mine, smiling like he just got great news. "Hey," he whispers in a deep voice that feels like a caress on bare skin.

I do my best not to shiver. "Hey."

"I have to give you a warning." I raise my eyebrows and he continues, "I'm going to dance us under the nearest mistletoe."

"Oh, good," I say curtly. "I would expect no less."

He missed most of this season, but the team supported him in prioritizing a proper recovery rather than a quick one. Thanks to that, he's almost brand new—if it wasn't for the surgery scars—and is poised to resume his career next season at the highest performance level of his life. Those were his doctor's words, not mine.

But one thing I discovered the moment he recovered, is how good of a dancer he is. Even though I only dance passably well, the subtle pressure of his hand at my back, the way his legs frame mine, the smooth sway of his hips against mine— make me fall right into his rhythm like I also know what I'm doing.

I slide my hands up his chest and to his shoulders, stopping to get on my tippy toes so I can kiss him. A hum vibrates through his chest, and he abandons his previous plan of the mistletoe to savor the moment. And by the moment, I mean my mouth.

Glad I wore waterproof lipstick.

"Why are you laughing?" Lucky asks against my lips.

"Nothing. Just a little aw-shucks that I ruined your plan."

He runs his thumb across my jaw. "Nah, you didn't ruin it. You made it better."

"That's right." I give one nod.

"Cam?" he asks with sudden gravitas, using the nickname that he has permission to use now.

My eyebrows rise. "Lucky?"

"The cookie sisters texted me again."

My lips twitch. If that's the sequitur then this can't be about bad news. "What now?" Billie, Val and Nellie have also become our friends. We exchange regular updates about our lives, and they're still lobbying pretty hard to be the maids of honor of my hypothetical wedding to Lucky.

He continues, "They want to know if we're going to have a Christmas wedding too. Billie said they can visit their parents another time next year."

I shake my head. "Geez." It's been only the millionth time they bring up the topic.

"And that got me thinking…" He presses his hands over my waist a little harder. I'm wearing a burgundy velvet dress that is warm enough for the season but isn't bulky, and it allows me to feel his touch perfectly. "Should we get married on Christmas next year?"

I trip on my own feet, one of the heels catching on the hem of my dress. Thankfully he keeps me upright. My eyes pop as wide as they can be. "Wait, what?"

"Or does that make you think of Rudolph?"

"The reindeer?" I ask, suddenly dizzy.

"No, your evil ex."

"Oh." I shake my head once, hard. Then again. "No, I don't ever think about him anymore."

That pleases him. Even though his expression stays calm, his eyes have an extra twinkle. "So does that mean you'd like to marry during the most wonderful time of the year?"

"Lucky, is this a proposal?"

"Kind of. But I'll give you the ring another time, I haven't quite found the right one yet." He pauses. "But also, it would probably be rude to steal the newlyweds's thunder if I kneel in the middle of their wedding party."

I inhale a shaky breath. "Lucky…"

"I mean, I'm also cool with marrying you in the summer. A PR summer wedding would be perfect too. Or in the fall or whenever. My point is"—he breaks himself off to grin—"I love you, Camila Puig. I want to build bear shaped snow-women, snuggle on the couch with you, go on roadtrips, walk barefoot on the sand, wake up next to you more than we have to Face-Time, and I want to see all your smiles, dry all your tears, and have the right to hold you in my arms every day. I want to spend the rest of my life with you if you'll have me."

I circle my arms around his neck and bring him down for another kiss. I'm so giddy and fluttery that I have no finesse, I half miss his lips even as I grab onto his hair for purchase. "Yes, I want you in my life forever, mi osito."

AND THEY DANCED HAPPILY EVER AFTER

*

Turn to the next page for a bonus scene preview at what the third and final book in the SPORTY *Christmas series is about!*

BONUS SCENE: RACHEL

SIERRA'S BACHELORETTE PARTY

"I can't believe I'm getting married." Sierra plops on my living room couch, the margarita in her hand slushing dangerously. "And to a co-worker."

I tease, "One you hated for two years, to boot."

"Bah. Don't remind me about my dark past." She waves her free hand and then takes a sip of the too strong eggnog that she made herself.

Cam seems to be having work withdrawals. Her eyes keep switching to the handsome leather folio that contains her iPad and her phone. Or perhaps it's not so much work what has her mind drifting, but the stunning boyfriend she got herself during a wild trip home just before Christmas last year.

"At least no one's gossiping about you two anymore," Cam adds to Sierra, right before she catches me keeping a hawk eye on her.

We agreed to have a chill bachelorette party for Sierra because not only we're all busy women—one planning her own wedding, another running a whole company, and me trying to prevent my son Adrian from getting into more trouble than it finds him—and thus, we're tired. Instead of going to a bar downtown, or traveling to a city for more exciting shenanigans, we settled for a boozy pajama party and enough food to tide us over for the next five years.

Cam was in charge of the beverage selection, and I'm not surprised to note that she bought the top shelf labels of everything. Meanwhile, food was my responsibility. I'm not much of a cook other than what's needed for survival, but I'm a damn fine baker. My coffee table is loaded with a gorgeous margherita pizza, an apple pie, and tequeños. Do they match? No. But they're delicious and dare I say, looking more popular than the creamy drinks.

With the two of them, at least. I'm looking forward to getting plastered. I pour just a tad more Cacique Añejo onto my eggnog cup.

Sierra's eyebrows lift off as I take a particularly big gulp. "Uhh, what's up with you?"

Cam scans me from head to toe. "You look like someone who's trying to forget her sorrows."

Bingo.

"I'm just glad to have a quiet moment with you guys. This year has been difficult for kiddo."

"Yeah, puberty's rough," Sierra says with a sympathetic cringe.

Ever the sharpest, Cam asks, "But is that really what's making you hit the rum so hard?"

The problem is that, yes, that season of Adrian's life has officially started and is hitting us both like a wrecking ball. I've gone from being the slightly uncool Mom who wouldn't let him leave his dirty socks strewn all over the place, to the biggest villain that has ever existed. Step aside Lex Luthor or Thanos, it's me—a tiny second-gen Venezuelan American who had him when she was a kid herself and has had to figure everything out on her own since.

But…

That's not the real reason why I'm hitting up Mr. Cacique. I'm not much of a drinker but I'm honestly at a loss with how to deal with my life these days.

Because I have a big secret—actually *big* is too mild a word for it.

I've never told anyone who Adrian's father is. Not even Adrian himself.

In my defense… No, I have no defense.

The plain facts are that I hooked up with the most popular guy in my high school class after senior prom, and that's how Adrian came to be.

Before that, we'd barely exchanged more than an occasional greeting in our neighborhood—since we lived right next door to each other—but never at school. He had his crowd of popular football kids who gravitated around him, being the quarterback and all. I hung out pretty exclusively with the girls in my soccer team.

We of course had different dates for prom, but somehow we ended up sharing a dance together, and he teased me saying that *his* football was the superior one, and I had to explain how *mine* is actually played with the feet, and that I hated that I had to call it soccer here.

Next thing we knew, we were making out in a corner, and it was so hard to tear apart from each other that we decided to leave. Together.

It clicked well after the deed was done that he'd had a hotel room reserved all along, and that I was never supposed to be the one who shared it with him, but his actual date.

That was the first and last walk of shame I've ever done, leaving that hotel room in my half zipped prom dress, shoes in my hand so that I wouldn't wake up the guy who didn't care who he slept with.

He wouldn't miss me, and with graduation three weeks away, we were going our separate ways already anyway. So I acted like absolutely nothing had happened and went back to ignoring him at school. The only difference was that every time I caught sight of him around the neighborhood, I'd do whatever it took to hide—even going as far as jumping into a garbage can.

It worked so well that we didn't cross paths again, and graduation came and went.

When the morning sickness started, right as I was supposed to start college with a fancy soccer scholarship, I figured there would be no point in giving him the news that he was about to become a father. He was already clear across the country playing football.

My dad was too busy being disappointed and angry at me to even ask who the other side of the blunder was. After all, he'd rather kick me out of the house than deal with my mess. I had more important worries than the biological father of my son.

Years later, even though Adrian asked a few times about his dad, I think he could sense that the story would break his heart and he didn't push it. Until puberty started, he seemed to be fine with me being both his dad and his mom.

I would've continued like this the rest of my life if it wasn't for Adrian's dad appearing again. Here, in Mapleton. And even worse, as the focus of the biggest project I've had assigned at *SPORTY* ever since I became a Publicity Talent Manager.

I've had a few PR campaigns with some of the top athletes in tennis and golf already, but all of them pale in comparison to the height of sports celebrity that Aiden Tyler has achieved as one of the best QBs in the game right now, and certainly the most photogenic one.

That's who Adrian's father is. And nobody can now—especially not Aiden himself. Just thinking about that secret leaking out is making me break into hives.

The silence has stretched far too long and their patience is even more dangerous than if they were peppering me with questions. Clearing my throat, I say, "I'm just kind of bummed that I'm going to be the odd woman out."

"What do you mean?" Sierra asks.

"I mean…" I squirm a little. "I'm not complaining, don't take me wrong. And it's quite normal for things to be this way. But Sierra, you're getting married and moving into Conor's cabin in the woods, and Cam has her hands busy enough being *SPORTY*'s new CEO while also keeping her relationship with Lucky happy and healthy. I feel kinda lonely," I admit with a sheepish smile when I realize that even though I said all of this to throw them off the scent, it's all true.

Then Sierra declares, "The solution is to find a man of your own."

In contrast, Cam rolls her eyes. "Don't listen to her." She pauses. "Unless you want to."

"Nah, I'm good. The last thing I need right now is to further complicate my life with a guy." I reach for a slice of pizza. "But anyway, tonight isn't supposed to be about me. Sierra, I want you to know I'm really so happy for you."

Sierra lifts her reindeer-shaped mug full of eggnog. "Cheers—to this Christmas being the magical time we all need."

"Cheers," Cam says now that she has become a big fan of the holiday.

I make a noise that sounds a lot like the word without actually saying it, because I have a strong feeling that all that awaits for me this Christmas is trouble.

*

*Thank you for reading **Cheerfoul**! I hope you can take a brief moment to leave a review on Amazon.*

Stay tuned for Rachel's story, the third and last book in the SPORTY *Christmas series, coming out in December 2027.*

But before that, **I'll come back in 2026 with a brand new series of soccer romance!** *Please anticipate it ;)*

My other works are available on Kindle Unlimited if you're craving more closed door sports romance. You can also sign up to my newsletter at mariloyal.com to get my free volleyball novella, **Set Me Up** *and be the first to find out what's next from me.*

Merry Christmas!

MORE FROM THE AUTHOR

Upcoming Soccer Romance Series · Book 1* ·
Wild Baseball Romance · Wild Pitch · Wild Catch · Wild Hit ·
St. Cloud Hockey Series · Faceoff · Overtime · Shutout ·
SPORTY **Christmas Romance** · Mistlefoe · Cheerfoul · Book 3* ·
Volleyball Romance Novella · Set Me Up** · Set Me Up 2* ·

*Coming soon.
**Newsletter exclusive.

*

Find my closed door romantasy, paranormal, and sci-fi romance books as **MC
Loyal**.

GLOSSARY OF SPANISH VOCABS

Chapter 2

- Mierda (see also Chapter 23): crap/shit.

Chapter 4

- El Frontú: Puerto Rican slang for something like main character energy.
- Anda pal carajo: go to hell.
- La madre que lo parió: the mother who birthed him. This is a mild form of a way spicier insult.

Chapter 5

- Qué mucho apesta esto: this stinks so bad, in Puerto Rican grammar.

Chapter 6

- Entonces: so…

- Puñeta (also Ch8, 17, 24): Puerto Rican semi-spicy slang for surprise or anger.

Chapter 9

- ¿Qué?: what?

Chapter 10

- Mala mía: my bad in Puerto Rican grammar.
- Perdón: sorry.
- El Bro: Spanglish for the brother.
- Más te vale cabrón: you better, asshole.
- La chancla (also ch17): famous disciplinary blunt instrument that parents wear on their feet but love to throw at their unruly children.

Chapter 11

- Carajo: Venezuelan semi-spicy slang for surprise or anger.
- El que no lo conoce que lo compre: a saying that goes along the lines of "whoever doesn't know him shouldn't buy him."

Chapter 12

- Tenemos que hablar: we need to talk.

Chapter 13

- El Niño Jesús: Baby Jesus.

Chapter 14

- ¿Qué dijo?: what did she/he said?

Chapter 16

- ¿Qué? Yo——: what? I—
- Buenos días, mi osa: good morning, my (female) bear.

Chapter 18

- Para: stop.
- No te emociones, cabrón. Solo se habían acabado los cuartos, no significa nada: don't get excited, asshole. There were just no more rooms, it doesn't mean anything.
- Pendejo: semi-spicy word for someone who is dropping the ball.

Chapter 20

- Media naranja: "half orange" aka other half.

Chapter 21

- Le rompo la cara: I'll break his face.

Chapter 23

- Mami (see also Chapter 29): in theory it means mommy, HOWEVA when used in adult settings, it's more like "hot mama."
- Quinceañera: 15 is the Latinos version of Sweet 16.
- Osa: (female) bear.

Chapter 24

- Lechón (see also Chapter 33 and 34): roast pig.
- Epa mano: hey, bro.
- Mielda: crap/shit but with a different pronunciation.
- Cabrón: asshole.
- Está bien: fine.
- Brodel: brother pronounced in Caribbean.
- Chupacabra: mythical monster in Latin America. For some reason, it was a whole sensation in the '90s talk shows.

Chapter 25

- ¿Qué estoy haciendo?: what am I doing?
- Jajaja: hahaha.

Chapter 31

- ¿Qué estás haciendo, Camila?: what are you doing, Camila?

Chapter 33

- Hallacas: typical Venezuelan Christmas food like a big corn dough tamale, filled with different stews among the various regions of the country, wrapped in plantain leaf, boiled, and sprinkled with ancestral love.

Chapter 34

- Arroz con gandules: rice with pigeon peas.

- Angelito: little Angel.
- Dame un permiso: excuse me.
- Pórtate bien o te voy a dar: behave or I'll hit you (implied: with the chancla).
- Pan de jamón: ham bread.

Epilogue

- Mi osito: little (male) bear.

Bonus Scene

- Tequeños: cheese sticks wrapped in dough and deep fried. You know you want some.
- Cacique Añejo: aged rum from the Cacique brand. The good stuff for the connoisseurs.

PS. It has been truly an honor to write a Puerto Rican MMC and a Venezuelan FMC, and I hope you can tell by the abundance of slang from both Caribbean nations!

Feliz Navidad in José Feliciano.

ACKNOWLEDGMENTS

"I wrote this book in December last year, surely I'll be able to edit it with plenty of time and give it the launch it deserves," I told myself while thoroughly botching the launch of Wild Hit, which I finished writing way too close to the publish date.

And then, surprise! Mari goes through *another* life changing event.

2025 has been a highly impactful year for my family and I. It has included high stakes medical procedures, unpredictably long workload peaks at the day job, mental health episodes, home construction, insurance beef, small and big heartbreaks, new family members, and a sprinkle of burnout.

Choosing the lesser disappointment—between not releasing as promised *at all*, or failing to make each release feel special to my readers and to the books themselves—has seriously left me wrapped up in an itchy and smelly blanket of shame and guilt.

I'm trying to toss it away by simply forging on, because ultimately if my books are able to reach <u>one</u> person this year and abstract them from the terrifying chaos of existing in 2025, it will all have been enough.

As the year winds down, I hope this book is a soft blanket to shelter in as we transition to 2026, that it feels like Christmas and cocoa in your heart.

So this one goes to my family, friends, you, and also myself for forging ahead no matter what. May the Lord reward our efforts in 2026.

ABOUT THE AUTHOR

Mari Loyal was born and raised in Venezuela, a baseball country that only cared about another sport, football soccer, every four years. As such, she decided to make hockey her whole personality because she had to make a point of being different. These days she no longer suffers from Not Like Other Girls syndrome and is very happy to be in the sports romance fandom. She writes closed door romance with a Latin American flair and an abundance of cinnamon rolls heroes. She also enjoys eating cinnamon rolls (the confections), in her spare time.

Find her:

Website & Newsletter mariloyal.com
Instagram mariloyalauthor
Threads mariloyalauthor